CW01024603

1914: The King Must Die

About the author

Jamie Camplin was born in 1947. His first love was history and, after winning a place at Corpus Christi College, Cambridge, when he was sixteen, he went on to take a Double First. After a period working for the textiles and fibre company Courtaulds, he embarked on a publishing career at Thames & Hudson, where he was Editorial Director 1979–2005 and Managing Director 2005–13. He is the author of *The Rise of the Plutocrats: Wealth and Power in Edwardian England* (1978).

Reviews of *The Rise of the Plutocrats*

'Mr Camplin has a convincing thesis and writes of it all with skill and a wry romantic wit. I can see he is playing brilliantly' – Michael Holroyd, *The Times*

'Gossipy and lively' – C.P.Snow, *Financial Times*

'His research has been exhaustive, yet the hundreds of anecdotes, quotations and statistics have been subjected to the discipline of a coherent narrative' – Gordon Brook-Shepherd, *Sunday Telegraph*

'There is a real feel for the period, interesting light shed on it and questions raised about it' – *Times Literary Supplement*

'An absorbing account of Edwardian financiers and industrialists. Their rise to power, influence, pastimes, demise and place in a social revolution are resurrected with a digestible wealth of telling detail' – *Sunday Times*

'He is at his best not only in telling their stories but in collecting *obiter dicta*. Some of the millionaires really did talk in the way Shaw expected them to talk. They philosophised in public' – Asa Briggs, *The Guardian*

'Fascinating… Camplin has done an enormous amount of work and his answers to the whys and wherefores deserve attention' – Marghanita Laski, *Country Life*

'Excellent' – *Daily Mail*

'Crisply authoritative' – *Publishers Weekly* (New York)

1914
The King Must Die

Jamie Camplin

php

PARK HOUSE PRESS

First published in the United Kingdom
and the United States of America in 2015
by Park House Press, 10 Perrers Road, London W6 OEY

1914: The King Must Die © 2015 Jamie Camplin

All Rights Reserved.
No part of this publication may be reproduced or transmitted
in any form or by any means, electronic or mechanical, including
photocopy, recording or any other information retrieval system,
without prior permission in writing from the publisher.

Contents

The story that has never been told

WHEN my greatgrandfather, Walter Ransom, died on the 24th of August, 1931 – the day Ramsay MacDonald's government fell – there was a certain ambivalence in the tributes paid to him: nothing, perhaps, that one could define, but none the less a curiously restrained assessment of both his achievements and his weaknesses. *The Times*, in its obituary, remarked upon the diffidence with which he had assumed – and exercised – power in the many and varied offices of state which he had held over a long period. There was a hint, or so it seemed to me when I came to study his life, that a full perspective of the man's life and career was not being presented.

Many years later, when his private papers were at last revealed to the family under the terms of his will, many things became much clearer. Some of the events my greatgrandfather recounted in his detailed chronicle are familiar to all, or to most of us; others appear in a new and quite startlingly different light and reinforce the sense I have always had that historical truth is (to put it gently) a subjective matter.

'The English', Winston Churchill once observed in the House of Commons, 'never draw a line without blurring it.' In our amiable and in one sense admirable ability to see all sides of a case, and in our instinctive desire (for the best of motives) to keep secret what we believe might embarrass or hurt, we often weave a far more powerfully propagandist view of the past than the shrill recorders of authoritarian regimes.

In this volume my greatgrandfather covers no more than seven weeks in the summer before the outbreak of the First World War. I confess that I have shamelessly introduced into his account additional evidence from a wide variety of sources, not least modern historians. Notwithstanding what I have said above, I must express my deepest thanks to all of them in helping to fill in the lacunae, and something of the broad background, of this tale.

They will forgive me, I hope, if I have striven to make their 'version of events' consistent with the story that, in a century, has never been told. Until now.

James Ransom, London, 2015

CHAPTER ONE

The night of the Buckingham Palace Ball

IN the early morning of the 5th of June 1914, Walter Ransom slipped quietly out of the front door of No. 11 Berkeley Square, London W1 – an imposing house in that age and any other – and walked quickly past the wonderful, tall plane trees in the centre of the square towards a silent Berkeley Street.

As he reached the great mansion of Lansdowne House, for four generations the London home of the Lansdowne family, he paused briefly and looked over his shoulder. The large cast-iron link extinguishers on the railings outside his own house, once used for putting out powerful street torches, stood out prominently against the white façade. He fancied he saw a slight movement of the curtains to his wife's bedroom on the second floor, and turned hurriedly back to face the direction in which he was walking.

To his left were houses and stables, some converted, belonging to the mansions of Dover Street. A few more paces and he turned right, negotiating the iron bar which had impeded highwaymen in the days when Berkeley Square had been as lawless as it was fashionable. Down a few steps, and he entered the narrow, below-ground passage between the gardens of Lansdowne House and Devonshire House, which had its frontage on Piccadilly.

Emerging at the east end of Curzon Street, he had speedily arrived within close distance of his objective. At No.19 Benjamin Disraeli had spent his last breath. He passed a few modern buildings, but the closed alley at either end of the street, used for carriages, was a fitting reminder of the past.

Within a stone's throw, it was as if the eighteenth century had survived intact, continuing a London tradition in which the very rich rubbed shoulders with the very poor. In narrow streets that had not changed for two centuries, shopkeepers went about their trade from early in the morning, while servants of many kinds enjoyed each other's company, and the publican's ale, much as they had in the long-forgotten era of England's first Prime Minister, Sir Robert Walpole. In Hayes Mews, running northwards between Charles Street and Hill Street, *The Running Footman* continued to invite servants in their few spare hours to express good-natured indifference to the fleet-footed, enthusiastic figure on the signboard, swinging silently in the breeze.

On the other side of Curzon Street, down side streets, the frantic, noisy traffic of Piccadilly passed by day oblivious of what lay close by its side. Ransom's goal lay in one of Curzon Street's intriguing offshoots. First Bolton Street – once the very western edge of London and provider of secret lodgings for the Young Pretender. Then to Clarges Street, with dead men's history in reach of every glance he made. Dr Johnson's serious lady friend, Mrs Elizabeth Carter, had died here, at a very great age. Macaulay, Daniel O'Connell, Lady Hamilton, Charles James Fox…each had once found a home in this street.

He waited for a moment in the shadows as several men clattered somewhat unsteadily into a waiting cab at the far end of the street. They had emerged from a house on the corner of Piccadilly, originally the residence of the Dukes of Grafton. The Turf Club had moved there from Grafton Street when he was a child and he had no wish to meet a group of late-night card players who might, possibly, recognize him.

His footsteps seemed unnaturally loud as he proceeded some steps further before halting again. He turned the key in the lock of the door of the modest building he had reached, pushed his way into the dim passage beyond and climbed the narrow stairs to the attic. Here he had to bend to avoid the sloping roof. His eyes passed from the peeling whitewash of the rough walls, to the newly cleaned skylight, which eerily revealed the distant stars, then to the dusty fireplace, still full of winter ash; and finally to the ancient iron bedstead.

In this Anna lay sleeping.

After no more than a moment's pause, he methodically began to remove the evening dress that he had worn to the Buckingham Palace ball some hours before. He made a tidy pile on the one simple chair in the room and, when quite naked, slipped into the bed beside her. The springs creaked, but she did not move.

He rested on his back and peered in an unfocused way through the semi-darkness at the ceiling, on which intruding damp from the previous day's downpour had traced a peculiar pattern. At least the ceiling was at rest; a pleasant change from the furious dizziness he had felt as he had left the Palace and stumbled on the path before the car.

He had picked himself up to the sound of his wife rustling past with unstated disapproval, his eye catching sight of the bright new façade of the Palace. From its balcony in the centre, the King could look down on a patriotic and enthusiastic people, the model of unchanging loyalty when they gathered in strength on state occasions. But this was not the house built for the Duke of Buckingham in 1703, nor even Nash's masterpiece of a century or more later. The previous year he had been among the spectators who watched as scaffolding and platforms, electric-powered lifts and vast cranes came on the scene. An army of workers had laboured by day and night for three months to give brilliant life to the designs of Sir Aston Webb in bright white stone.

Through his befuddled senses, he was struck by the grandeur of it all. The Royal Standard flew at full mast. The National Monument to Queen Victoria braved the front of the chief façade, while any hint of domesticity was well hidden in the King's private apartments on the north side, overlooking the gardens, with their chapel, lake and great pavilion. Inside, miles upon miles of red carpet acted as the link between the host of formal bedrooms and sitting rooms, and between the majestic picture galleries, the throne room – hung with crimson satin – and the ballroom itself.

Only those who knew could see the feet of clay. There they all were, the earnestly complacent rulers of the greatest empire the world had seen, fresh from the Whitsun recess. David Lloyd George, the Chancellor of the Exchequer, had been at Brynwhelion, his home at Criccieth on the coast of Caenarvonshire in his native Wales, content with his family and his favourite dogs: not so content, however, that he did not allow himself to be photographed as he studiedly addressed his fellow countrymen in the vernacular, wishing to goodness that he never need come back to London. 'I found time for some golf,' he said. And then the Prime Minister, Herbert Asquith. He had been a happy refugee at Lord Sheffield's country retreat at Penrhôs near Holyhead, where he had played…golf. Even the leader of the Opposition, Mr Bonar Law, had found time for that while also indulging in more dangerous sport in troubled Ireland.

Standing with his back to the giant fireplace was a red-faced gentleman dressed in the uniform of the Scots Guards, who looked as if he was slightly the worse for wear, but wasn't, who laughed heartily at the worst jokes and whose voice boomed in imitation of the most advanced foghorn. It was difficult to comprehend that this was one of the best-connected men in the world – cousin of the Emperor of Germany, the Tsar of Russia, the Kings of Spain and Norway, nephew of the Kings of Denmark and of Greece. Ransom found himself staring at the rather slight figure of his king, slight at least in comparison to his corpulent father, Edward VII. George V had always seemed to him a rather shy man, with an apprehensive air, though never so apprehensive that his essential ability to order his life was in jeopardy. The same could not be said of his cousin Tsar Nicholas II, whom he so closely resembled in physical appearance.

George V's self-indulgence was not taken in the form of alcohol, but expressed in his plodding, black-and-white directness. There was no subtlety, no detachment in this King: bluff common sense, applied to the facts, was the approach to all problems. He did not recognize passion in others and could not feel it himself. At most there was a sort of lacklustre affection. What was it that Margot Asquith – the Prime Minster's wife – had said to him?

'Sir, your great fault is that you don't enjoy yourself.'

'Yes, I know,' came back the reply. 'But you see I don't like Society; I like my wife.'

The bejewelled but still somewhat dowdy figure of Victoria Mary Augusta Louisa Olga Pauline Claudine Agnes, Queen of England, looked, as ever, rather fatigued. She tried hard in her nervous way to put nervous people slightly more at their ease. She must be the only woman in Society, it had been observed, who was not a Society woman. Margot railed at her false piety and sanctimonious pomposity. All that, 'There is simply nothing one can't do when duty calls.' Well, it was not done to support someone so quiet, so reliable, unassertive and steady.

Ransom mused on whether the Queen's unspontaneous and rather suffocating love for 'my own darling Georgie' was preferable to the moody unpredictability of his own wife, Rosalind. Fifteen years of marriage had left him with a frustrated distaste for her self-evident unhappiness, the dreams she had for objectives which were never quite real, despite the frantic concentration with which they were temporarily pursued. It was ironic that a woman with such conventional tastes – in this she was at one with the Queen – had a face so revealing of extremes: swelling like a ripe fruit when her dark eyes showed joy, only to shrivel into a thin, white, lined parody of itself on other occasions.

She was 44, a year older than him, and an incongruous three inches taller. From a distance he supposed that he appeared relaxed in a slightly formal way, with a full head of brown hair. A closer look would reveal a criss-cross patchwork of lines, especially around the eyes, which gave him prematurely the look of someone much older. He often thought, to his irritation, that it was as if the stresses of life had been etched on a face which was otherwise that of a child.

His wife was bored, certainly – her most arduous task to check, one by one, the weekly accounts from Harrods which itemized all her housekeeper's purchases, from a tin of this, to a pair of that. These months, the months of the summer round of social occasions, were usually her best, perhaps because they were the busiest. The hectic rush back from the pleasures of the 4th of June at Eton to prepare for the Ball at Buckingham Palace left no time for expressions of anguish. Besides, Rosalind was enormously proud of their one son, David, now in his second year at school.

Ransom's own love for his son was unstated but understood by his wife. He had made sure that they arrived in time to watch the school walk out to field against the Ramblers on Agar's Plough.

Rosalind, ostensibly watching the cricket, was the object of more than a few glances: much thought, and doubtless expense, had gone into her choice of clothes – the amethyst and black taffetas, the fine old lace used to soften the corsage. For once he enjoyed Rosalind's delight as much as she did herself.

Everything about this occasion was sheer spectacle. Soon there were the 'Speeches' at Upper School, as the busts of Eton's former progeny – Canning, Wellington, Fox, Hallam – looked down on their successors, David among them, while they proved their prowess in the Classics before the Provost. David's delivery of Pitt's speech on the Abolition of the Slave Trade seemed greatly more stirring than anything Ransom himself ever managed in the House of Commons. He felt secure about his son's promise, and that was very reassuring. One could not be certain, of course. How curious it was that his remarkable colleague Winston Churchill could have had a remarkable father who saw nothing special in him as a child. But since Ransom could not have conceived of not wanting an heir any more than he could have imagined the sun not rising the next day, he rested content in this part of his life.

There was just time to watch the beginning of the procession of boats in the early evening, the crews in white ducks and flower-decked hats, the captains in admirals' uniforms – all an exquisite ceremonial reminder of the joys of youth. For Rosalind at least it was an unforced pleasure to be entertained by the Headmaster and Mrs Lyttelton in the company of such old acquaintances as the Shaftesburys, the Wallersteins and the Bacons. Besides, a number of these faces transplanted themselves with a seasoned lack of breathlessness to Buckingham Palace by the required time of ten o'clock.

Lady Shaftesbury, indeed, was the object of much informed comment that evening. What exactly was the significance of the enormous emerald and diamond pendant, which she displayed so prominently and which had been given to her by the bachelor tea-king, Sir Thomas Lipton, at the launching of his new racing yacht, *Shamrock IV* ? But if Lady Shaftesbury heard any of this, she did not show it: she was as oblivious to gossip as the plentiful supplies of asparagus and early strawberries clearly had been to the late May frosts of the week before.

Ransom sat back contentedly at a small table with Rosalind and the Asquiths. Margot was, as ever, playfully provocative. 'The trouble with Queen Mary is that she's such a Tory,' she said carelessly. While this remark was meant for all of us, only Rosalind seemed to be listening, and it was to her that Margot turned directly as she continued: 'You can imagine what it was like being brought up in the White Lodge, and then ever since – constant complaints about what the Liberals are doing to encourage Socialism. Have you been in her sitting room?' She did not wait for an answer. 'It refuses to accept the idea that the least bit of disorder might exist anywhere in the universe. The writing table shows no sign of human activity at all: just neatly stacked paper, untouched, untouchable envelopes.'

A pause for breath and then the diatribe continued: 'And then when she talks…all the false piety about social distress, underpinned by the same old faith in order. "There are no slaves here," she said, "only the King and Queen: they are slaves to duty." When I quoted this to Crewe, all he would say was, "Her Majesty likes to feel that she is custodian for the nation."' Margot gave a gesture of mock despair, and spoke with hands clenched in clever imitation of Crewe's awkward search for the right and safe sentiments to express.

The Prime Minister, secure in the knowledge that his wife was too much the social animal to allow her indiscretions to be heard by the wrong people (at least, not *too* often), commented affably: 'So Crewe makes a good leader for us in the Lords. His judgment is sound and based on long experience – we don't get support there by trying to be radical.'

'It also depends on whether you think attention to duty and

courtesy condemn one to be a Tory,' Ransom added equally un-
heatedly. 'I remember my mother telling me of her first sight of
the Princess Mary – attentively listening in the ladies' gallery on
the afternoon Gladstone introduced his first Home Rule Bill.'

'The best I'll give you', retorted Margot, in something less
than a compliment, 'is that when she laughs, she does laugh. In
fact her whole body shakes…. Why Rosalind, are you all right?
You're very quiet.'

No one was allowed to be silent in Margot's presence, though it
helped to be a good listener, too. One of the reasons for Rosalind's
refusal to participate in this last exchange was the romanticism in
which she tended to take refuge as an escape from the disappoint-
ments of her own life. None of Margot's comments could destroy
her own memories of the King's Coronation Day – not as an
important constitutional occasion but as a romantic celebration:
the excitement in the Queen's eyes, the way she looked at the King
when the Archbishop placed the Crown on his head. Margot, on
the other hand, remembered the darker side of it all, the Queen
Mother's regret that her darling dead son, Prince Eddy, could not
succeed to the throne. 'Eddy should be King, not Georgie,' she
had said.

A worried look from Rosalind alerted the group to the fact that
the King was moving within earshot. 'Here May,' he was heard
to say, 'now you can help the Ambassador over this.' It was plain
that he did not refer to M. Paul Cambon, the relaxed Frenchman
whose snow-white hair and prominent blue eyes added to his
look of distinction. Cambon stood next to the jewel-like Chinese
Minister's wife, her exquisitely embroidered robe set off by a tiny
coronet of roses on her head. No, it was Walter Hines Page, from
the United States, who had wanted to know how the monarch who
held absolute sway over whether the lowest button of the waistcoat
was to be buttoned, or whether pearl-coloured spats were to take

the place of tan-coloured spats, spent his daily routine.

Queen Mary's earnest desire to answer any question was matched in this case by the Ambassador's earnest thirst for knowledge. 'If the weather is fine, a ride in the Row before breakfast makes an excellent beginning to the day,' the Queen affirmed. 'But if the clock does not chime at 9 o'clock as the King arrives for breakfast, then it is the clock's timekeeping that is at fault.' She smiled. 'We do so like to keep it an unelaborate family affair – the King has to be in his study by thirty minutes past nine, and those bulging red boxes bring so many problems. Then there are audiences with Colonial Governors and Ministers Plenipotentiary and [she smiled again] Ambassadors. The hours before luncheon pass quickly. Later, there are more audiences, more dispatch boxes; it is an exacting existence.'

The Queen broke off, though it was difficult to judge at this and at other times whether the rather laboured explanation was to continue. 'But pleasurable, too,' the King interjected. 'The Ambassador must come for an hour or two of rackets.' He turned to Page enthusiastically. 'We have a full-sized court, you know, which was at one time a rather large and useful conservatory. I am sure that you would like it.' The Ambassador's age and physical shape seemed an appropriate answer, but for those who liked it, and those who were deferential to it, the King's boyish delight was infectious.

Ransom was well used to this sort of polite chatter. He lived each day with the protocol, that enervating discussion in the Cabinet, for instance, when the King had wanted to wear the Crown rather than the Field Marshal's cocked hat – a tradition begun by his father – at the opening of Parliament. Some said that it killed every fine instinct, or at least emasculated it. The gossip was that the King had agonized over sending a bland telegram to Ramsay MacDonald, the Labour leader, when his wife was very ill. Toying with anarchy, they said in the Conservative press when MacDonald published it. A King had to listen, Ransom supposed – when she died a month later, there was no message of sympathy.

A conscientious man, yes, even a tenacious one. 'Busy with boxes' – one could imagine a typical diary entry. But there was something too deliberate about the way he would sit on edge in his high-backed chair, tapping the table with his pen as he talked. People would advise him and he would listen, but he was never able to extract information from them. 'Well, we never did that in the olden days,' was the strongest admonition Ransom had heard him muster, though for someone so content in his life style, it had some force. It was said that a housemaid at Windsor had lost her job for tampering with the furniture in the room in which Prince Albert had died – more than half a century before. The homeliness, directness and simple humour were not always allowed to be reciprocated, even if the American Ambassador was discovering to his amazement that he was able to chat to the King as if they were merely 'two human beings'.

Mr Page, who had become the Page of Doubleday, Page, the American publishing house, at the beginning of the century, had been rewarded with the Ambassadorship after his close support for Woodrow Wilson in the 1912 elections. He was said to be close to the President, to whom he recounted in some detail the perplexities of the English way of life. Already that evening he had been the object of an outburst from the Dowager Lady Chortleton. 'What would you do and what would you wish your son to do if you were me?' she asked, not expecting or desiring an answer. 'My husband's family has had a seat in the House of Lords for 600 years. My son sits there now – literally "sits", for a peer can do nothing else. All their power has been taken away. They are robbing us of our property. When they can they will abolish the monarchy itself. The King knows that his house is doomed.'

The Ambassador appraised George V's overall demeanour as

closely as he dared and as bravely as the representative of a great democratic country should. The King did not look doom-ridden.

'So many public engagements must be a great strain on Your Majesty,' Mr Page said politely.

'Oh, not so much,' the King replied kindly. 'One does grow up with it. I suppose the first public appearance is the one that sticks in the memory. Mine was more than twenty years ago, but I recall every detail. Poor Clarence – my brother, you know – had died in January and at the end of the year I acted as my father's deputy, opening the Royal Eye Hospital in Southwark. Even then I had Uncle George – the Duke of Cumberland – to support me.'

'My colleague, the former Ambassador, spoke warmly of the privilege he enjoyed in attending your Coronation,' the eager statesman continued.

'It was a great occasion for me,' the King commented. It was not quite clear whether he was humouring Page, or vice versa: probably there was an element of both. The Ambassador, dressed in what he liked to call 'my distinguished waiter-black', had not shown similar respect for the gaudily dressed representatives of other governments. 'We left the Palace not a moment later than half-past ten,' the King continued. 'The Coronation coach was drawn by eight horses and there must have been 50,000 of Kitchener's troops on the route, together with five or six times as many of our people. The service was frankly an ordeal, but beautiful too. I nearly broke down when dear David came to do homage to me – it reminded me so much of when I did the same thing to the late King, he did it so well. May looked wonderful – a great comfort to me to have her by my side, just as it has been every minute since' – the Queen merely nodded – 'but these things don't go on for ever. It was all work that afternoon, answering telegrams and letters.'

The King's last words were spoken with a finality, the unjarring abruptness that always indicated that he had become aware, perhaps by the workings of some mysterious inner clock, that he should move on to other guests. He caught the Prime Minister's eye, and Asquith's group rose respectfully to greet him. The King did not seem wholly at his ease, at least to the four pairs of practised eyes that faced him, probably because he was at his best with complete strangers rather than those who had come closer to him. Asquith was reminded of the sight – across the room – of the King at the buffet of the Hôtel de Ville not two months before: perfectly natural, enjoying a revivifying *sirop*, cheerfully fraternizing with those around him, none of whom had he met before.

Queen Mary preferred it that way. She disliked the easy familiarity his father had had for his rich, noisy friends and applauded the King's dislike for the games and gambling that had accompanied Edward VII's relationships. If George did occasionally go to the races, it was only because he was expected to; and if, above all, he enjoyed shooting, the arm's-length socializing that went with it was perfectly acceptable. She looked fondly at him: how strained he looked – his face had never found its natural colour since the typhoid attack. He must take care: the thimbleful of whisky with milk or soda that he allowed himself on such occasions was probably for the good and the compensating indulgence in creams and sweets could do no harm, surely? In private, she was happy that he should smoke, and that – she knew – he enjoyed.

The King greeted Margot and Rosalind with the courteous indifference that he displayed to all women. Nothing was more unlikely than – as an early rumour had it – that he had secretly married the daughter of an Admiral while he had been serving with the Mediterranean fleet.

'I gather that you had an exciting time, Sir, while the rest of us were trying to find some Whitsun peace,' said Margot.

'I trust your "peace" was pleasurable,' replied the King, not immediately responding to her comment. 'Yes, it was very embarrassing,' he continued with assurance. 'The fellow climbed over the railings and the wall at the bottom of Constitution Hill. It was dark and there were no sentries or policemen. Worse, he found a basement door open. We were lucky that it wasn't someone more dangerous – I wouldn't want the Suffragettes to know how easy it is to penetrate the Palace. We have already had windows smashed.'

This last remark was made with some gravity. If there was a species of woman about which the King was by no means relaxed, it was the Suffragette. Lavery's portrait of him in the Royal Scottish Academy had been slashed by Suffragette hands and it was not clear that future violence would be confined to property. Already a deputation had tried to force its way into the Palace to petition him against forcible feeding and it had taken a police cordon and more than sixty arrests to break up the demonstration. He hated the idea of force feeding and was worried at the effect it would have on public opinion; but they couldn't expect sympathy by calling him 'a Russian Tsar', raining inflammatory literature on law-abiding citizens, or by indulging in the thousand and one other disgraceful antics, scenes and outrages that had marked the Spring.

'I fear that it is we who may be in danger,' the Prime Minister said. 'I hear that Mrs Pankhurst is threatening to starve herself to death on the steps outside the House of Commons.'

'When a Hindu wants to do a really bad turn to someone,' Ransom murmured, not quite sure whether he was saying something foolish, 'he dies at the enemy's gate – and haunts the house for ever.'

Rosalind shivered. 'What an unpleasant idea.'

'Violence is always unpleasant,' Ransom replied.

'These are anxious days for all of us,' said the King. 'We must be prepared for violence from wherever it comes: please God it will not, but it threatens everywhere.'

'Yes, it seems strange to think that our grandfathers talked of "dear little Germany",' observed Asquith.

'Oh, but Prince Henry seems very nice.' Ransom glanced at Rosalind sharply, thinking that she had – not for the first time – rushed in too quickly, but the King too felt warmly about the Kaiser's brother, who was in England that summer with his sister Sophie, the Queen of Greece. 'With that I can agree,' George V declared. 'I have done my best to assure him that England will remain neutral in the event of any Continental conflict.'

When still a boy, the King had gone to Heidelberg, where he had stayed at the home of Professor Von Ihne in an attractive environment overlooking the Neckar, but his knowledge of the language remained rudimentary. His cousin, the Kaiser Wilhelm, had actually complained to the British Military Attaché that the Prince of Wales, as he then was, seemed reluctant to come to Berlin – the German regiment of which he was Colonel had taken great offence. Strange for someone whose surname might plausibly be Guelph or Wettin, but it was plain that he much disliked the studied histrionics of the Kaiser – the sort of man who would feel he had to put on the uniform of the Dragoon Guards just because he was eating English plum pudding. Since Queen Victoria had made him an Admiral, a Knight of the Garter and a Grand Commander of the Victorian Order, and Edward VII had given him a Field Marshal's baton, in addition to appointing him Colonel-in-Chief of the first Royal Dragoons, he had plenty of English ceremonial games that he could play. George's mother, Queen Alexandra, had helped to form his view of Wilhelm: she had spoken privately, and sometimes not so privately, of 'the fool' and ridiculed him for including in his entourage Herr Haby, whose sole daily responsibility was to train the Imperial moustaches upwards.

The King retreated into a momentary silent rehearsal of all his dislikes of Germany, but recovered himself quickly, and said: 'I'm very much afraid that Prince Henry is not typical of his country. They seem so rigid and aggressive, don't you know. Look at the trouble Reid had in Berlin.'

None of those present had any knowledge of any difficulties encountered by Sir James Reid, the King's doctor, in Germany and, in response to their puzzled looks, he continued. 'When we went to the wedding – the wedding of the Kaiser's daughter last year. Well, Reid took the wrong turn at the Opera – I forget the name of it: something inspired, if that's the right word, by the Kaiser. Would they allow him through the cordon around the box? Not a chance – not even when he waved the Kaiser's very favourite Grand Cross of the Red Eagle. The poor fellow was pushed into the crowded street and manhandled there: he was quite shaken, I believe.'

The King had the full attention of the company now, and he showed no sign of stopping. 'I must say it makes me feel that England is good enough for me. I like my country best, climate or no, and I'm staying in it. I'm not like my father: there is nothing of the cosmopolitan in me. I'm afraid', he finished with some satisfaction, 'that I'm insular all the way through.' This was true, in the broadest sense: George's deepest beliefs were in the invincibility of the Royal Navy and in the unequivocal rectitude of everything English.

The Queen, who was beginning to feel that the conversation was getting dangerously out of hand, asked a little abruptly: 'Have you seen my David this evening?' Why she should use the very last of the future Edward VIII's seven Christian names, Rosalind did not know. 'I saw the Prince of Wales dancing most energetically, with Princess Maud, a little earlier,' she said.

'If only he had attended to his studies at Oxford with the same diligence,' the Queen replied, almost (but not quite) with a sigh. The President of Magdalen, the Prince's college, had put it succinctly: 'Bookish he will never be'; and it had just been agreed that he and Oxford had had enough of each other, that he would spend the remainder of the year travelling before joining the Grenadier Guards the following January.

'Keep your hair on,' said the King, using a favourite expression acquired when he was with the Navy.

'That young man must be watched,' Queen Mary declared, and prepared to leave in search of him. Rosalind saw none of the dowdiness as she curtsied: the Queen's front was ablaze with diamonds, including the famous Koh-i-Noor; her gown was of Indian cloth of gold with a woven design of flowers and the corsage embroidered in gold. Surely this was majesty.

Margot Asquith would not have agreed, while the King took it all for granted. He returned to his topic of the moment without further pause. 'You see, none of the Continentals, certainly not the Germans, properly understand the dignity of monarchy.' He seemed oblivious of the fact that he was complimenting himself because he did not believe he was: it was the Englishness of England that he was applauding. 'In Berlin my cousin the Tsar handed out 600 decorations. We managed a mere 35. You can imagine the result?' It was impossible, Ransom discovered, not to nod. 'Of course! Everyone wanted an English order. Stamfordham told me that burglars left behind the Stanislaus when they were stealing from the house of one of the German generals: apparently the police decided that they must have got it already: enough people have!' The King guffawed.

Despite his situation, Ransom allowed his mind to wander. There was the Princess Maud, in a perfect gown – a mixture of pale pink and pale blue. There were the Yeomen of the Guard, on duty as the King's bodyguard. From the picture gallery came, faintly, the sounds of Tchaikovsky's *La Belle au Bois Dormant*. It really was all rather grand….

Now rather drunk, he could still hear the King, without fully taking in what he was saying on some new subject. On droned the voice: 'These women are too morbid. Here we are, having memorial services year after year. There I was as a boy, buying a new pair of black gloves every time and going to memorial services for the Prince Consort. And I never even saw the man. And here I am now, with one room in which my father slept, kept with a dressing gown over the chair, and my brother's room with his toothpaste undisturbed. If it went on we'd have no rooms left to live in. I've put it in my will that there are to be no memorial services for me. I wouldn't have it.'

Wills? Memorial services? What was all this about, Ransom pondered in an unagitated sort of way. This King was not going to need those for an age, surely?

It was something, perhaps, to be able to hold polite conversation with the King of England. In some ways a strain, too, but the endless champagne certainly helped: faces, sentences, postures, pictures passed rapidly through his thoughts as uncontrolled reminders of the evening's events.

Beside him, in Clarges Street, Anna stirred, signed and opened her eyes. She smiled and kissed him lightly on the lips.

'Back from feudal times at last,' she murmured, without malice.

'It's hard work,' he replied, 'even if Margot does help to liven things up.'

'I don't know why you bother,' she continued playfully.

'I'm not the one who wants to change everything. You, on the other hand, have to be very careful not to be tainted by our evil ways.'

There were times when Anna Kinsky could be as taut, as acerbic and as unyielding as all the anarchist tracts that she spent long hours compiling or writing or distributing. Now was not one of them. It was a genuinely happy moment – the last they were to know in the weeks ahead.

Her eyes flashed before him, as rich and as varied in hue as all the browning leaves of autumn rolled into one. She pushed him onto his back, her nose quivering in a sort of dance of delight, while her mouth broke quickly into a smile that was in perfect, sparkling union with the rest of her features.

In a gesture that managed – without effort or skill on his part – to be both strong and gentle at the same time, he pushed her off him and they rolled over, tightly together, until he was on top of her.

Anna gave him the spontaneity he otherwise lacked, and he was grateful.

'Your heart beats like jungle drums,' she said immediately afterwards.

'It may not always. I need you, and its beat would cease at the thought of life without you.' He was serious, but she shrugged it off and said, not without warmth: 'Don't spoil it with silly words. I wonder at what I feel for you. That is enough, I think. Death will end it, as death ends everything.'

'Why, what a solemn girl you are!' Anna said nothing. He added: 'If I can have you until death, then I can be content – it is tomorrow, next week, next month that frighten me.'

'Death comes quickly enough' was the enigmatic reply.

Then, in silence, they lay together in a spent tangle of limbs, only to be momentarily startled by the ringing of the telephone. At first it seemed that neither of them would move, but suddenly, in a pandemonium of flying arms and legs and bedclothes, they both made for the telephone.

Anna picked it up and Ransom settled down onto the bed, revelling in the shape of her body, its back towards him, patterned by the light from the window in the ceiling above.

'Yes,' she said. He thought he caught a note of anxiety in her voice.

'Not now. I don't know why you telephone me here.'

Then, in response to the voice at the other end: 'Later, it will have to be later.'

She put the telephone down and returned to the bed. His ex-

29

pectant look was not rewarded with an explanation. So he asked, not unkindly, 'Who was that?'

'Someone.'

'Yes?'

'You don't own me, you know.' And then: 'I'm sorry. I didn't mean that. But it isn't always so easy, consorting secretively, slyly even, with someone who is a part of everything that would like to destroy you.'

'It isn't like that.'

'No. But ... you understand.'

He nodded. Reality came sneaking in. 'Time to be going, in any case. In four hours I'm meant to be the Prime Minister's first appointment of the morning.'

He dressed quickly, kissed her once more, and turned just before he reached the door. 'I don't want it to be like this any more than you do. You believe that, don't you?'

'Yes,' she said, though perhaps she did not mean it – how could she really know? And then he was gone.

* * *

Anna lay still for a long time, the covers pushed in a pile to the end of the bed, her legs slightly apart as she rested on her back, her eyes closed. Eventually, she slung her legs to the left, down to the floor, and walked, silently, to the telephone that lay on the mahogany chest to the left of the door.

She spoke to the operator. 'Central 6124, please.'

Just near Old Street Tube Station, in City Road, was the German-owned City House Hotel. At this hour, 6 a.m., only a single figure could be seen at its reception. He sat rather still. To the right, above his head, a sign proclaimed: 'Rooms from 2s 6d. Lift – Steam Radiators – Electric Light – Newly Built. Für Familien wie auch für einzelne Damen und Herren.'

The telephone rang. 'Ja.'

'It's me,' said Anna. 'We don't have to argue. I've decided. You know I don't like it, but I have no choice. I'm ready to do whatever you want.'

The man grunted, smiled and carefully replaced the receiver.

CHAPTER TWO

A mission for the
Prime Minister

IN this June of 1914 anger and discord lay in every direction. In Ireland, Curse-the-Pope-put-your-foot-in-his-belly Orangemen were irreconcilably divided from the race of Catholic Nationalists. There was no politics as Ransom knew it, only two peoples bent on self-destruction. In that crazy country, James Larkin the Syndical-ist, William Murphy the laissez-faire capitalist, Joseph Devlin the Radical and John Redmond, one of the most deeply conservative men he had ever met, all managed to be Nationalists.

While leading statesmen of the day played golf, the Member of Parliament for Dublin University, Sir Edward Carson, had rushed off to Ulster over Whitsun 'to make arrangements for the final scene', reiterating Lord Randolph Churchill's old cry: 'Ulster will fight and Ulster will be right.' If his face, as Baron Franckenstein of the Austrian Embassy had observed, was hewn out of granite, the same might be said of his ideals. Mr Page, the American Ambassador, said grimly to Ransom at the Buckingham Palace Ball: 'Somehow it reminds me of the tense days of the slavery controversy before the Civil War.' And he was right. Protestant clergy in full canonicals blessed the colours of the armed Ulster Volunteers as they paraded to the accompaniment of prayers and hymns.

> One Law, one Land, one Throne
> If England drive us forth
> We shall not fall alone

The Catholic Nationalist counterparts of the Protestant men, with a Volunteer army growing by the hundred daily, were fast proving that they were no novices when it came to running arms and ammunition.

How could it happen? The Catholics wanted Home Rule. The Liberal Government of which Ransom was a part had introduced the necessary legislation. It was the third time since Mr Gladstone's Bill in 1886 that a government had tried to introduce a measure of self-rule for the Irish. The Ulstermen would not have it, and – more important – the Conservative and Unionist Opposition in Westminster would not have it. In this topsy-turvy situation the party whose creed was synonymous with loyalty, with law and order and with traditional authority encouraged riot and rebellion, the corrosion of constitutional forms of behaviour.

'I utterly deny that the Army is the instrument of the Government,' Lord Robert Cecil had asserted, in an unconvincing historical analysis. 'The Army is the instrument of the nation, and you have no right to use it as the instrument of a mere party body like the Government.' When, in March 1914, a group of officers in the military camp at the Curragh, near Dublin, made it clear that they would rather be dismissed from the service than take part in Ulster's coercion, the War Office in London gave them an assurance that they would not have to enforce the Home Rule Bill. An angry Asquith insisted on – and received – the resignation of his colleague Colonel Seely, the Secretary for War, but there was little doubt that the Army had successfully pressurized the Government.

Nothing, it seemed, could end this power Ireland had – as Winston said – 'to lay her hands upon the vital strings of British life and politics and to hold, dominate and convulse, year after year, generation after generation, the life of its people.'

Others learned the lesson. Just three days before, the Norman Church at Wargrave had been burnt out in the early hours. They had saved the Parish Register – that had survived all threats to it since 1538 – but outside the blackened church lay Suffragette messages. If even churches could be set on fire, would life itself be taken next?

As it was, the railwaymen's leader had already threatened that if wage negotiations failed, he might go to his people and – like the Ulstermen, like the Suffragettes – organize his forces. There were half a million pounds waiting in union funds which would buy enough weapons to kit out an army. Miners, railwaymen and transport workers talked of a Triple Alliance to win their demands.

In this new world there was a vital awareness of the strength that comes from banding together – and a vital ignorance of the destructive lunacy let forth when human beings combine their strength.

Only the very poor seemed, as usual, to have missed the message. Anna taught Ransom that, made poverty real to him. When she had softened him through the power of her own account, she made him read the reports he had always ignored. Alexander Paterson, journeying *Across the Bridges* from comfortable London, found the unemployed man of thirty who had given up playing games, given up making love to his wife, given up the dream of a better future. He did not even shudder as he went out into the darkness and cold of the street; he would shuffle along, no sign of anguish, no sign at all in his eyes. And as Arthur Ponsonby, someone despised as a traitor to his class, graphically described: 'Man of no occupation. Married. Two rooms; two children; parish relief; ill; incapable; two little girls, one consumptive. The rooms are miserable, badly ventilated and damp. The house shares one closet with six other houses, and one water tap with three others.'

The poor were unmoved by the German menace, but many others felt it keenly. Each year in Germany there were hundreds of thousands of new Germans born, eagerly learning from their parents that their country's might and vitality must be acknowledged by the rest of the world. The alliance system had become over-rigid; instead of acting to stifle conflict, it threatened to encourage it to develop into general war. Fear and mistrust had produced an arms race; public opinion – excited and organized through a new popular press – was not allowed to respect compromise. If the Irish and the Suffragettes and the militant trade unions did not destroy the British way of life from within, there was more than a chance that everyone else would join in the destruction of the peoples of Europe in the war that had been so narrowly avoided for so long.

Problems on all sides. And yet still the British (Ransom would not have excluded himself) put their bets on inaction. They had learned that the way to strength lay in keeping calm: *solvitur ambulando* had been the great Queen Elizabeth's motto – everything at walking pace. If men paraded their arms in Ireland, they surely would not embark on civil war. If workers went on strike in England, they surely would not riot. If nations bristled with armaments, sharpened their knives and ground their teeth in Europe, they surely – the diplomats confirmed – bore no seriously unfriendly feelings towards each other.

It sometimes seemed as if the frantic pursuit of the pleasures of Society was a response to suppressed fears. One should enjoy oneself while one could, as *Punch* understood:

'Do come to dinner tonight and afterwards to Diana's dance.'

'But I am not asked.'

'Nonsense. Come with me; we have all been counting on you. Since lunchtime.'

Ransom knew this kind of life well enough. London was the largest city in the world; no other capital, Paris always excepted, sucked up, sponge-like, so much of the life around it. The four-mile radius from Park Lane enjoyed an unearned social increment of such prodigiously increasing value, a popular paper quipped, that Ransom's colleague Mr Lloyd George should have taxed it. This was the last city to set the Thames on fire: it was dilettante, anaesthetizing, sterile; it treated politics as a minor offshoot of social activity, despised intellect, babbled and blathered but did not shape events. It revelled in dinners, balls, receptions, parties; in polo and ballooning and automobile racing and now aviation; in Henley Regatta or the tennis at Wimbledon…anything but seriousness of purpose.

That, at least, was how Ransom felt some of the time, as Anna influenced him. She herself was clearer. If it was terrible that violence threatened, in a sense it was worse that it was suppressed. From all directions the traditional way of life was under siege; but everything in England dictated compromise, half-measures, peace from fundamental disagreement. How typical it was that the only casualty of anarchist violence in England was a Frenchman – Marcel Bourdin, who blew himself up by mistake in Greenwich in 1894. All he managed was to provide the plot for a novel – Joseph Conrad's *The Secret Agent*. In England literature seemed more plausible – more satisfying – than real life. The ultimate complacency, Anna said.

* * *

'Real life', on the other hand, was about to show a will of its own. Back in Berkeley Square Ransom lingered slightly longer over breakfast than usual. He was not due to see the Prime Minister until ten o'clock and – since he was not sure what the meeting was for – he was too unsettled to begin on anything else. In *The Times* he read of the failure of Chaplin, Milne, Grenfell & Co. – with liabilities approaching £2,000,000. His Cabinet Minister's salary of £5,000 a year would not have been much comfort had he involved himself in the City in a big and reckless way, but his inherited wealth – not an inconsiderable sum – was wisely, and cautiously, put to good use. Risking scandal through his association with Anna was one thing; risking financial ruin another – and unnecessary. Besides, however much everyone remembered what had happened to Dilke and Parnell, it was far more likely that a political career would be threatened by financial than by marital difficulties.

So far as he knew, Rosalind did not know of Anna's existence, and he supposed that she must think he found a sexual outlet by paying for it; that would not have been unusual and was perfectly acceptable, provided no affection was involved. He had told her firmly that he wanted no more children and that if she wanted a fuller physical relationship she must be prepared to use the contraceptive device she continued to find 'not decent'. She was unlikely to risk divorce, even if she were the innocent party: no woman ever quite survived that with her reputation totally intact. No, Rosalind was a moody, difficult but fundamentally realistic woman, whatever the circumstances. Apart from her son, she was probably closest to her widowed mother, who would descend on Berkeley Square at frequent intervals with a mountain of luggage, since it had been many years since she had had a home in town.

'Will you take some more tea, Sir, or may I clear away?' Elsie asked.

'Yes, clear the table by all means,' Ransom said. Elsie was a helpful sort, a month or two over the age of eighteen, and though he was rarely conscious of her existence, he could not help musing contentedly this morning on the pleasant, plumpish girl before him. Anna for passion, Rosalind for good order's sake, Elsie for pleasure? Perhaps not: he was not a man who sought more complications in life than seemed already thrust upon him. There were Elsies enough to be had if the occasion demanded: one in three of all the girls in the country between the ages of 15 and 20 was in domestic service, so Blunt's paper had told him.

It gave them, usually, a good home – better than they had known – and security, he supposed. But not an easy life: he was just sufficiently tinged by the 'radicalism' that had made him a Liberal to be conscious that cleaning grates, lighting fires, washing steps, polishing brass or boots, carrying water, turning heavy mattresses, waiting at table, fetching coal for upwards of 14 hours a day was an exacting vision of paradise. It was surprising that Elsie and her companions remained, in the main, so cheerful: there was a warmth about them – except for Travis, David's former nanny – that he did not often find among his peers. Perhaps it was because of his upbringing: ample indications of being part of a superior clan, and yet a coldness too – education at first at home, then the rigours of Eton; frequent experience of the cane – never from the servants, always from his father; no freedom to deviate from the norm. Be silent, eat all that is on your plate, stop slouching…. It taught him how to give orders, and that did for most of life. Still….

He rose noisily from the breakfast table and walked thoughtfully into the hall. He passed Elsie, busying herself with cups and saucers, without a glance and, at the door, another servant handed him his hat, his Malacca cane and his gloves. Upstairs, Rosalind – recently emerged from bed – scowled at the grey hairs visible in the mirror of her dressing table.

Outside, he hailed a passing cab, which took him through

Trafalgar Square; between here and Parliament Square close by, the entire administration of a great Empire was concentrated.

Inside No. 10 Downing Street, he was ushered to the Cabinet Room, where Asquith sat at the green-covered table round which so much history had been made in such unelaborate, almost austere surroundings. Even at this hour, it seemed ill-lit and in the dimness, as the notes of Big Ben boomed in the distance, it was not difficult to imagine his distant predecessors shaping the future.

Asquith, Gardiner remarked, was the finest product of the Balliol system – which avoided excessive zeal and 'distrusts great thoughts even if it thinks them'. He looked up slowly as Ransom entered, in that quiet, detached way that would be taken for incurable laziness by anyone who did not know that he had the capacity for fast, concentrated thought. A year or two over sixty, he was at the peak of his prestige, presiding over a Cabinet which had crusading genius in the shape of Lloyd George, wonderful gravity in Sir Edward Grey and creative brilliance in Winston Churchill at its call: more than enough to compensate for the declining powers of Burns, Haldane and Morley.

Asquith had before him a map of Ireland and a sheaf of figures produced by civil servants on the mix of population and religion in the same country.

'Ah, Walter. Good of you to come,' he said. 'I expect you are wondering why I asked you.'

Ransom smiled, concealing his inner unease. As the only member of the Cabinet without a specific portfolio, it was often difficult for him to know what would enhance, and what would harm, his position.

'These are not easy times for the Government. I don't need to remind you of what has been happening in recent by-elections. Losing a single seat would not be good, but Bethnal Green, Leith, Derbyshire North-East and Ipswich is too much to ignore in such a short period. You won't see any by-elections resulting from the next Honours List, I can assure you!'

'It's the Labour vote that worries me for the long term,' Ransom commented. 'The working people now seem to be prepared to use politics in pursuit of their individual ends.'

'"Our trade, our politics". Yes, it's a pernicious doctrine. But if the Labour Party meets them on the idea, then the Labour Party will have their votes.' The Prime Minister sat back in his chair. 'It saddens me, you know. I do not know how we could have gone further or faster in all our reforms. I am, frankly, proud of them – and so are all the great working-class figures, the Burts, the Fenwicks, who have given us such support.'

Asquith would not allow himself more than a moment of such reflection, Ransom mused, and he was right. 'And yet we must be practical,' the Prime Minister continued. 'There is another factor in this, and we would not be proposing an electoral pact with the Labour people if it were not so.'

'Ireland?'

'Precisely. Ireland.'

Asquith relaxed slightly. 'For a long time after our great landslide in 1906 we could well afford to ignore the Irish and the Catholic votes, but not after 1910. What we now have is a very nasty post-dated political cheque presented to us – and we have to listen to the Nationalists. If we give more to the Protestants than Redmond and his supporters can vote for, then Redmond will release his English supporters from voting Liberal. That might mean – at a guess – 80 seats lost to us, and more will go to the Tories if we quarrel with Labour.'

'You can never ignore the Irish in safety,' Ransom retorted. 'I am no great enthusiast for the work of Mr Bernard Shaw, but this time he is right. "If you break a nation's nationality it will think of nothing else. It will listen to no reformer, to no philosopher, to no

40

preacher, until the demand of the Nationalist is granted." Besides, with Dublin having the highest mortality rate in Europe, it was surely a great mistake to allow the trade unionists to channel their grievances through the Nationalists.'

'Perhaps. What worries me more is this. If we do get the Royal Assent to the Home Rule Bill, the chances are that Carson will set up a Provisional Government in Belfast on the same day. And that will mean Civil War.'

'Even Bonar Law is saying that there are things stronger than Parliamentary majorities. It's incredible.'

'All too credible, I'm afraid. It is all very well to proclaim in public that Ireland is one nation not two – I have done so myself. But we must ask ourselves: would public opinion support a war waged to suppress a million loyal British subjects protesting against their subjection to a creed they detest? The Tories have a gift, and they would win an election on it, I'm sure. Moreover, these are the facts: all the power, the political power, the social power, the economic power in the north of Ireland is concentrated in Protestant hands. Belfast's economic ties are to Glasgow and Liverpool, not Dublin.'

Asquith paused. 'Now listen. We've known about an arms build up for some time through some slick work by Kell's men at MI5, but the really bad thing is that the Germans seem to be involved. And I don't merely mean that they have some clever businessmen.'

'You mean the Kaiser?'

'Possibly. That's what I wanted to see you about. I need you to find out.'

Momentarily startled, Ransom managed: 'An Irish matter is for Birrell, isn't it?'

'I don't think he will do in this case. He never wanted the Chief Secretary's job; he said as much. Besides, the civil servants seem to have persuaded him that things are not nearly as bad as they seem. I don't think he realized what a gaffe he had committed when he said that Ireland had not been so peaceful for 400 years. Until I sent him over in the Spring, he hadn't been near Dublin or Ireland for months.'

Augustine Birrell had never been an adequate Chief Secretary for Ireland, and it was Asquith himself who had always been in effective charge of Home Rule negotiations. Birrell was too indolent, in the nicest sort of way, to want to tackle their complexities. He was the 54th Chief Secretary since the Act of Union and took the job, he said, 'because the Prime Minister asked me to'.

'I don't want to mislead you,' Asquith said. 'I wish that all our colleagues were as good-natured and witty as Birrell – and I wish even more that the Irish responded to those qualities. They don't.'

'Birrelling', Ransom reflected, had passed into the language – at least into the language of the political establishment in their London clubs – as a synonym for superficial judgment, agreeable games-playing. By comparison the Prime Minster seemed an intellectual giant, as Ransom had been able to observe when he sat, with Birrell, Churchill and two others on the Cabinet Committee on Ulster, which Asquith had set up in March.

The Prime Minister rose from his chair and walked over to the window. Turning back to Ransom, he said: 'The Ulster Volunteers have been landing arms. At Larne. At Donaghadee. Perhaps elsewhere. You may recognize the name of the chief conspirator, if I may call Major Frederick Crawford that.'

'The lunatic who once tried to kidnap Gladstone?'

'The very same. He's getting huge quantities of new rifles through Hamburg. There's a fair assortment of older stuff as well, and no shortage of funds. They charter steamers for the purpose, and change the names. Carson is involved up to the hilt – he sits in Eaton Square, but the telegrams we've intercepted leave no doubt.'

'And why do you suspect the German Government may be involved?'

'They don't really hide it. Traffic has been stopped in the Kiel Canal to let the steamers get round Denmark into the North Sea, out of sight of our own navy. Carson's followers brag that a powerful foreign monarch, initial 'W', will help them. The damning thing is that the Germans are helping the Nationalists too. They have a man in New York, Albert Sander, who has been very successful in getting the support – and the money – of the leaders of the Clan-na-Gael.'

Ransom looked blank.

'You know how Ireland is riddled with secret societies. The Clan is the American controlling end of the Ancient Order of Hibernians. We have watched things closely there and we know that the US representative of Krupps has placed more than one order for dynamite and detonators: Krupps don't need that for home consumption.'

'Surely the Irish Nationalists can't see Germany as a friend?'

'Don't be so sure. They may not want to exchange English for German domination, but they wouldn't disapprove of an Anglo-German war: they could expect better Home Rule terms from the Kaiser, I don't doubt.'

Asquith paused again. 'This is not something that can be dealt with through normal channels. What I want you to do is go to Germany and talk to the top people directly, find out what's going on, and what can be done to stop it. We've gone as far as we can behind the scenes.'

'They'll respond?'

'Oh, the details can be quickly arranged,' he said in a surprisingly cavalier tone. Perhaps he was relieved that Ransom had not demurred. 'We shall say nothing to the Germans for a few days yet, and I shall arrange for you to have a full briefing. Meantime, of course, speak to no one of this.'

'Not even our colleagues?'

'Especially not them,' said Asquith, as he smiled for the first time that morning.

His face quickly returned to its clouded expression. 'Walter, this is important. Whatever happens on the Continent we can probably ignore; but Ireland is different; and if Germany meddles in Ireland that is worse. We cannot absolutely count on the loyalty of the army, and the Germans saw the potential of the situation some time ago: Von Bode, from the Embassy, made a lengthy visit to Ulster a year ago. So…our future might well depend on what you can do.'

As Ransom was leaving, he encountered Lord Stamfordham, the King's Private Secretary, and stopped to talk briefly to him. He seemed brusquer and more direct than usual, probably because he was asked if he would forgive the Prime Minister for keeping him waiting – alas, Asquith would not be free for another 15 minutes.

'This Irish business is damned serious,' Stamfordham said, almost fiercely. For a moment Ransom thought he must be referring specifically to the conversation he had just had with the Prime Minister, but he quickly realized that the other man must be making a reference to the whole question of Home Rule. 'Asquith is absolutely constant in his assurances to the King that everything will come right in the end,' Stamfordham continued. 'And I get exactly the same from Lloyd George. "We lawyers", he told me the other day, "know perfectly well that the most critical cases are often settled out of court at the last moment."' He snorted. 'As if Mr George was a leading member of the Bar!'

Ransom nodded. 'He might as well have said, "We financiers" for all his understanding of the intricacies of economics,' he observed mischievously. 'Still, we must hope that he is right. The Prime Minister, in any event, steers a very firm course.'

'And takes a very long time about it,' Stamfordham replied impatiently, glancing at his watch.

* * *

After Ransom had gone, the Prime Minister had waited a moment and then said to his secretary, 'Send in Kell.'

It was fortunate for his peace of mind that Ransom did not hear the conversation that followed.

Captain Vernon Kell, late of the South Staffordshire regiment and now in his early forties, listed his interests in *Who's Who* as 'fishing and croquet' (later in life, he dropped the croquet). Perhaps it was these profoundly ungentlemanly pursuits that gave him the obstinate ruthlessness he employed to such good effect in persuading his peers of the importance of something so dishonourable as spying. Besides, as Baden-Powell had said, 'though the agent, if caught, may go under, unhonoured and unsung, he knows in his heart of hearts that he has done his bit for his country as fully as his comrade who falls in battle'. As it happened, Kell's father, Major Waldegrave C.F. Kell, had been a member of the same regiment, but his mother was the daughter of a Polish Count with friends and connections all over Europe. It was no fool who stood before Asquith and listened alertly to what the Prime Minster said.

'But we know he's a risk, Sir. I don't understand why you're so indifferent to what I've told you about that girl, Anna Kinsky. The trail leads straight to her from all those foreign plotters and anarchists in the East End. You should ask Ransom to resign.'

'In time, perhaps,' said Asquith defensively. 'But not while he can be useful. You forget that, while we know a lot, we don't know everything. There are too many missing pieces in this jigsaw. Watch him – and her – by all means. But make sure he has all he needs in Berlin. There's nothing like letting those who might destroy you work for you instead.'

Asquith became slightly cooler. 'I trust you have no doubts about my other colleagues?'

'You should tell me if I should, I think.'

'Yes,' said the Prime Minister tartly. The meeting was at an end.

Kell's task was an uphill one. The Boer War had helped to show up British deficiencies in the field of intelligence, but when Kell's 'department' had been set up five years before, it consisted initially of himself, supported by the tiniest of budgets and allocated one small room in the War Office. The existence of British counter-espionage was not recognized at all in law and until 1911 an antiquated Official Secrets Act did not even allow for action against spying in peacetime. But 'K', as he became known, was well suited to the challenge. In his view, war with Germany was bound to come: he had visited the country in 1908 and even then felt that the signs were clear.

The Captain would have been an interested eavesdropper had he heard Anna talking on the telephone to the City House Hotel earlier that morning: the man she had spoken to, who seemed to have some hold over her actions, was Karl Gustav Ernst – in charge of communications for the German Secret Service in London. But despite what Kell had said provocatively to the Prime Minister, it was precisely because he did not – yet – have a full picture of the German activities, and how they might relate to the anarchists, that he was not ready to act. When the time came, he would call on the efficient help of the ambitious head of Scotland Yard's Special Branch, the extraordinary Old Etonian Basil Thomson, whose busy life had already included periods working for the Kings of Tonga and Siam, as well as being Governor of Dartmoor Prison.

Despite everything, 'K' looked to the future with some confidence. He had managed to gather a staff of fourteen, and that was a beginning only. To some extent he had freed himself of the bureaucrats by moving out of the War Office and was happily ensconced in the basement of the Little Theatre in John Street, off the Strand. If Asquith and his colleagues were not always as helpful as they might be, he would stick at it. He had at least one good ally in Winston Churchill, who had got him the necessary authorization to open the correspondence of suspects. He was enjoying himself more than at any time since the Boxer Rebellion, in which his courage, and his knowledge of Chinese, had been put to good effect. Enemies of England should be on their guard.

CHAPTER THREE

Anna

WHILE the Prime Minster and 'K' talked, Ransom went to find Anna. Past the taxidermist, with its rhinoceros heads and tiger-skin rugs, situated a few doors from the junction of Piccadilly and Clarges Street. Then a discreet entry into 'their' house, where he found a brief note: 'Back in two days. Love – A.' Nothing more. He cursed and felt much in need of her. After going over to the bed, he flopped down, tiredness catching up with him.

A strange woman, Anna. Through her the lives of the broken, the helpless, the shiftless failures had been given a reality to him for the first time; and yet her vitality was proof that out of misery came forth joy. We spend our lives coming to terms with our formative experiences, he thought; but when did those formative experiences begin and when did they end? Why should memory count for so much? Why couldn't we just change the past by an act of will? The most radical never questioned or reconstructed the mere version of events that is their memory of their own past, however dismal – as if to do so was a sort of self-mutilation.

So much had happened on the day he had first seen Anna, more than three years before. Winston Churchill's excited telephone call, asking him to join him, had been followed by a frantic dash through the traffic into the East End to Sidney Street – there to find the mysterious figures wanted for the triple murder of policemen some weeks before. They missed the gunfire that wounded Sergeant Leeson, who was bravely holding a site opposite the house by the brewery wall, but the arrival of two squads of Scots Guards fully prepared to fight helped to alleviate the danger. As lunchtime approached, smoke began to seep from behind the barricade of bedding and furniture erected by the defendants. No one could tell whether the fire, which had quickly spread, had been started from outside or in, but in the ruins the remains of several bodies were found – Joseph Marx, a bullet through his brain, and Fritz Svaars, apparently the victim of suffocation. These men were identified as political refugees from Eastern Europe, but rumour persistently identified them with the anarchists who had made the East End the centre of their activity.

Fifty yards from the house in Sidney Street, in a road which lay parallel to it – Jubilee Street – was the Anarchist Club. Peter the Painter, one of those said to be connected with Marx and Svaars and of whom there was no sign after the siege, had acquired his nickname by painting the stage designs for the anarchist political dramas performed there. Whether his name was Peter Piatkow or Peter Straume, as he was variously called, or whether – as Kell suspected – he was really the Tsarist agent Serge Makharov, would never be known, and further muddied some very muddy waters. In this strange environment, Churchill and Ransom, with the police and the soldiers, temporarily gathered in the aftermath.

In a large, mainly empty room, which had a gallery above it and contained only a few old pieces of wooden furniture and seating, the only colourful feature was the wall posters and slogans in Yiddish. A tall, thin girl with jet black hair and eyes whose passion could not quite disguise their tenderness, was taking the opportunity – bizarrely – to try to sell the Club's newspaper, the *Arbeiter Fraint*. Stung by curiosity, but without exchanging a word, Ransom bought a copy. In it he read:

'We have entered a period of mass-murder such as the world has not known before. All the crimes of the past will pale before this, will look like child's play against it. No one knows what awaits us. Those of us who will live to see the end of it will tell of experiences such as no human tongue has told before.'

It meant nothing to him, but later – lying restlessly awake in bed that night – he thought again of the girl and the intensity with which she had set about selling her papers and pamphlets. In his life people did not have that look in their eyes; it was not to be seen in Westminster, still less in the drawing rooms of Society; nor even in his wife, whose emotional torments seemed to be without purpose or direction.

Of the communities of the East End of London, the Jews, the Irish, the native working class, he knew little. In Bethnal Green he had once visited the tall blocks of model dwellings, constructed like prisons or military barracks as if to impose order on those who did not understand self-discipline. Individuality lapsed into public squalor in the wash-houses in the yard, for use by everyone, the shared lavatories on the landings, the fetid communal rubbish shoots. There he was told that the people enjoyed destroying the chance that had been given to them, and he probably believed it.

With sanctimonious innocence, he followed Thomas Holmes in his study of *London's Underworld*. Up six flights of stairs – dark and greasy – along narrow passages, slimy moisture on the walls, past the semi-darkness of the landings, to where the match-box-maker lives: the beds covered with little boxes, the floors too; 1 – 2 – 3 – 4 over his shoulder they go; there – horrors – one dead child and one newly born sharing the room with the living.

Yes, the image lingered. But he had felt something closer to revulsion than compassion. Why did people choose to live like this?

It was emphatically not to answer such a question that he set out for the East End again several days after the Sidney Street siege. Rosalind and he were not on speaking terms and whether for that or deeper reasons he wanted to find that face again – the face of Anna. He had no idea of what he wanted to say to her; that, perhaps, would take care of itself. In the Whitechapel Road he passed a baby's funeral: a single carriage, with a tiny box for coffin, a driver with white hat band, no bearers. Posters announced the efficacy of Himrod's for asthma, Benger's for 'Digestive Rest' and Biomalz as the tonic food. A gang of scruffy schoolchildren banged improvised drums, made out of tin cans, and sang:

Mrs Pankhurst
She's the first
And Mrs Lily with a nine-pound hammer in her hand
Breaking windows down the Strand
If you catch her
Lay her on a stretcher
Knock her on the Robert E. Lee

Above their heads, the largest of posters proclaimed: 'Life is service. Ye are the salt of the earth. Ye are the light of the world. A city that is set on a hill cannot be hid. Let your light so shine before men that they may see your good works, and glorify your Father which is in heaven.' At this Salvation Army hostel a farthing would buy you a cup of tea and a large slice of bread and jam. Those who ran it did indeed serve, but children strong and loud enough to sing irreverent songs fell outside the definition of service. He watched as the last of them, far faster than her uniformed chaser and resplendent in boy's peaked cap and ancient lace-up boots, lifted her voluminous skirts in insult before disappearing round the corner.

Not so far from here, in a small neighbourhood containing perhaps the most densely packed urban life in the world, was the area to which the Jewish immigrants had flocked in previous decades, to adjoin – but not to join – the Irish.

This unique landscape, which was later subject to scholarly analysis by Lloyd Gartner and William Fishman, was quite different from the new slums of Bethnal Green. The immigrants came to what were once the homes of relatively prosperous skilled workers, or even traders and merchants with sufficient material worth to aspire to gentility. But the original owners had long gone. A mass of little homes and lodgings, with too many foul culs-de-sac and narrow passages, unattended refuse in ugly heaps, monstrous piles of stinking rags from the small-time garment manufacturers – and, here and there, struggling businesses and storehouses, or railway tracks and their attendant constructions.

He travelled on foot, down the pot-holed roads, past blocked, smelling gutters. Here there were rows upon rows of terraced houses set below the pavement, so that he might easily have stepped directly into upstairs rooms. Shops no larger than a small room offered a limited range of goods – fuel or dried fish, sour brown bread, unpleasant-looking sausages and salt herrings. Decrepit buildings announced the possibility of 'loshings' or 'bekrum' being available. Next door to the Anarchist Club, passers-by were offered coffee and 'tie'. On the pavement, a pale, consumptive Jew, his hair cut so close as to make him nearly bald, sat idly with a companion. 'That your life may be a long one.' He spoke unprompted.

'I remember you,' she said. The smile was genuine. There was no need for formality, no need, it seemed, for explanation. It was almost as if she understood his need to know everything about her, his search for a reason for being there.

The world revealed to him was a strange one. In it, even the strongest did not stand upright and acquired a deathly white complexion; tailors, shoemakers, furriers, hatmakers, seamstresses, working together – when there was work – in a dust-filled, stifling atmosphere for all the daylight hours and more. All the lung diseases, the 'white plague' of tuberculosis, found homes here. Sweaters and sweated existed on cold coffee and bread and cheese, working without a break, with unlimited application, in the fierce heat from the stove – oblivious or uncaring of their surroundings.

Nowhere, not even in death, was there privacy: in the *hebra*, in tiny places of worship – in homes or shops or even churches abandoned by the Gentiles – shrill, clamorous services almost without cessation, and readings from the Talmud, were only one aspect of the total togetherness. Disease, death and its aftermath, not just prayer, were causes of gathering, with the *shammash* in command. Outside, the squalor seemed unaffected, the *hebra* appearing as another wretched home or workplace in minimal disguise. Little wonder that the East End was always a *freie Medinah*, in which the luxury of an Orthodox Rabbi was out of the question. In Whitechapel Road, on a Saturday, the dealers were always busying themselves to find machinists or pressers: in the evening a new week's work would start, if only there were orders to be satisfied.

One image, especially remained with her. 'I remember them in the snow,' she said; 'in the dark of January, before dawn, a jumble of men like big black insects, Gentiles and Jews, in a back street behind the Town Hall. For an age we waited, myself in the shadow of my father, the snow whitening the blackness of our coats. Our bodies were too frozen to move; our feet no longer belonged to us. Not until after eight did the authorities acknowledge us and the first hundred from ten times as many more were hired, a few pence for each hour worked on whatever unsavoury labour would be for the public good, and nothing until a full day's torment was complete. Many dropped as the day wore on – among them my father, carried home by the combined efforts of my mother and two friends.

'The man in charge said: "Even if you give these people a job, they don't do it."'

Quietly, she asked: 'Do you begin to understand why you find me at the Anarchist Club?'

In the London of 1914 there were, perhaps, 180,000 Jews, seven times as many as sixty years before. Anna's father, who had dealt modestly in furs in Hamburg, seemed devoid of the energy to try again when he arrived with his wife and daughter in the summer of 1900. Their first experience of an 'English' home was a room in Chicksand Street at a shilling a week, next door to them a Gentile couple whose prize and practically only possessions – a clock and a china tea-service – had been pawned the previous winter: they were something of a Gentile island in a Jewish sea, but lacked the will to move.

The anaemic wife, Tilly Bowden, was in any case prematurely old, and had less than a year to live. Anna's childhood memories of her were, in retrospect, almost a medical diagnosis: her gums were tinged faintly with blue; she seemed to lose her sight for short, and soon for longer, periods and would bump into objects around her; and she would sit with aching head in her hands, or vomit onto the floor, too weak or tired to go into the street, with its water tap. Much to her father's annoyance, she had once, fascinated, shared a bowl of Tilly's soup: carrot and onion and cabbage, a free bone from the butcher, a few herbs, not much else.

Anna had watched her die: a thin, pale-faced girl of twelve, peering with enormous, startled eyes, frightened but still childishly inquisitive, through the open door as the convulsion spread from limb to limb, until the whole body was in movement oblivious of its unconscious owner.

She had run from the house, run until she could run no more. Late in the afternoon she wandered wearily down Petticoat Lane, which – after a long history as a street market – had all but been taken over by Jewish traders in the previous two decades. Those who were displaced made the same complaint that was made the world over about Jewish thrift and industry: the newcomers had used unfair, dishonest, vile methods. If this meant that the pub at the end of the street was empty of Jews, it was true: drunkenness was a common feature of many poor areas of London, but not where the Jews congregated. On either side of the pub, through the open windows, Anna could watch the white faces of the garment workers, as weary as herself, as they worked to produce cheap clothing.

She pressed her nose to the engraved glass of the pub window and saw a cheerful, disordered scene in the large bar. By the light of the already burning gas lamps, she could see a group of men playing cards; a solitary figure with a small glass of beer reading, or pretending to read, a newspaper; women, happy to exchange their depressing homes for an unruly environment of a different kind; their children, dipping dirty fingers into the beer or drinking it with the encouragement of parents who knew it would quieten them and help them find sleep. Outside, a few of the smallest played marbles in the gutter.

The sound of a small brass band heralded the arrival of a march of members of the Temperance Movement. Their espousal of 'the cup that cheers but does not inebriate' – tea – was finding many supporters, even with beer at 2d a pint, but not here. A scuffle developed and Anna found herself in the midst of a frightening mob; pinned to the pavement by the heavy body of a drunken labourer, his breath a foul mix of the smell of beer and more noisome elements.

In a moment she was free, running again, past the stalls, past the garment workers, the furniture makers, the little shops, the public baths – and on home, to find another death. Frank Bowden had slashed his wrists no more than an hour after his wife died. Already the bodies had been removed, negotiations in train for re-letting the room.

Images of death haunted Anna's puberty. For a short time things seemed better. Her mother, a stronger character than her rather feckless father, organized the Gentile women to take in washing. When there were not enough to fulfil a contract she would wash herself, scrubbing once the whole night through, covering everything around them with the wet, hanging garments. They had three rooms now, and through the open space which led into her tiny bedroom, Anna could see the elements of their material universe: the hooks behind the main door, on which their clothes hung for want of anything else; a tiny fireplace more full of ash than coal; the torn, loose lino on the floor; the patterned oil-cloth – brought all the way from Hamburg – on the table; two shelves of ill-assorted crockery. Her mother and father talked endlessly of the life, the relatives, the comforts they had left behind them, and of poor Georg, Anna's brother, who was still in Germany.

Anna was a solitary girl, who would sit for hours patiently combing the tresses of her shiny black hair. Her mother gave up asking what she was thinking about: she would not, in any case, have been able to give a satisfactory answer. She seemed to be waiting, but for what she could not say. Her only friend proved to be her saviour when her parents fell ill of some sort of bronchial disease and died within a few months of each other. Martin Burns was a teacher, a proud working-class Englishman who had in effect educated himself: Anna's parents decided – not without endless debate and anguish, but circumscribed by their illness – to give her to be one of the *englische Kinder*, to be fostered by Burns and his wife. She adapted surprisingly well to this; Burns's environment was in many ways as closed as the one she had left, but – simply by being different – it offered a curious species of hope.

Martin Burns was a voluble man, who told her everything about himself. His grandfather had come from Suffolk as a brick-layer: only one of his eight sons – Martin's father – had survived, and he had worked, when he could, as a dock labourer. These last were in a terrible position: in Hamburg they were at least employed by the week, in Antwerp by the day, but in London it was only from hour to hour that they knew that they still had a paying job.

Martin had a purpose in telling Anna all this, a purpose which she could not have discerned. She listened patiently, interestedly, because her new 'father' seemed so wise in the ways of the fright-ening world around her. She did not resent his bitterness about the employing classes who had organized their lives as they were, because she could see – every day a little more – something of the political vision he had. From the few years of formal schooling he had had, he told her, he remembered only one thing that was important – sitting in the front of the hall, hearing one of the Governors saying as an aside to the Headmaster, 'It is pleasant to see the small and dirty boys reading the labels in the shop windows. It is one of the signs of the happier future.'

The poor man did not, yet, share that happier future. Martin spoke without emotion. 'We have one enormous advantage over those patronising bastards, you and I, Anna. We know birth, death, starvation at first hand: we know them, and we understand them, in a way they never will. That gives us strength.' Despondency broke through for a moment: 'But we still lack money, and money is power. Our people cannot buy newspapers or write letters, or go to concerts, buy clothes or pay the doctor or give their children marbles or dolls. All wealth is concentrated in the hands of no more than a fifth of our fellows. The rest are never removed from the threat of slipping into the abyss.' Then strength: 'Yet listen, Anna. The tide is turning. We'll never destroy them by using their own instruments. Parliament holds out nothing for the working man – years of striving by Labour men and what's to show? They're demoralized, all of them; they've lost the sense of what it is to be a working man. Who do they choose to lead them? Namby-pamby Ramsay MacDonald – a man who's scarcely seen a day's manual labour in his life. That's not our way. It's not our way because the whole damned system is on the run – even the Unionists can see that: if they don't get their way in Ireland, they'll forget such constitutional niceties as Parliamentary majorities and use the army. You'll see. What we must do is this: get at the wealth – direct action against the employers, wring the profits out of them. We have the power because we have the numbers. Stick together and we can cripple the lines of communication, cut off the electricity, the coal, force them to give in.'

It was a tempting vision, not very well rooted in the facts. Sectarianism ruled. When the miners secured the terms they wanted for themselves, they went back to work, and hanged be all the others. But for Anna, there was a seed planted, a seed of a peculiar kind, for in the years ahead it did not grow into the Syndicalist flower of English working-class politics. What could that mean to a Hamburg Jewess, uprooted, but sharing in the experience of so many of her kind? Instead there was fertile soil of another kind close at hand.

The power structure against which Martin Burns so vehemently inveighed was, relatively, tolerant to the anarchist clubs that foreign immigrants began in England: foreigners did not understand, and therefore would not meddle in, English affairs, and could be safely left (most of the time) to indulge in their crackpot schemes. For Jews who had fled pogroms all over Europe, it was a dubious privilege to take up residence in London sweatshops run by other Jews. Most accepted it; some gravitated to the International Club in Berners Street, Whitechapel, where the German exile, Rudolf Rocker – ironically, a Gentile himself – led the campaign for the propagation of anarchist ideas. Burns had supported their work in running a communal kitchen, which provided meals for the very poorest, but he was too English to enjoy the cosmopolitanism that prevailed.

For Anna it was different. Within a few months of the opening of the Jubilee Street Club, which also served to print and publish the Yiddish *Arbeiter Fraint*, she began to spend all her time there: a mass of eighteen-year-old passion and energy, the past all behind her, the future to be won.

* * *

A small crowd was gathering in the central hall of the Club as Anna spoke of these things to Ransom – the stranger, richly dressed, who had sought her out. She could not have said yet why she so patiently explained to him fact that – by the expression on his face – he did not understand. For his part – well, for his part he was suppressing his sense of incongruity in these surroundings. Often he had thought back to that day – there is no one like the person who has never been in love before to be so ripe for plucking when the time comes.

'Now you must listen again – more carefully than before,' Anna said. She hauled herself onto the platform with the litheness and agility that he had already recognized as one of her attributes, and called the meeting to order. Her voice, though not loud, seemed to fill the hall:

'Fellow Workers, We come before you as Anarchists to explain our principles. We are aware that the minds of many of you have been poisoned by the lies which all parties have diligently spread about us.

'Belief in submission to authority is the root cause of all our misery. The remedy we recommend – struggle to death against all authority, whether it is that of physical force identical with the State or that of doctrine and theories, the product of ages of ignorance and superstition inculcated into the workers' minds from childhood: religion, patriotism, obedience to the law, belief in the State, submission to the rich and titled....'

This is treason, a voice in Ransom's head told him, but he sat still and listened, or rather watched Anna – fascinated by the movement of her mouth and her hands and her arms, and the flashing of her eyes as they darted back and forth across her audience. She continued in more moderate tone:

The fact that a great number of persons is in favour of something is no guarantee that it is right. New discoveries, new lines of human activity are first found and practised by a few, and only gradually adopted by the many. The majority that makes the laws or abides by them will almost certainly lag behind progress, and the laws made by it will be reactionary from the very beginning.

She was dressed entirely in black and now threw the shawl from her shoulders as she spread wide her arms. The passion came to the surface:

'We Anarchists are internationalists, we acknowledge no distinction of nationality or colour. The workers of all countries suffer as we do here, and our comrades have everywhere to fight the same battle for freedom and justice.... It is in the interest of all governments to uphold patriotism, to have their own people ready to fly at the throats of their fellow workers of other nationalities wherever it suits the employers to open up new markets, or draw the attention of the people away from the contemplation of their own misery, which might drive them to revolt.

'We shall be asked what we intend to put in place of the State. We reply, 'Nothing!' The State is simply an obstacle to progress; this obstacle once removed, we do not want to erect a fresh obstruction.

'These are our Principles – and dynamite and assassination are our means. Feel no shock. Feel no compassion for the people who, by colliery disasters, the running of rotten ships, fires in death-trap houses, railway accidents caused by overwork, daily massacre more people than the Anarchists of all countries ever killed. These people have no voice when the question of Humanity is considered.'

Rhetoric would not feed the masses; it did not impress those who had attended the meeting for the warming food and drink that would follow. But for Anna herself, and for at least some of those around her, it was exhilarating.

After everyone had at last departed, she took hold of Ransom's hand and led him up the stairs to the gallery, off which – in a tiny room – she was for the while making her home. What was it about Ransom – tense and awkward, into middle age, his face fleshy and lined, his perfectly fitting clothes impeccably cut to build an ice barrier around his emotions…was she tempted by the idea of toying with corruption, risking the contamination of her ideals, the excitement of that?

In no more than a moment, or so it seemed, she slipped out of all her clothes and stood naked before him. She seemed to notice his eyes, become conscious for the first time – as she later told him – that they were attractive to her. She kissed him lightly on the lips.

They did not speak until, as he was about to enter her, she pulled him closer with a firm clasp. 'You may have my body', she hissed; 'but you will never possess me.'

CHAPTER FOUR

Dinner at Downing Street

A challenge this, he thought. After three years not just with a mistress, but with one who spent much of her time denouncing the system, the society, the government of which he was a part, there were no visible results, none. His marriage was drearily intact – at least, as intact as it had ever been; his career was untouched – it had moved itself, with no more than automatic support from him, to the heights of second-rank grandeur beyond which it might not ever go. And he was no nearer understanding Anna: it was easy to relate what she said, what she believed, to what she explained of her background, but that answered everything and nothing.

It was the passion he did not understand, the passion she always carried with her, which he could always sense but which was only communicated to him as a feeling when they made love or when he had not seen her for some days.

Sometimes, indeed, weeks went by without a meeting. He was busy; she was – somewhere. Always there was a mystery. Where had she been? What had she been doing? She would not be questioned.

She would manage to be playfully imperious and vulnerable at the same time: the two qualities were irresistible. He had insisted on buying the little house in Clarges Street so that – as far as possible – they could meet each other with ease; she had insisted that it was left more or less as it was bought, with no more than the impersonal necessities that furnished the bedroom. It was not a home, she said, and it should not look like one. At times it served, it seemed, as just a means of conveying messages, left by one or the other of them by the bed.

'Dearest Anna,' Ransom wrote, and then paused immediately. Suddenly conscious that the day was passing, and quite unconscious of the indiscretion in what he wrote, he scribbled quickly: 'I am summoned to Germany on a mission for the Prime Minister, no less. Why do you disappear when I need you? Telephone. Please telephone and then, at the least, I can hear your voice.' This note he left unsigned.

Three hours later, at about teatime, Anna returned a day before her own message had suggested. She saw what he had written, and – after a moment's thought – reached for the telephone. But it was not to telephone Ransom.

'I think you should get Von Bode to arrange a meeting with him.'

'That's dangerous.'

'Everything's dangerous. It's important that he should be talked to before he goes to Germany.' Anna's tone was insistent, but not friendly; it was plain that she did not enjoy the apparent need to be so persuasive.

'I'll do what I can.'

Thus it was that, as Ransom was preparing for dinner that evening at 10 Downing Street, his own telephone rang.

'Mr Ransom?'

'Yes.'

'Forgive me for bothering you. I would not do so if it were not a matter of some urgency. This is the Baron von Bode at the German Embassy. You will perhaps recall that we have met several times at Prince Lichnowsky's. I would very much welcome the chance to have a few words with you – this evening, if at all possible.'

'Would you mind telling me what this is about? I have an important dinner engagement which will keep me until late.'

'I gather that you are shortly to take a trip.' Ransom did not respond. 'It is of that I wish to speak to you,' Von Bode continued. 'If you were to come to the Embassy after dinner, I could explain. No need for over-much secrecy, of course, but I suggest that you don't use the main entrance. There's a little door you may have noticed on the right-hand side as you go down the Duke of York's steps to Pall Mall.'

He did not seem to expect Ransom to refuse, or so it appeared to the Englishman at the time – the latter could not see the sweat glistening on Von Bode's forehead.

Ransom pondered. 'All right, I'll come,' he said decisively, feeling better, 'though I cannot promise at what time.' This was too intriguing to miss.

'I shall be waiting.'

* * *

Ransom said goodbye to Rosalind in good humour. At least a little excitement was gently intruding into his life, and it did not seem, so far as he could yet see, to carry any threat with it. He told his wife not to wait up and, while normally she would not have considered doing so anyway, she responded warmly to his jauntiness. He imagined she hated his brooding moods, which weighed her down, but it took as little to restore her to a temporary well-being as it would later to upset her again.

Rosalind was content that there was no place for her at the Prime Minister's: she was intrinsically not nearly so dull as many of those she met who tried to be clever, but was easily intimidated. This dinner at Downing Street was a special, and all-male occasion – an election anniversary which brought together most of the members of the Cabinet, many of whom would not have dined together by choice.

Usually the Prime Minister left the list of guests to his wife and often his first introduction to those for whom he was host came as he joined them after their arrival in Downing Street. Margot, in her fiftieth year, liked a mixed and cosmopolitan crowd at her parties and only Winston Churchill and John Burns of her husband's political confederates were usually invited.

Officially, there was very little entertainment at 10 Downing Street, but when half London's police force was detailed to guard the place, it was not for reasons of national security; it was to keep out those who wanted to eavesdrop while the exuberant Margot Asquith smoked and behaved otherwise outrageously in semi-public. Of her rivals as Liberal hostesses, even the formidable threesome of Lady Mond in Lowndes Square, Countess Beauchamp in Belgrave Square and Pierpont Morgan's niece, Mrs Lewis Harcourt, in Berkeley Square, could not match her slightly scandalous panache.

Margot had summarized her own approach to life: 'I hope to die in debt.' It was said that no one thought her more sensationally admirable, or her conceits more sagacious, than she did herself. Queen Victoria, certainly, had not approved, pronouncing her 'unfit for a Cabinet Minister's wife' back in the days when Herbert had been Home Secretary. Ransom's knowledge of her was more recent, but he had always been wary of her theatricality and stinging asides. Her marriage to Asquith had given her what she wanted – not someone chic and popular in Society (she could take care of that herself) but someone who would be seen to be successful.

For him there were great advantages in finding a classically good-looking wife who did not endlessly want to question him about his private life. This was friendship or, at any rate, companionship, without the need for a sexual spark. Besides, he was for the present in love with Venetia Stanley, the pretty young friend of his daughter Violet. Venetia's father was the Liberal peer, Lord Sheffield, and who was to say that the Prime Minister's Whitsun stay at Penrhôs – one of Sheffield's country houses – had not been genuinely for the golf and the politics?

He was late for his guests this evening because he was writing to Venetia, after having spent part of the afternoon in his new Napier – chauffeur driven, if not chaperoned – driving out to Richmond with her. On his writing desk was a tidy heap of books: *The Wars of the Roses*, *The Jews in the Middle Ages*, Green's *Prolegomena to Ethics*, Kant. Could these really have been the inspiration as he wrote: 'To see you again and be with you, and hear your voice, has made a new creature of me. You are the best and richest of life-givers'? It may have been so – like his speeches, his love letters were the tidy expression of thoughts that had been subject to an inquisition of high feeling and intellect. What passion was left was not the passion of ignorance or carelessness: the thin line of his mouth seemed proof of that.

Yet Herbert Asquith did not make a graceful or distinguished figure: for twenty years he had become steadily more stout and, in the face, puffy cheeked; he dressed without distinction, maintained at best an air of self-satisfied, benevolent complacency, at worst something close to untidy bad taste. His detachment was interpreted by some as laziness. This Prime Minster enjoyed his weekends and his holidays, and could not be persuaded to hurry his dinner or the brandy that followed it.

The House of Commons became well used to a figure that had dined a mite too well, but whose authority did not seem to be impaired. If his body swayed, the mind that was supposed to be directing it was otherwise very much in control. Asquith, for the moment, knew where he stood; his attitudes had deep roots, and this gave him strength. He distrusted rapid decisions, yet benefited from his calmly realistic approach to politics – as someone who could remember the Rosebery-Harcourt discords, he could be satisfied with the unity of his colleagues. No one had yet resigned from his Cabinet on grounds of principle, but he was not without Ministers of strong opinions.

Strong opinions, yes. But principles? Ransom wondered, as he surveyed the others. In one sense they were a mixed crowd. For pleasure Asquith might study the classics, Haldane – the Lord Chancellor – might read the German philosophers, and Lloyd George sing Welsh hymns. Yet it was ironic that, in the great age of political cynicism, the eighteenth century, politicians went to the guillotine, but in Ransom's time – when politics at home often seemed to be Society's plaything and international affairs were played at, like an elaborate game – they all died tucked up in their beds.

Birrell, who had been told by the Prime Minister of Ransom's mission, seemed to bear this out. 'He seems so unconcerned about everything,' Ransom said in an aside to Lloyd George. 'Oh,' replied the Chancellor, 'he cares nothing about the rights or wrongs of a public matter – his sole concern is whether the Irish will accept it or not. He wants a quiet official life and will throw away money or principles like water to get peace. I cannot stand the man's dilettante sarcasm.' Ransom remembered the one piece of advice Birrell had given him: 'Nothing in Ireland is explicable: everything of unimportance is known.'

Still, Lloyd George was one who would not recognize a principle. As the poor boy from the Welsh village with an instinct for the dramatic, Mr George, as he properly was, had learned early the virtues of combating social injustices and supporting small nations, but from there on it was all impulsive opportunism. No one could persuade him to concentrate on reports or files or papers, to analyse the details; he fed on conversation, loved talking, grasping the essence of the matter from that. At the least, there should be no theorizing: if you did not understand, you must go and find out, on the spot, how the thing worked. But facts must never be allowed to interfere with enthusiasm; even on such an occasion as this, he would not feel inhibited from turning to Margot (who greeted the company before dinner but then withdrew, as she said, to more important things) and speaking as he would to friend or foe, great or poor alike.

Lloyd George focused his blue eyes on her, running his hands through his thick, greying hair and leaning back in his chair. 'You know, Margot, there is one little quality that my little race has that gives everyone peculiar offence, especially the dullest, and that is the gift of imagination. It has pulled me through many a fight, and it will pull me through the future, because, when insults hurtle through the air, I can always see a vision on the horizon that sustains me.' To what new battle he might be referring, Ransom could not even guess, but that was irrelevant.

'In all my career', the Chancellor went on with an unstoppable torrent of words, 'I do not remember a hand being held out to me from above, and a voice saying, *Dringifyny yma* – 'Climb up here', you heathens. But don't misunderstand me: there have been thousands of hands which have pushed me up from behind.' Twenty years before, Lloyd George had learned from Gladstone what he knew in his bones already: it was better to do most of the talking if you wanted to lead. Besides, as he said himself, the Welsh peasant saw more of heaven and earth from his hillsides than the shrewdest man of the world could see from his fog-enveloped club windows.

For all his lecturing and hectoring, Lloyd George had the great gift of making you feel that you too were important, someone with whom he was enthusiastic to share his ideas. He could talk of golf or Criccieth or women in passing, but only to carry you with him, to find his eyes drowning in tears or his voice shaking with wrathful passing at some vile tale of suffering or oppression. It was almost as if he could see into the minds of those to whom he spoke, at the least identify their mood, know how to calm or to encourage them. He could judge what was demanded of the occasion – and work on the assumption that he would provide it.

Asquith, Ransom fancied, was a little afraid of all this charm. Probably he, Lloyd George, was a little afraid of Grey, the Foreign Secretary, but of no one else. He did not like Margot's mad social whirl, and he disliked McKenna, the Home Secretary, for his icy and industrious, methodical and logical approach to everything: McKenna was a man who read Burke's speeches aloud every day for not less than forty-five minutes, purely as an exercise in oratory.

As for Winston Churchill, he was treated in patronizing fashion, like a wayward schoolboy, and Winston, for all his belief in himself, could not be expected to get to the top. The English, renowned for their distrust of intellectuals, disliked wild schemers the more. They would applaud anyone who could charge, without thought for himself, with the 21st Lancers at Omdurman, as Churchill had, but that did not mean they would want the same man to shape their political future.

Churchill was good at managing an air of crisis, but had no talent for feeding off the humdrum, as Lloyd George did, and turning it to his own uses. Without the facility to pass the time of day, he too often blurted out what was uppermost in his thoughts, and that was often wildly implausible, rude or sour, or – more likely – an unnecessary reminder to everyone of his great abilities.

Introduced to Rosalind for the first time at a party Ransom had given some years before, Churchill stood in painful silence for what seemed a long period, then abruptly – as if noticing her for the first time – enquired how old she was. Rosalind replied, politely, that she was 39. 'And I', he said a little desperately, 'am 32 already. But', he added, 'that's younger than anyone else who *counts*, mind. We are all worms, but I do believe I am a glow-worm. Your husband kindly lent me the *Ethics* of Aristotle. I thought it good, but am bound to say it is extraordinary how much of it I had already thought out for myself.'

That was the year of his first big political appointment – as Colonial Under-Secretary. It had not hurt his career to abandon one political party (the Unionists) for another (the Liberals): President of the Board of Trade, Home Secretary, now First Sea Lord, and still not even on the edge of middle age.

Here was a man who would, without hesitation but with a great instinct for survival, desert a sinking ship. The question was, would others benefit? How different from Sir Edward Grey, who spoke only words of patent sincerity, though not many of those: he could be thought handsome if it was not for that thin, silent mouth. His features had been cut from steel and polished into a glinting but unyielding toughness, reinforced by his deep-set eyes.

A look at the Continent from a railway-carriage window en route to Paris with the King that very Spring was the total extent of his experience outside the British Isles in equipping him for the post of Foreign Secretary. His Northumberland house and his Hampshire fishing lodge were quite far away enough, without venturing to foreign parts, or even the Celtic extremities of Britain. Was he joking, Ransom wondered, when he said to Prince Lichnowsky, the German Ambassador, at lunch with the Ambassador's family: 'I can't help thinking how clever those children are to talk German so well'? He spoke no German himself, and when he spoke French – well, his latest conversational object, the Greek Prime Minister M. Venizelos, had found it impossible to understand.

In no other part of the world would Grey have become a prominent politician: he fulfilled his official tasks as a dutiful penance – the only time he kept a diary, Margot whispered maliciously, was at the weekend, when his attention could return to his roses and his fishing. Yet he was certainly effective when it came to dealing with the many complicated, but usually solvable, problems of peacetime diplomacy, in which you needed good sense, give and take, tenacity to work out concrete solutions to concrete problems. No one could say that he was unable to master a complicated brief.

The drawing-room gossip was not so friendly. 'Sir Edward's enemies may say all they like about his ignorance; only his friends know how deep it really is.' Like many of his contemporaries – Ransom was a relatively studious exception a decade later – he had not worked at Oxford and had been sent down. At home in Falloden, in wonderful countryside just two miles from the Northumberland coast, he was back where he had been brought up – where he had spent long hours learning the ways of sea-birds that lived in the burns which made their way from the heather moors to the sea. Both his wife and his brother had died in appalling accidents, reinforcing his desire to be alone.

He was not happy with the gathering that evening. No one could find anything in common between him and Churchill and Lloyd George. 'Grey is a good colleague because he never takes any risks', Sir Hugh Bell – a fellow director of the North-Eastern Railway – had said; 'and he is a thoroughly bad colleague for the same reason.' Besides, he had little interest in party matters, and only knew the names of all those present because they were perforce thrown together so often around the Cabinet table. He could not even see them very clearly, for his eyesight was deteriorating apace. Rest, the oculist advised, but what chance was there of that? And was it even desirable? 'Work, incessant, peremptory work, relieves nervous strain,' he advised Ransom; 'it allows no vacant house in which anxiety can prey upon an unoccupied mind; it wearies, but by that very weariness helps to ensure sleep sufficient to restore; unless or until it causes exhaustion, it stimulates.'

So there was Sir Edward, the model, modern aristocrat, but there too was John Burns, the first working-class man to reach the Cabinet, seen by the flickering light of candles like those he had started working life by making. He had come a long way since he had been imprisoned for leading a mob of workmen against the police and, if he was only a member of a Liberal government because he could not get what he wanted through the Labour party, he had none the less an agreeable personality.

Not everyone agreed.

John Burns was the workmen's M.P.
A friend of the toilers was he
Till he made it his game
To win Cabinet fame
At the head of the Local G.B.

In February, after more than eight years as President of the Local Government Board, he had become President of the Board of Trade, and spoke relatively good-humouredly this evening of the motion that was expected to be put down against him in the House of Commons to reduce his salary: he had faced something similar for each of the previous three years.

Now nearing the end of his career, John Burns had a red, lined face, a beard which grew a little too intermittently, strikingly clear eyes and a voice that was startlingly gentle and powerful at the same time. Ransom liked him, though they were never close. He did not show fatigue, was always ready for work and harried everyone at the dinner table as if it were an extension of a Cabinet meeting. Colleagues were blamed for their weak-kneed attitude to Carson and the army officers who supported him; they were blamed for their failure to tackle the Suffragettes, against whose attacks his home on North Side, Clapham Common, was heavily protected by the police. Only on the German question was he strangely silent: was it pacifism, Ransom wondered, or was there a hint of pro-German sympathy?

'We have only to think of the importance of the Rhine', Winston was saying, 'when we envisage the possibility of a German attack through Belgium or Holland.'

'But the Rhine is a German river,' Grey intervened.

'Quite so, Sir Edward,' said Asquith. 'The Rhine lives in Germany, but it is born in Switzerland and dies in Holland.'

Morley, the seventy-five-year-old Lord President of the Council whose roots lay in the classic age of British Liberalism fifty years before, looked disapproving at this joke at the Foreign Secretary's expense. He remained the philosopher-king, and the conscience, of the Liberal party – and was nickname 'Priscilla' for his pains.

Haldane was irritable for a different reason; he had studied philosophy in Göttingen and, as perhaps the hardest working man Ransom had ever encountered, was anxious to mend English relations with what he called 'my spiritual home'. 'I would remind you', he said a little pompously, 'that Britain and Germany are each other's best trading partners. We have close connections through our royal families and there is no desire, on the part of many of those who voted us into power, to be seen to consort with Tsarist Russia.'

'You miss the point, my dear Haldane,' Churchill abruptly retorted – always ready to rush in, whatever the mood of the opposing troops. 'Russia is weak because the Tsar is weak. His Minister, Stolypin, was assassinated in front of him; Rasputin has taken hold of his family; his wife is openly libelled in the newspapers. France is far too divided and feeble to act as a useful ally. What would have happened if the Balkan crisis had got out of control, while the

French spent their time gabbling about the cherry red trousers of their absurd army? "Le pantalon rouge, c'est la France."'

Winston allowed himself a short pause to gain the full effect of his ridicule, which was heightened by the undisguised ineptness of his own French accent, but he waited only so long before continuing:

'Make no mistake. Germany is a great and rich country. Great and rich countries do not sit quietly at home for long. They begin to look around and soon they begin to march.'

Haldane, to Churchill's annoyance, did not give the company time to savour these words. 'If there is a threat – and I do not accept that there is – we have nothing to fear. The Kaiser knows our language and our institutions as we do. You forget that he has guided his people through nearly a quarter of a century – and preserved unbroken peace in that time. It is a record of which any monarch might be proud.'

Churchill snorted. 'You wish to espouse absolutism?' His lisp was pronounced, but if it was nervousness that had produced the speech defect originally, the nervousness had long ago been conquered.

'Democracy is rapidly finding its feet in Germany under his aegis,' added Haldane.

'It will gain little if it loses its head at the same time,' retorted Churchill.

'Really, the Lord Chancellor's flights of fancy are quite as remarkable as Nijinsky's exit in *Le Spectre de la Rose*!' It was plain already that the Russian season of operas and ballets at Drury Lane was going to overshadow in spectacular fashion the summer at Covent Garden – and in the far-fetched analogy of drawing-room gossip, no less than in the skill of performance.

With some informality, those present began to drift away from the table into the adjoining room, with its more comfortable chairs.

Haldane distanced himself from Churchill, with relative graceless-ness, to join the Prime Minister. Their friendship, the friendship of contemporaries, went back longer than that of anyone else in the Cabinet, though Asquith was not often to be seen these days in Haldane's own home in Queen Anne's Gate. Possibly Margot shocked the Lord Chancellor, with her insistent concentration on the joys of the present as against the obligations of the future. The only way he might revel in what he called her 'superabundance of animal vitality and spirit' was as a philosophical concept – he had not studied Goethe for nothing.

Asquith was reassuring. 'Oh, Winston is in high spirits at the prospect of war, which to me shows a lack of imagination. All froth, born out of foam: that's how he thinks. But, frankly, one does not have to share your view of Germany, Haldane, in order to be more relaxed.' Asquith in command: 'They could not hope to attack us with less than 70,000 men, and the Navy would thwart any such attempt. And if war should break out on the Continent, I see no necessity for our involvement. We are more in danger from those ninnies in the City than from military defeat: if they panic, they can bring us all down.'

Across the room, Lloyd George – having applauded Churchill for his chastisement of Haldane and launched into his own criti-cisms of Asquith's detachment ('The spirit was less mighty than the expression,' was how F.E. Smith had put it) – would not let Winston have it all his own way. He was not with the pacifists, with Morley or Burns, but it no longer seemed likely that England would be dragged into a conflict between Austria (and Germany) and Russia (and France). 'Our relations with Germany are very much better than they were a few years ago,' he observed. 'We begin to realize that we can co-operate for common ends, and that the points of co-operation are greater and more numerous and more important than the points of possible controversy....'

Churchill made an indefinable sound, muffled by taking a large gulp of his drink. Grey, who had not heard the previous interchange, intervened with the magisterial, apparently sanctified certainty that he invariably displayed. 'Now let me say this,' he began, and paused in ritual acknowledgment of interruptions that would not be forthcoming. 'German strength is by itself a guarantee that no other country will desire to seek a quarrel with Germany. That is one side of the shield, and one of which Germans may well be proud. But there is another side of the shield, and that is: if a nation has the biggest army in the world, and it has a very big navy, and is going on building a still bigger navy, then it must do all in its power to prevent the natural apprehensions in the minds of others, who have no aggressive intentions themselves – save defence.'

Ransom had always been both attracted and repelled by Grey's mind. The historical tide moved onward, with its own motive force, until exceptional individuals acted to modify it. In nature man lived at peace: if Germany seemed ever more warlike, then she must be deterred – and she would be. Her army could defeat a weak France, but she would know that the British Navy, with France and Russia as allies, was ultimately stronger. Anything could be made to sound rational – even Ransom's love for Anna – and the belief almost made it so.

Grey's unremitting seriousness seemed to relax the company: the nervous reaction of tired and slightly drunk men in important positions in the world of affairs.

Churchill, who had sat down heavily next to Ransom, waved a piece of paper he had just withdrawn from his pocket with some satisfaction. 'Here is Ramsay MacDonald's speech at Dundee. He describes me as the worst First Lord of the Admiralty in history. I'm so pleased that I'm having copies printed as a testimonial!' He leaned forward, his brandy and cigar precariously held in one hand. 'How little they understand history. How did we defeat the great Armada of Spain? Or the trading power of the Dutch? Or the mighty land armies of Napoleon? It costs so very little to be the mistress of the seas.'

'Don't complain. You won your battle this year over the Estimates – much to L.G.'s annoyance,' Ransom said.

'But we shall have to find reductions for 1915,' the First Sea Lord commented sharply. 'That was part of the deal.'

At that moment, Lloyd George, who had gone out of earshot, ambled over to join them, Birrell at his side. Winston's tone changed. 'Ah, L.G. – I was just saying to Ransom here, about you and I: our friendship. A wonderful thing! For ten years there has hardly been a day when we haven't had half an hour's talk together.'

'How awfully bored you must both be by now,' interjected Birrell, with tart good humour.

Lloyd George ignored the comment, and said playfully to Churchill, 'Now then, how is your "surprise" mobilization for the fleet coming along? A "surprise" exercise which is given five months' public notice will be a surprise indeed.'

'Precisely,' said Churchill, unabashed. 'Since you will not allow us the money for grand manoeuvres, we shall have to make a splash of a different kind.'

'From what I hear,' Birrell said, 'our aggressive First Lord is in danger of making his own splash: from a great height.'

'Birrell, my dear chap, you must have heard about my photograph,' a pleased Winston said. Turning to the puzzled company, he continued: 'Yes, there is a very tolerable picture of myself in this week's *Illustrated London News* after a flight from Salisbury Plain to Portsmouth. I am quite determined to earn a pilot's certificate. These Grahame-White biplanes are perfectly safe in the right hands: if we could parachute our way out of political difficulties as easily, life would be much more congenial.'

Ransom's turn. 'Yes. Much as we love you, it seems to me that the risk of an election is somewhat greater than the risk to your own very splendid person by taking to the air.' They were all at their most astute in their particular roles.

CHAPTER FIVE

Von Bode offers
some advice

SO the hours passed, the physical positions of the members of the Cabinet changing as naturally as their intellectual stance. Now Asquith and Lloyd George stood by the fireplace, their hands encircling two identically large glasses of brandy. Total opposites in both temperament and – so far – in achievements, the one a careful cataloguer of the precise, the other an endless stream of possibilities. The popular press suggested that the difference was the reason that they worked together so well: like two drunkards standing upright by leaning against one another.

Asquith sighed. 'Another Bridgeless royal evening to look forward to on Saturday.'

Lloyd George grunted. He had never liked the game.

'One does so need it after a dinner with the Queen. Last week – at the Crewe's – I sat next to her. There was not a subject under Heaven – dress, the Opera, sea-sickness, the Suffragettes – that we did not exhaust. By the end of dinner I was more exhausted than after a debate in the House. Then, at least, there was Bridge of a mild kind with Lady Kerry and Lady Selborne.'

The Chancellor grunted again.

'Margot has to present Elizabeth at Court this coming Thursday. I fear that the poor girl has strong competition – all the talk is of Clarina. You know Clarina, I believe?'

A third grunt. If the truth had been told, Lloyd George cared little for Asquith's daughter, Elizabeth, and knew less of her cousin, Miss Clarina Tennant – daughter of Margot's brother, Lord Glenconner.

'If only the King were more subtle. One might be able to be more sympathetic to some of his views if he were able to mask them a little – he responds to anyone who appears to be offering a clear-cut solution.'

'Yes,' said Lloyd George, at last turning his attention to the conversation, 'and many of the Queen's closest friends are ultra-Unionists. The Duchess of Devonshire. Lady Shaftesbury. Just like the plots of a court cabal. The King should not listen to her, or to them.'

'I have told him plainly that the Cabinet is responsible for policy and for the advice it offers: as a constitutional monarch, he must accept it. He talks of a "residual" right to dismiss his Ministers, but I think he will draw back as he watches just how far down the road to anarchy the Unionists are going. Bonar Law has the mind of a Glasgow Bailie: I never liked the man. Raymond says that he combines the uncivilized vocabulary of the schoolboy with the unbalanced temperament of the schoolgirl – a clever phrase.'

Raymond Asquith was full of clever phrases – cleverer, perhaps, than his father could manage. But it was certainly difficult to see any common ground – save their interest in bridge – between the dour Unionist leader and the Balliol scholar who had become Prime Minister.

Lloyd George did not disagree. 'They are trying to persuade themselves that "Bony" is a big man, but they must know in their hearts that he is not. The trouble is that, on the Home Rule issue, the Unionists may have the best man to lead them. I had my introduction to Parliament, you know, when Gladstone's second Home Rule Bill was thrown out – twenty years ago.'

'Today it is different. The matter has always aroused strong passions, but when the Leader of the Opposition connives at demonstrations in the Chamber…you heard what he said when he was asked if he gave his consent to the shouting and the clamour? "I will not criticize what you consider to be your duty in asking the question, but I know mine and that is not to answer it." A scandal!'

Carrying a half-empty decanter, Ransom poured more brandy into both men's glasses. 'Winston is remarkably calm on the subject. He is firm that both Ulstermen and Catholics must have what they want, as if that was compatible.'

'We should not forget that our colleague was once on the other side of the House – he still has good friends among the Unionists,' said Lloyd George.

'A wicked comment, L.G.,' Asquith observed mildly. 'No, I think he is persuaded – wrongly – that a European war is coming, and that it is vital to settle the Irish question because of that.'

'He is a good man to have on one's side,' Ransom added. 'You would understand that if you had heard him at Bradford – there are worse things than bloodshed, he declared. It needed saying.'

'Yes, but what did he mean?' Lloyd George countered.

'You cannot discount people's deepest beliefs,' Ransom said, surprised but happy to find himself lecturing the cleverer man. 'The Ulstermen would rather accept the Kaiser as their king than obey a Dublin Parliament. Redmond and Carson did not create the violence – they are merely pale reflections of it. The people of Mayo speak of the people of Connemara as if they were the inferior natives of another planet, and yet they are as close together as Croydon is to Charing Cross.'

'Walter, I see you are becoming an expert,' Asquith commented. (Was he being patronizing? Ransom couldn't tell.) 'But don't let's get carried away. The situation is grave: it is bound to be with an army that is impregnated with the strongest Tory prejudices, that – as Carson believes – cannot be relied on to shoot down the loyalists of Ulster.' (How beautifully he puts it!) 'We shall yet find a way: there will be compromise.'

Asquith was not as certain as he sounded, and Lloyd George for once spoke for them all. 'Well,' he said, 'whatever we do – if we compromise, if we fight – history will only listen to the results. We either win this one with the biggest victory of all time – or we stand condemned as the blindest, incompetent government in a thousand years.'

The room was momentarily quiet. It was time to go, or so Morley evidently thought. The old man, a small but robust figure, rose energetically to his feet, his eyes darting rapidly from side to side, his head moving with them. A few quick words with the Prime Minster, a solid 'Good evening' to the rest of the company, and he was striding through the door, swinging his arms, keeping them straight – almost as if he were on one of the military parades he so deplored.

Churchill, for one, did not look up. He was again in full flow, describing the German army: that terrible engine of war…marches sometimes 35 miles in a single day…its number as the sands of the sea…supported by all the nightmarish technology of the modern world…. It would be a while before he made his way back to Eccleston Square and his wife. Once, before they were married, he had written to her: 'I am a solitary creature in the midst of the crowds. Be kind to me.' Whether there would be kindness, or not, he would make sure that the crowds would notice that he was in their midst.

With Morley, perhaps, he had one thing in common: a dislike of Asquith's reluctance – as Morley said – 'to grasp the nettle'. 'With Asquith,' the older man had declared, 'it is not only a constitutional disinclination to anticipate events, but a reasoned conviction that in nine cases out of ten a decision is best deferred till the last moment.'

Meanwhile, the Prime Minister stood nonchalantly by the door. It was difficult to know whether this was an indication that everyone should leave, or a measure of politeness to those who wanted to – a perfect summary of the man: govern by asking people their opinion *and* by showing them the way. Passion and ignorance were his twin political enemies, Ransom concluded. How different from Margot, who never got beyond personal judgments of a 'Lloyd George cannot see a belt without hitting below it' kind. It was strange how two people could share the same views from utterly different standpoints: Margot disliked particular Suffragettes; for her husband it was simply a case of not understanding what the emotion was all about.

Ransom had not had an unhappy evening. The food and wine had been – had seemed – exceptional, and there was satisfaction of a kind from scurrying through the great issues of the moment as part of perhaps the most powerful decision-making body in the world. Why didn't it always feel like that?

* * *

Shortly, Ransom found himself outside 10 Downing Street, with – as Margot said – its 'liver-coloured and squalid' façade. Few cabs ventured here and he decided to walk to the German Embassy. The visit had added spice after the evening's events and, as he set out, he felt curiously light-hearted. If one wanted to be gloomy about it, there was plenty of gloom to be found in the political history of the immediate past. Labour troubles. Suffragettes. Ireland…. And yet it had been a convivial few hours – the most convivial time he could remember with his Cabinet colleagues – and it seemed to have helped to have put all these problems into a more relaxing perspective. If it wasn't for Germany, that is….

His step slowed. Was Anna right? She made out a powerful and – as always with her – impassioned case. Partly a sickness, she said: an unbalanced preoccupation with waiting for *Der Tag* when Germany would come into its own. Throughout Europe a glorying in the arms race, which also bred hostility and mistrust, a retreat into the safety of military might in the Pan-German League or Action française. No one immune: there was Churchill proclaiming that 'The world is arming as it has never armed before' in justification of yet another increase in the Navy estimates. And a shaping up for the coming conflict through alliances of small groups of nations, rigidifying into concrete commitments the fears of one and another country. None of them understood what it would mean, what carnage would result from trying to behave like the romantic knights of old – these knights would be caught in the death trap of modern warfare.

'Sometimes, Walter,' she had said, 'sometimes I yearn for it: an end to quiet endeavour, meaningless virtue, petty corruption. All blown away with the first blast of the bugle. See, read this here, and deny that it is so: "War is a glorious thing. Array as you please the loathsome horrors, the awful miseries, the inhuman cruelties, the blackened fields, the ruined homes, it remains true that the call to arms so stirs men's blood as to fling all else out of thought."'

Anna! A mass of contradictions. Revelling in and hating life at the same time. How he loved her!

Yet was the fever in the peoples of Europe really so deep-seated? Signor Marinetti and his Futurists found beauty in war and strife, but could the same be said of the nameless masses?

'Look around you, Walter. Open your eyes.' She chided him. 'In England, in France and Germany, all the children are taught to value patriotism and military strength.'

'So we are strong. Who dares challenge us? Who has more powerful industries, greater colonies, a mightier navy?'

'Strength comes from unity. You will find no Ireland to rip the heart of Germany apart.'

That, at least, was true. Complacency, a rule of life that Ransom had followed far too much, no longer seemed to serve him well.

A quick glance around, and now he took special care in slipping unobtrusively into the large Embassy building as he approached it by the side entrance.

Of the Ambassador there was no sign, but the Chief Secretary, the man he had come to meet, always seemed very much in command. Tall and good-looking, Von Bode had a deceptive air of straightforwardness about him, which he took care to encourage as he talked. A large Imperial eagle over the fireplace was almost the only decoration in the room, clearly not his office, in which they sat.

He knew little concrete about Von Bode, though Grey had indicated in passing that he had not been unhelpful in negotiating colonial agreements in Baghdad and Africa. Margot Asquith had also suggested that any German civilized enough to take afternoon tea could not be all bad.

'Let me be frank with you, Mr Ransom,' he said. 'For since I am taking a very great risk in trusting you, it is vital that you should trust me.'

A little weakly, he nodded. 'I'm listening.'

'It may be apparent to you that our Foreign Office does not altogether approve of Prince Lichnowsky: we are not, as a people, overfond of rich and liberal-minded dilettantes: we find them too – too impressionable. But, for the present, he fulfils a role here; he keeps you amused, and – while you are amused – you do not worry.'

'We worry a great deal about German ambitions,' Ransom said quickly.

'I want you to understand them. I – we – have no quarrel with the British. Let me put it in personal terms. You have a relaxed approach to life; you enjoy your social charades and would not want to destroy these pleasures by going to war. I can understand this, even if I do not want to be a permanent part of it. I am a rich man, Mr Ransom. My father was a railroad entrepreneur and my wife has her own business fortune….'

'Made, I believe, from the manufacture of armaments.'

'Yes, yes, but with profit, not war, in mind. The future of Germany lies in peaceful economic strength and we don't want anything to upset that. Unfortunately, something does threaten to upset it.'

'Not England.'

'No, not England, except indirectly. But you are close to Russia, and she is the menace to Europe, with her vast population and re-actionary ruling classes. All competent analyses suggest that Russia will be ready to fight within a few years. Then she will crush us by the weight of her soldiers; then she will have built up her Baltic Sea fleet and her strategic railways.'

'The Tsar is weak. His family live under the spell of a mad-man. He merely shuts himself away in the Peterhof or plays with his feeble little haemophiliac son. You fear that man? Dreamers, with melancholy smiles and timid gestures, don't make successful warriors. Alexandra can tell him to "be an autocrat" in her best Hessian accent, but it will have no effect.'

'None of this worries Sukhomlinov. Now he has yet another wife – the fifth – he can enjoy himself, and he is perfectly prepared to march in the same spirit, knowing that he has one limitless resource: expendable manpower.'

Von Bode neglected to mention that the debt-ridden, extravagant Russian Minister of War was having secret discussions with German intelligence. But his next assertion was indisputable: 'And the Grand Duke Nicholas Nicholaevitch, who commands the army as well as being the Tsar's uncle. Could anyone be more anti-German? While Russia grows in strength, our group becomes weaker. We have to put up with that disintegrating heap of nations beside the Danube as allies.'

'It was your poet Busch who said, "If no longer you like your company, look for another..."'

'"...if any there be",' Von Bode completed; 'you British cannot replace Austria, but you can at least keep out of any little Continental difficulties.'

'You have still given no proof of Russian intentions.'

Von Bode was silent for a moment. 'Let me show you how much I'm prepared to take you into my confidence. For one thing we are fully conversant with Russian preoccupations through our spy in Benckendorff's Embassy in Chesham Place. You may know him – Basil von Siebert, the Second Secretary there. A shy but genial fellow.'

The man was wonderfully cool, Ransom had to admit: it made him the more suspicious of his motives.

'What Von Siebert gives us is not only worrying in what it tells us about Russian aggression, but also about the benevolence of the British towards it.'

'Germany need not worry. You believe you know the English. Our national pastime is inaction: problems solve themselves if you leave them alone. You can trust us. Do you suppose that we would continue to export gold and grain to Germany if we expected to be at war within a few months? Besides, we feel utterly secure. The idea that any force could land upon our shores, march on London, and bring the country rapidly under subjugation is absurd.'

'Your expenditure on armaments does not bear out the image

of a peace-loving people. You have your new naval base at Forsyth – your fleet in the North Sea is enhanced. And yet your Mr Bennett describes Germany as a military despotism threatening mankind and England as the home of freedom. Northcliffe even runs your most venerable newspaper as an anti-German propagandist sheet: what happened to *The Times* of old? What happened to fair play?'

Von Bode took advantage of Ransom's silence. 'By comparison we are a peaceable people. For two years now we have not increased our naval budget: can you say the same? We have even had due regard to British commercial interests when it comes to negotiating over the Persian Gulf: can you deny it? Yes, we want our place in the sun, too – but what is wrong with that?'

'Everyone is bound to view the situation from their own point of view,' Ransom said in conciliatory tone. 'But what I have been trying to say is that war is in no one's interests. It would mean the bankruptcy of Europe, perhaps revolution.'

He caught a strange glint in Von Bode's eyes as he said the last word, but did not pause. 'Half the world's coal comes from European mines; three-quarters of the world's merchant shipping is European. We all have vast investments to protect and we – Germany and Britain – are each other's best trading partners. No one, at least very few of us, love Russia.'

'And the French – and their aggressions? They affront us with the most strictly guarded frontier in the world.…'

'Actually a measure of their weakness. Even if France's armies were a military match to your own, she could not call on anything approaching the same human reserves. Frenchmen have not talked seriously of *La Revanche* for a generation. Remember what Gambetta said: "Never speak of it, always think of it". What power does France have? Ribot. Viviani. Ministries falling like ninepins. More than forty Ministers for War in forty years. An army that still believes in the mad charge, attack at all costs.…'

'And has the *soixante-quinze*, the most impressive gun of our times. Besides, you are allies. Your King and Queen visited Paris not two months ago – even the cartoonists show France seeking to change her engagement with England into a formal marriage.'

'We have our own problems.'

'Yes, and you should concentrate on them. Lichnowsky thinks that the Conservatives will support your government in the end, but I believe you will have civil war over Ireland.'

'Which you are doing your best to encourage.'

'The arms?'

'You admit it?' Ransom said, taken aback.

'We cannot afford to have Britain involved in Continental disputes. We can cope with the Russians by themselves – perhaps; and even with the French and the Russians together. But you must remain neutral.'

'And why don't you make this plain through official channels?'

'Come, come, Mr Ransom. You know that would not work. Too much distrust has been created. But when I heard of your visit to Germany, I thought I should prepare you to make the best of your trip.'

'I made no mention of a trip. It was you who referred to it on the telephone. How do you know of this? What have you heard?'

Von Bode was unperturbed. 'The answer will puzzle you. The fact is that I am in close touch with Anna Kinsky.'

Ransom gasped. 'Anna!' He was incredulous and did not stop to think of what it meant that Von Bode, of all people, should know of their relationship. 'But she abhors all that you and Germany stand for.'

'I dare say,' said Von Bode, cutting Ransom short and continuing with all playfulness gone from his voice. What Von Treitschke pointed out over thirty years ago is undoubtedly true: 'The Jews are a German misfortune.' But I cannot imagine that she approves of you and your beliefs either. It is a little hypocritical, is it not, to rush from the respectable life of a Cabinet Minister into the arms of someone so destructive?'

Ransom ignored the insult. 'But why should she help you?'

'That you will have to find out for yourself. You could try asking her when she last saw her brother; I am only concerned that you should understand that she wants you to listen carefully to all that is explained to you when you go to Germany. And now I suggest that we both need some sleep.'

He would not be drawn further. With much to think about, Ransom walked back to Berkeley Square. Not far away, at the same time, a drunken intruder was discovered within Buckingham Palace, provoking renewed fears for the safety of the Royal Family.

CHAPTER SIX

A visit to Germany is arranged

THE next week, on Tuesday the 9th of June 1914, Parliament reassembled after the Whitsun recess. Ransom was relieved that the House of Commons had nothing more controversial than two Milk and Dairies Bills with which to grapple; it gave him full freedom for his mind to wander.

As he had passed through the lobbies and passages to the Chamber, familiar scenes had seemed to be charged with something sinister: he wanted to talk to someone about his conversation with Von Bode and yet feared, absurdly, that everyone was already talking about it. As ever in the Commons, groups of men conferred, whispered, grumbled, protested, consulted on matters which appeared – and in some cases were – both secret and important.

Since the Parliamentary session had begun in February, the House had not once sat late or on a Saturday; until Easter, Government business had occupied only three days a week. For all the fears about the German menace and the build-up of arms, Sir Edward Grey had shown little sign of wanting to talk about foreign affairs and the Opposition even less sign of wanting to question him.

Immediately before Whitsun Grey had managed a curious speech in which he explained that he had come not to speak but to listen and – as if to elaborate on his lack of a theme – apologized at length for being late. Other Members discreetly withdrew or, in a few cases, fell asleep as he seemed to get into a private conversation with Sir Gilbert Parker about the New Hebrides. The scene was not unfamiliar.

He habitually ignored the Reporters' Gallery behind the Speaker's chair and – with one elbow casually leaning on the dispatch box – he would read, clearly but without modulation of voice, from the carefully prepared text in front of him to the captive members of his own party below the gangway. The journalists were fairly kind, none the less, and even when one of their number, Ransom's friend Michael MacDonagh, described him as a self-conscious schoolboy reading an essay, rather than England's Secretary of State for Foreign Affairs determining the fate of Europe, no one noticed very much.

Only one issue was ever-present – Ireland. And that, perhaps, because of the powerful physical presence of the leaders of the respective factions. Carson, who had led for the prosecution twenty years or so before against Oscar Wilde, always seemed like a giant of a man: his face rather brutal, with dark eyes brooding over a long jaw and heavy, jutting chin; a straight, unyielding nose and curving, mobile mouth which threatened all on whom his glance alighted. Ransom disliked the scowl of self-righteous defiance to be found on Carson's public expression, but would not have told him so. One had to admire what he had done, Ransom grudgingly supposed: a Southern Irishman – a Dublin Protestant of the Church of Ireland – Carson had turned to the north as the spearhead of resistance to Home Rule and had trained rioters and street rabbles to the discipline of a movement.

That at least was what one was bound to think. Ransom knew from his own more pedestrian contribution to politics that what fired men to march was not necessarily what took some to political power. The imperturbable Captain James Craig, the Member for East Down, was Carson's greatest asset: Carson led in the Westminster Parliament, but Craig organized in Ulster, and no one could discount that role in mobilizing a people. Polite, even kindly in manner, this red-faced millionaire director of the whisky distillers, Dunville's, had a mind that was keen, cold and as narrow as the narrowest eye of a needle.

If anyone understood that the Ulstermen's campaign against Home Rule was no sudden outpouring, it was the Catholic leader, John Redmond, though it had only been the events of the Spring that had finally convinced him of the seriousness of the military preparations of his opponents and persuaded him to encourage his own people's Volunteers. 'The face and figure of a Roman Emperor,' was what Wilfrid Blunt had said of him and, as usual when someone sounded as if they were being clever, Ransom had to join the applause. But the description was not very apt: light blue eyes, ruddy-faced, firm mouth were the sum of it. Most things about Redmond were very un-Irish; he was careful, conventional, rather fussy in his dress; lived quietly, avoided invitations, was 'Yours very truly' to friend and foe alike in the few letters – all of them to a purpose – that he wrote. When in London he dined most evenings at the Commons and lived in an unostentatious flat in Kensington with his wife.

There would not be much to be gained by talking in confidence with him – his quiet implacability was, in a way, even more frightening than Carson's passionate showmanship. He sat that day, as any other, on the top bench below the gangway on the Opposition side: with his wary eyes and prominent nose, MacDonagh said, he was like an eagle.

Redmond was purposeful, but took nothing for granted. 'Is there anything that can rob us this time?' a Tipperary priest had asked him. 'A European war might do it,' was the cautious reply. In Ireland, at Anghavanagh in Co. Wicklow, he bided his time in the rather forbidding building he used as a shooting lodge and which had originally been built as a barracks at the time of Wolf Tone's rebellion in 1798.

Now, with the new, and almost certainly decisive Session well under way, he was prepared for anything. Next to him in the Chamber sat his confederate, and one-time enemy, James Dillon, a melancholy, aging figure, with a white beard and moustache and spectacles that did not suit him, but with a toughness, a severity and an integrity that was exactly the same as it had been when as a young and intense Irish patriot, he had confidently gone in search of his aims.

Before this sitting in the Commons, the Speaker's Chaplain, Archdeacon Wilberforce, had said prayers for God's light and guidance. Whether God was thinking of Carson's crowd or of Redmond's rabble was not clear. Afterwards the thin, other-worldly Archdeacon, dressed in black silk gown with scarlet bands, retired to the Bar according to custom – backwards, bowing to Speaker Lowther, who presided from his dominantly positioned high chair. Asquith was on the Treasury bench, Grey to his left, Lloyd George in turn to the left of the Foreign Secretary.

Seated at the end of the bench, Ransom was interrupted in his thoughts by a note passed to him. He read: 'Dear Mr Ransom – I would appreciate a word about your travel arrangements. Now, if at all possible. I shall be sitting to the left of the entrance to the Members' Lobby. Yours truly – V. Kell.'

With some sense of unease, he left the Chamber to find Kell.

He had never met the man and knew only distantly of the work of his department, which was treated with scant seriousness by the political establishment. Kell evidently recognized him, for he came straight over and held out his hand. Taking it, Ransom said, 'I'm flattered that you should come yourself.'

'To be honest, there aren't very many of us,' was Kell's retort. 'Not nearly enough, given the perils ahead. It may be, as your distinguished colleague, Lord Haldane, told the House of Commons, that there are those who look about for useful information when they're abroad. He said: "That is a different thing from coming as spies" – he was right, but not in the way he meant. We badly need professionals, not snobbery, when it comes to intelligence-gathering. As it is, we're all very stretched, the police included.'

'You won't have heard, but already there's been trouble this morning at Court with the Suffragettes: just one young lady this time. I gather that the King managed not to notice, but the Queen was furious. Still' – he glanced at his watch – 'the real militants will be getting it in the neck at any moment. You know Tothill Street, not far from here? There is a raid in the hornets' nest about to take place.'

Here was useful babble to put one at one's ease, even if – in Ransom's case – it did not quite succeed.

They burrowed deep into the House of Commons, down passageways and stairs, past historic busts and paintings, to one of the interview rooms. Ransom was not happy with so public a place, though he knew how many private conversations that stayed private took place there. Kell, by contrast, was relaxed.

'Let me tell you a story, Mr Ransom,' he said. 'Fifty years ago, during the American Civil War, an important state politician in Ohio publicly sympathized with the Confederacy. Ohio had not then been invaded. Vallandigham – for that was his name – was tried by court martial and convicted of sedition and supporting the Confederacy. The Supreme Court would not interfere – rightly so. *Our* enemies do not so clearly identify themselves: while the gentlemen of the House of Commons engage in slanging matches, much of Europe is getting ready to march.'

'You mistake the surface for the reality,' Ransom countered firmly. 'The members of your department have no monopoly of insight.'

'Quite so,' said Kell, who was nevertheless clear that the publicly seen manipulators of opinion, the Prime Minister among them, were too easily swayed by naïve assertions and by their own vanity. 'I simply want to convey to you my own view of the situation and of what is needed. You will then judge for yourself.'

Ransom nodded, and Kell continued. 'When the Kaiser last came to England, for the late King's funeral, he brought with him at least one secret intelligence specialist – a spymaster, if you like. He was identified and followed, but not exposed. It gave us a very good picture of what was happening. Much of the work of the Germans here is innocuous enough and more directed towards the Navy than anything: their communications chief – working from a hotel in the East End – is on the grand retainer of £1 per week. You will have been party to Mr Churchill's decision to allow us to open suspect letters on a general rather than a special warrant: that has given us a rather good idea of the quality of information – or rather the lack of it – being supplied.'

Ransom had nodded again, though in fact he had known nothing of Churchill's action three years before as Home Secretary. 'I believe the system is only used for proven spies,' he said wryly: it would not do for his own correspondence with Anna to be scrutinized. 'Naturally, we are scrupulous,' said Kell, who – it later transpired – had already been working on a means of keeping closer tabs on the relationship. Apart from anything else, he had some evidence that German Imperial funds were being used to aid extremists and their organizations in England.

'What, then, is the problem?' Ransom asked.

'The Germans, like us, are given too few resources. They still have a potentially impressive system: you can make a grand tour from Ciro's in Monte Carlo to the Royal at Dinard, to Maxim's in Paris, the Grand at Rome or the Hotel Hungaria in Budapest – they're all part of a network. A tribute in the main to one man: Colonel Walter Nicolai, the head of the German Secret Service. A Prussian, worldly, but not brutish: I expect you will meet him.'

Kell poured himself a glass of stale water from the table at which they sat. 'None of it would matter if it were not for German intentions, and whether or not we are prepared. The French have their fortifications at Maubeuge, for example – proof against anything "short of the heaviest siege artillery": the kind of artillery that needs properly prepared and sited gun platforms able to take the strain. Well, we happen to have observed that Frederic Krupp bought 600 acres of land in the woods of Lanières, no more than 4 miles from Maubeuge, three years ago. Do you suppose that he was indulging a whim? It doesn't matter that they don't know everything about our forces: it doesn't matter because they themselves are so strong. They will act, take my word for it. The question is when, and where.'

Kell allowed the words to sink in, and then began again in a different tone. He gave a clear and detailed account of when and how Ransom would travel, what he could expect to find out and whom he could expect to meet.

It was the last item that was the most startling. It seemed that he could gain access to the Kaiser. 'It's relatively simple really,' said Kell. 'Wilhelm doesn't discourage unofficial diplomacy, though he may treat it as a bit of a game. He likes the attention.'

'But surely it's the others that count. The military men. The Chancellor.'

'In part, sometimes in small part. But the Kaiser still rules and, what's more, if there is any mad scheme in train you can bet the Kaiser's behind it.'

'Remember this when you see him: in all his life only three people have been brave enough to stand up to him – his mother; Queen Victoria; and Edward VII. And they're all dead. "I follow my own course; it is the right one." "He who opposes my will, him will I smash to pieces." That's where the argument gets strangled at birth.'

'I shan't be arguing.'

'You shouldn't. But don't assume that all the histrionics mean that he's out of touch. He knows when to be a realist – knows, with respect, much more than any of your colleagues. The richest man in Berlin is Friedlander, the Jewish coal magnate: the Kaiser made him Von Friedländer-Fuld. It was the same with Von Schwabach, the head of the Bleichroder Bank.'

'I can see what you mean. What worries me is that the realism is mixed with a sort of lunatic obsession. I remember Grey telling me of the time Edward VII was invited to the Berlin Opera House to see one of the Greek tragedies. They made sure not only that the utensils, the clothes, the buttons, the weapons, everything was authentic; they even had a real funeral-pyre for the scene in which a monarch ended his life. Apparently the King was so alarmed that he thought the whole opera house was on fire.'

Kell smiled, but only briefly. 'The obsession goes right through German society: and you must expect most people to be supportive of the Kaiser. To begin with, the press is expected to be biased. Everything is designed to support the view of the Kaiser as cool, far-seeing, resolute, decisive. Bethman-Hollweg and the other politicians are probably more than a little afraid of him….'

'They're a little frightening themselves,' Ransom interjected. 'A foreign minister who, when asked how he would cope with the

Suffragettes, says with every sign of truthfulness, "I would beat them and I would kill them," is somewhat far removed from Sir Edward Grey.'

'Yes, Jagow is tough and confident. And there is also the army. Remember that the Kaiser likes to be seen as a military figure: one of the more useless pieces of information we have is that he is possessed of no less than 295 different uniforms. There's much clicking of heels, saluting and enthusiastic agreement with him from the military. They have their own courts of justice and, ultimately, answer to no one but the Kaiser. Nothing but contempt for the British army, by the way.'

'Is it unrelieved by nothing?' Ransom queried, in depressed voice.

Kell shook his head. 'Some might say the Empress. But she's German through and through. Bülow said so. All foreigners are unsatisfactory for one reason or another, and she feels she must work faithfully at her husband's side. He doesn't always want her there, but that's another story.' He paused. 'You see, right from the beginning Wilhelm was taught never to subordinate himself to anyone. Anyone. Even to talk about what he proposes makes you a *nörgler*, a grumbler, and it's a short step from that to traitor.'

Kell was efficient. Of that there was no doubt. He impressed on Ransom the vital importance of his mission, which was rapidly turning from dilettante dream into extraordinary reality. 'If they manage to help the Irish into Civil War, anything might happen. The Prime Minister told you, I think, about the German links with the Clan-na-Gael in America. If you're in doubt, I suggest you read the enclosed: it tells you what happens when that band of sweeties meets to admit a new member.'

Kell left first, and I slowly opened the crumpled paper. It read:

'Officers and brothers. We meet to perform a sacred duty. The cause of Ireland has been entrusted to our keeping, and we are here to protect and advance its interests. To rid Ireland of English rule, establish an Irish Republic and to elevate our race to its proper position is a task within our power if we are true to ourselves and to the glorious example set before us. By force alone can we win, as by force alone, under God's providence, our race has been preserved. As soldiers of freedom, we know that order, discipline and obedience to the authority of our brothers must guide our efforts and govern our conduct. May God direct our work and may the spirit of Tone, Emmet, Pearse and all the Irish martyrs animate us, so that this accession to our number may act as a tower of strength to our cause and a credit to our race.'

CHAPTER SEVEN

At the Lichnowskys

IN the early evening, in Rosalind's company, Ransom made a second visit to the German Embassy in Carlton House Terrace, just a few days after the first. The circumstances were very different. The air was warm, scented with unseen flowers. As they entered, they parted company for the cloakrooms, then rejoined each other to ascend the broad marble staircase, with flowers and greenery on either side. At the head of the stairs, by the first reception room, their hostess awaited them.

The Princess Lichnowsky was flanked by liveried footmen. The last time he had seen this comely, cultured woman she had been lying languorously back, idly stroking her dog and slightly more animatedly discussing the Italian Futurists before a concert by Mr Stewart Wilson. Margot Asquith had also been there: tea, like everything else at the Lichnowskys, was a social event. The Princess was a direct descendant of Maria Theresa and managed to project both nobility and dignity without their usual accompaniments: arrogance and pride. She loved impulsive behaviour and did not understand narcissism (which was why, according to Rosalind, she allowed herself to get overweight).

'Mr Ransom, Rosalind, how wonderful to see you.' In a moment, not in what she said but in her manner, she managed to convey that their coming to the reception was genuinely a matter of great importance to her.

Encouraged, Rosalind, too, was effusive. 'I did so admire your gown the other evening at *Prince Igor*.'

Further discussion of the sights of Drury Lane was cut short by the arrival of more guests. Rosalind and her husband passed on, to where two other reception rooms were en suite, with a music room beyond. Beneath their feet the floors were bare but highly polished; above them invisible electric lights, set in moulded ceilings, provided only the hint of a glow in rooms already well lit from large windows. Through one of them, across the hall, the trees of St James's Park could be seen gently swaying in the breeze.

In the music room a young man with a long name and longer hair played Chopin. Later, singers from one of the opera houses drew crowds round the platform, everyone staring hard at the soprano without for a moment abating their conversation.

Downstairs, in one of the dining rooms, flower-decked tables were well attended by correct, impassive waiters, ready to satiate appetites that in some cases had been satiated already, and would be again.

The Ambassador himself stood near the entrance to the third reception room. Margot Asquith, who seemed to be fond of him, had playfully summed him up: 'Pointed head, peevish voice, bad mannered to the servants.' 'How unfair,' said Rosalind, and for once her husband agreed. 'German governments appoint men of honour as ambassadors,' Walter observed, 'and', he continued, risking a glance at Von Bode across the room, 'they have intriguers as First Secretaries.' The jibe was not itself wholly fair: as it happened, more than one other member of the Embassy staff had written home hinting – even declaring – that Lichnowsky had been fooled by Grey and had become an inveterate Anglophile.

'Would that the same governments had their own sense of honour,' the Prime Minister said. He had joined them with Margot. 'When Metternich resigned because of "ill-health" everyone knew that Tirpitz had set out deliberately to discredit him.'

Metternich's successor as German Ambassador in London, Marschall von Bieberstein, had died before he could take office – though not before the Embassy had been redecorated from top to bottom – and Prince Lichnowsky was his rather surprising replacement. Lichnowsky behaved like the liberal grand seigneur, with an eighteenth-century demeanour to match – so different from the lesser nobility, the junkers from east of the Elbe.

'Dear old Lichnowsky always imagines that to gossip about something is the same as doing it. He doesn't seem to understand that Society is just the showpiece, at most the symbol of power; he thinks it's the reality,' Asquith continued in a satisfied tone.

Since anyone wanting to be a German diplomat – at any rate until a few years before – had to show an independent income of at least 10,000 marks, it was not so peculiar that the rich old families should continue to display their own particular values while in the service of the state. Lichnowsky himself owned extensive estates in Silesia and encouraged applicants to the German Foreign Office who had a similar background.

'Don't underestimate him,' said Margot. 'It isn't fashionable for a German prince to read Nietzsche, or to favour modern art.'

'Nor to talk with Jews,' Ransom added.

'Oh, yes, but in the main he's only carrying out the Kaiser's instructions. You can imagine. Give good dinners, show yourself at the races. Be a jolly good fellow. Wilhelm's shrewder than his own Foreign Office, who have always distrusted the dilettante.'

'I'm not sure that I understand what you mean,' said Rosalind, who seemed unusually anxious to see the point.

'Well, he's been successful in his way, I suppose. We are all *here*, aren't we? The English and the Germans may be ready to go to war, but it doesn't stop the German Ambassador and his beguiling wife' – he smiled at the Princess, who was out of earshot – 'from making the Embassy a social centre.'

'People like wealth and lavish entertaining,' said Rosalind, 'especially if it goes along with affability.'

'Precisely,' said the Prime Minister, his case made.

Margot, however, liked to have the last word. 'When he first came to London, he said to me that he had told the Kaiser at the time of his appointment that if he wanted trouble with England he was not the right man. I asked him: "And is there desire for trouble?" "No, it is all exaggerated. I have never observed ill-feeling." He uses an innocent smile well enough.'

'Finish the story,' said Asquith, a little impatiently.

'But, you know,' Lichnowsky added, 'Our Kaiser is a man of impulse.'

Margot smiled, unlike the rest of them.

The Ransoms wandered over to where Prince Lichnowsky was talking to Sir Edward Grey. 'However any such affair might come out,' Grey was saying, 'one thing is certain: that is, total exhaustion and impoverishment. Industry and trade will be ruined, and the power of capital destroyed.'

'Sombre words,' Ransom commented.

The Ambassador at once interjected in relaxing tone: 'When a money box is filled with gold it certainly does not clatter, but when there is not a penny in it, it does not clatter either. Now, some escapades of your colleague Winston Churchill make such a noise that they bemuse me with their sheer clamour; but when Sir Edward takes the box in his hands no one would know whether it was full or empty. And that is true bemusing.'

Lichnowsky did not believe, as many in Berlin did, that Germany was threatened by encirclement. Echoing Grey's sentiments of a moment before, he had himself written to the Kaiser that 'our policy should be guided solely and alone by the need of sparing the German nation a struggle which it has nothing to gain from and everything to lose'. He did not know that Chancellor Bethmann-Hollweg deleted such sentences from his dispatches – he merely received back hectoring notes of the kind Von Jagow, the Foreign Minister, had just sent him: 'We have not built our fleet in vain, and in my opinion people in England will seriously ask themselves whether it will be just that simple and without danger to play the role of France's guardian angel against us.'

Grey was looking a little uncomfortable; and Ransom could think of nothing sufficiently clever to follow the Ambassador's last remark. Rosalind rushed in where others did not want to tread. 'We have all benefited so much from having you and the Princess in London.'

Lichnowsky beamed, even bowed slightly. 'I am honoured to be so popular with so charming a lady. I had never expected to have the opportunity to come here, you know. I retired a decade ago, in anticipation of nothing but dinner parties and receptions for ever more, and my inadequacies as a diplomat are obvious – especially to my colleague, the Baron von Holstein.'

'Die graue Eminenz of the German Foreign Office,' Ransom muttered.

The Ambassador smiled. Frankness was his nature, and – at this reception – his diplomatic skill. His wife, who had heard the last exchange, commented: 'He was delighted to get the appointment, and I shared his delight. We were staying in that wonderful hotel, the Atlantic in Hamburg, and he rushed into my bedroom clutching an autographed letter from the Emperor. "I've got it!"

We had not even run a legation before.'

'Oh, well, I am just an old man keeping the post warm.' Lichnowsky's confession would have pleased the German Foreign Office's candidate, the young Geheimrat Wilhelm von Stumm, who had been distinctly displeased to have been passed over. 'But England is an agreeable place. You are all part of the same society, with common habits and a greater liking for a hospitable house than apparently profound general knowledge. Even if you do not always consort with each other, there is not the same unbridgeable gulf between, say, Mr Asquith and the Duke of Devonshire as there is between M. Briand and the Duc de Doudeauville.'

Coming from someone who had seen the abrupt departure of Lord Londonderry immediately after dinner with the King and Queen, in order to avoid being with Sir Edward Grey, this sounded unconvincing; but the Princess nevertheless added: 'We have a saying in Germany. "The Briton loathes a bore, a schemer and a prig; what he likes is a good fellow."'

It was difficult to resist such rich affability. 'You enjoyed your time in Oxford?' Rosalind asked the Ambassador.

'A wonderful occasion,' declared Lichnowsky, who had received an honorary Doctorate the previous day. 'Splendid tradition, and yet a typically English lack of formality. In a great chair sat the Vice-Chancellor of the University, murmuring (I have to confess) inaudible Latin words pronounced like English. Then the Public Orator delivered a long speech in Latin, praising (to my embarrassment) my supposed services to letters, and emphasizing amid applause that the honour done to me was a token of English admiration for German scholarship and for the German nation.'

'I bet that will go down well with readers of the *Berliner Tageblatt*,' Ransom observed under his breath.

Lichnowsky was more serious as he continued: 'It sounded very fine to hear this Englishman's voice ring through the ancient hall as he cried, *Totam Germaniam animo salutamus*. For a moment one had the feeling that an Ambassador could really form a link between two nations.'

Grey was staring awkwardly at the ceiling: he had had enough of this unofficial diplomacy. Noticing, Lichnowsky speedily adopted a different tone: 'And then there was the excellent lunch given by Professor and Mrs Fielder at Queens. Which reminds me that we are all overdue in attending the supper table.'

* * *

Afterwards Ransom invited the American Ambassador for a night-cap. Page had himself asked him to the Albert Hall Peace Centenary Ball, which was to take place the following day to celebrate a hundred years of Anglo-American peace.

Rosalind sat uneasily on the edge of her chair, while Ransom puffed a cigar and read from *The Times*. 'We have most grievously upset Congressman Mann from Chicago. Listen to him protesting about the peace celebrations. "Why not celebrate the day they burned the Capitol building? Do them honour; do it brown; tell them what great people they were when they marched up to Washington and burned the Capitol building."'

'Yes,' said Page, 'there was a scheme to erect Queen Victoria's statue in Central Park. I'm afraid it would have given full-time occupation to the police restraining the Celtic enthusiasts whose life's ambition it would have become to blow it up.'

'It would be no bad thing if the President could be persuaded to pay us a visit,' Ransom said. 'I gather he was asked when a public subscription was raised to buy the Washington family seat here.'

'As a matter of fact, except for a minute or two that President Taft spent over the Mexican border, no President has ever left the country. You see, we have to concentrate on being Americans. My infallible test of a genuine American is that when he votes or when he acts or when he fights his heart and his thoughts are centred nowhere but in the emotions and the purposes and the politics of the United States. We are not Europeans anymore.' He spoke firmly, but in friendship.

'Yes, but you cannot simply opt out.' Ransom felt suddenly a little drunk. 'I'd doff my own cap to Woodrow Wilson in preference to the Kaiser.'

'Herr Dr Hesamer would have his own ideas about that.'

'Doctor Who?'

'He is, by his own grace, "the acting ruler of all Germans in the United States".'

'Incredible. But presumably there's more to fear from the Irish Americans than the Germans?'

'Maybe. We hear wind, as you may, of money-raising efforts for the Irish Volunteers. But I don't think you will find the Clan-na-Gael are great enthusiasts for Mr Redmond: not in the person of Chairman Joseph McGarrity, you can be sure.'

Rosalind sighed. 'Was it always like this? Violence everywhere. When the Irish are quiet, the women take over.'

'You should live in a civilized country,' retorted Page in good humour.

'Mrs Pankhurst marches again tomorrow,' said Rosalind, happy to be involved in the conversation again. 'Another deputation to Parliament.'

'They'll stop it,' Ransom commented decisively.

'They must.' Page nodded, no longer joking. 'They must. Because this violence must stop. They don't seem to care whether the innocent are hurt. It was bad enough when the damage was only to property – quite why a chopper had to be taken to Mr Henry James in that most excellent painting by Sargent I cannot fathom – but now they seem to be all for the reckless use of bombs in public places.'

Rosalind cleared her throat. 'I do agree, but you would have to accept that the women have a good case. Their husbands will not involve them in their work and – when not working – retreat into their studies or into the company of their male friends. Shopping, charities, organizing the household bores them. But of what else have we to speak? What are we to do in our large, empty houses?'

The Ambassador did not appear to notice that she had begun with the generality and finished with a personal plea of her own. Her husband knew what she meant and moved uncomfortably in his chair.

'Women are kept in such ignorance,' Rosalind continued with a certain calm. 'One of the servant girls confessed to me that she and her friends were brought up to suppose that if a man kissed them on the lips, then, well then they would have a baby.'

Elsie, Ransom thought, flirting with images of her in his mind.

Page was content with this turn of the conversation and said: 'I do believe that it is our duty to improve the conditions of the women wage-earners: it will be a great issue for the future. And we shall have to face the political consequences of the suffrage. My friends tell me that in the recent Illinois elections, in which a high proportion of women voted, the influence may have been decisive in the vote for temperance.'

'I don't suppose that they influenced the Chicago bosses,' Ransom said, a little tactlessly.

'Oh, it wouldn't surprise me if you were quite wrong,' Page replied, quite unruffled. 'But will the vote come here?'

Ransom was non-committal. He knew that, in the Cabinet, Grey, Lloyd George and Haldane were in favour, Crewe, Samuel of the Local Government Board and Harcourt of the Colonial Office against. Asquith did not seem to understand what all the fuss was about, and that would probably mean that the women would have to wait. Ransom just said: 'It is a difficult issue. One of the many – as we have already noted.'

The Ambassador's careless arm swept his drink onto the carpet, and then – once the ensuing confusion had passed – he took his departure. It was late, he said, and he had drunk a great deal. Rosalind's expression did not reveal the fact that she could only agree.

Ransom sank back into his chair, his thoughts with Anna. One day he had teased her with *The Unexpurgated Case Against Woman Suffrage*, Sir Almroth Wright's extraordinary tract bemoaning the emancipation of the female sex from their traditional beliefs (and their traditional ethics) and their increasing role in public life – fast becoming 'one vast cock-and-hen show'.

At once she had turned on him, eyes blazing, putting the case for women exploited by men rampant with venereal disease, the women who could be liberated once they were politically free and economically strong. 'Votes for Women and Chastity for Men', as the Suffragette slogan had it, though Anna herself had scant faith in the power of the vote for the downtrodden of either sex.

However silly Wright's complaints about the moods of women, their recurring hypersensitivity and lack of any sense of proportion, it was odd, he thought, that the fastidious, neurotic, neuralgic, dyspeptic Mrs Pankhurst seemed to bear out the worst male prejudices. He was on the side of good order, wasn't he? He saw Anna before him and knew that the answer to that question could not be wholly yes so long as she was part of his life. What place could he have in Curzon's wretched League for Opposing Women's Suffrage, or even with the progressives in his own party? Anna was so much cleverer than either the pro's or the anti's, kneeling naked beside him, contemptuous not merely of his male friends, but of all those upper middle class, comfortable, so-called militant Suffragettes. Let them serve the life of a seamstress for six months, breathe the air of the workshop, before they mouthed their grand sentiments!

Let them throw off their clothes and take the man they want for the sake of their own unashamed passion!

In this state, he could not face Rosalind. It was a shame, because she was almost charming, certainly friendly after Page left. Then he asked her to go away and could not say why. That was the signal for her mood to change, and change rapidly, as if it had only been by a great effort that she had managed any warmth. She never knew where he was, she said, or what he was doing; and she didn't care. She never had.

He could not summon up the will to fight; it was too easy to retreat to his own bedroom, and he was too tired. Too tired, indeed, to sleep. There was much to be done before his departure, now set for the coming weekend, but after an hour or two of restlessness he opened the front door of his house, noisily amidst the still of the night, and walked into the street.

* * *

He wandered in quiet enjoyment of the London he knew so well. He thought of the grand mansions of Park Lane: Dudley House, Grosvenor House, Dorchester House, this last with its unforgettable central staircase. He imagined the daily spectacle of the riders in Rotten Row, the riches of Hyde Park with its summer flowers and its stately trees more than two centuries old. He recalled the Piccadilly goat, still to be encountered wandering the pavements of that esteemed thoroughfare when he was in his twenties. He watched the busy traction engines now thundering down it, carrying their fruit and vegetables to Covent Garden for the early morning market.

Over there was a cinema, a white-and-gold Picturedrome: a treasure house of delights, where for 6d or a shilling, a commissionaire with medals from the Charge of the Light Brigade (at the least) and grey-uniformed attendants would usher one past real palms to sit in front of thrilling dramas (each one preceded by Mr Redford's certificate guaranteeing its morality), while the piano or musical organ played.

What need was there for dreams, with all this freely, or almost freely, available? An end to dreaming was the beginning of real hope.

And yet…if the stones of London gleamed with lines of gold, their base was the most enervating greyness. So it seemed when he arrived in Clarges Street, without Anna. She had dropped her handkerchief and he clutched it until the sweat from his hand made it damp. She had told him the truth often enough: London listens to birth or wealth. Rosalind would have agreed – certain things were immutable, unquestionable: brown boots could not be worn in London, any more than blue-spotted ties could be worn in the country. He had no desire to question such rules, but he would argue with Anna, as he would not with Rosalind, for the sheer joy of watching her talk.

'Anything goes now,' he had said. 'The more poisonous your taste, and your accent, the better.'

'Explain that to the Earl of Derby, or the poor people who cannot even watch him spend at the rate of £50,000 a year,' she retorted. Head thrust forward, not play-acting this time. 'The old order is alive because it understands power and its realities: new traditions are being created daily in order to reinforce it.'

Misreading her mood, he said bluffly: 'We pay income tax seven times greater than just forty years ago….'

'*We*', she said – the word almost spat, he was alarmed to find himself observing. It was true, he supposed, that he spoke only on behalf of those who for generations had never needed to worry about money. With the lawyers, they – and not the businessmen, still less the working class – controlled the paths that led to political power. Ironically, Anna and her kind seemed a little easier in their minds about that than about the creators of wealth: the red-faced, hard-featured businessmen with their stubby fingers, gross bodies and gross habits. They were easier to caricature than those who appeared more certain about their position in society, but – thank God! – the world was a more interesting place than satire ever managed to divine.

What Anna had seen, and he had only considered under her influence, was the poverty that lay beyond the small band of rich – new rich or old rich – and the slightly bigger group of aspiring middle classes, polishing (or getting their servants to polish) their brass and their silver so that it might shine as brightly as their prejudices. Even so, he poured contempt on the 'isms'. Syndicalism, Feminism, Anarchism. The Pacifism of the members of the National Peace Movement, who were celebrating ten years of existence in a three-day meeting in Liverpool that week. And the Bohemianism of the middle-class refugees who lived in lodgings in the narrow streets and decaying squares of Bloomsbury or the studios of Chelsea.

'Anyone in your position', Anna told him, 'can afford to be sceptical.'

'Anyone in yours must believe.'

He lay down on the bed that he had so often shared with her and closed his eyes. 'And on the world goes.' Anna's handkerchief dropped from his grasp, a crumpled rag.

CHAPTER EIGHT

The Kaiser explains

AS Ransom prepared to leave for Germany, the domestic
political scene worsened. Bonar Law, speaking in Inverness
before a crowd numbered in thousands, accused the Government of
tearing open the old wounds of Ireland to keep in power. Asquith,
he said, had no mandate for Home Rule and was provoking law-
lessness by acting as a dictator in the name of the King. The absurd
cry of 'the Army against the People' was an inept disguise for the
Government's declaration of war against the Nation, and in that
conflict the Nation would win.

Meantime, the Opposition in the House of Commons warded
off accusations of fomenting rebellion in Ireland by condemning
the anarchical behaviour of the Suffragettes, and the Government's
vacillation and indecision in the face of it. The point seemed made
when, as the Home Secretary – Reginald McKenna – was defending
the Government's record, a bomb exploded under the Coronation
Chair in Westminster Abbey. This crude device, consisting of two
large domes from a bicycle bell filled with chlorate explosive and

iron nuts, represented almost enough of a problem for Ransom to cancel his trip. It would make his absence the more difficult to explain, he told Asquith; but – in a brief telephone conversation – the Prime Minister remained firmly against postponement.

On Sunday a great storm hit the south of London. Birds were killed by enormous hail stones. Children sheltering under a tree on the east side of Wandsworth Common were hit by a flash of lightning shortly after one o'clock; three of them died within the hour at the nearby Bolingbroke Hospital. John Burns, from his home in Clapham, was quick in helping to organize a relief fund for the families of the dead and for others who were injured.

The bad weather quickly took itself across the Channel. At Diedenhofen, in Germany, an army airship was wrecked. In Paris there were many serious subsidences; sewers burst; gas mains broke. At the Place St Augustin a taxi fell through a hole that opened up in the road; driver and fare were found dead in muddy water at the bottom of the pit. Fifteen people slipped through the crust of the street by the Place St Philippe du Roule and no more than four of them survived.

Thus it was that when Ransom left the security of the marble-columned Great Eastern Hotel in Harwich to board his boat at Parkeston Quay, the squally winds threatened to keep him on English soil. There followed a desperately uncomfortable journey (though at 58s 9d First Class not an inexpensive one) on the Danish Royal Mail Steamer. All but twenty-four hours in length, it took him via Esbjorg to Copenhagen. He could, of course, have sailed to Hamburg, but Kell had suggested this rather roundabout route, made even more unpleasant for him and the other passengers by news of the collision of the US liner *New York* and the Hamburg-America steamer *Pretoria*.

For him it seemed a meaningless inconvenience. Copenhagen felt full of conspiracy for some reason. He had been there only once before, to Christiansborg Castle just outside the City, at an official reception marked mainly by the presence of royal familiars: Queen Alexandra and her sister, the Dowager Empress Marie of Russia, the Queen of Denmark and her husband's cousin, the King of Greece.

His hotel, the Palace on Rådhuspladsen, was full of Germans; the servants spoke German as if it were their first language; and much of the babble of debate around him was in German too. It was, as ever, difficult for a small nation. Many Danes had not forgotten that their powerful German neighbours had forced them to give up Schleswig-Holstein in the 1860s – though a hundred years had not erased the viler infamy: the British destruction of the Danish fleet, accompanied by the burning of parts of Copenhagen, in the Napoleonic Wars.

He wandered thoughtfully through the Copenhagen streets, along Vester Voldgade from his hotel, down Studiesstrade to Nørregade; a pause there by the statue in front of the Bishop's Residence across from the Vor Frue Kirke Cathedral; too uneasy in his mind to take in anything in great detail.

Two trains daily carried several hundred passengers to Berlin. First there was a land journey, then a boat to a seaside village; train again, though for a shorter period, followed by transfer to a large steamer and a crossing of the Baltic to Germany. Theoretically, an overnight stop might be made here, but the town of Warnemünde was full of German soldiers on manoeuvres: it was almost a military camp, offering little in the way of hospitality.

And so to Berlin, Europe's third city in size, much of it newly built in the ostentatious style of the self-confident generation that preceded his own. The architecture, everything about it, celebrated a nation displaying its rather recently acquired status in the world. Three million people lived in this, the capital of Prussia and the home of the Imperial Government. Diplomats from each of the twenty-five states in the German Empire overfilled the place with their noisy and often petty presence. As he arrived in the late afternoon, many Berliners were still busily engaged in the work of the new week, looking forward, perhaps, to an evening in the local *Kneipe*, the pubs that cheered otherwise rather grim lives. If it was true that the workers' slogan *Berlin gehört uns* – Berlin belongs to us – was not a mere aspiration, it was equally true that the territory over which they ruled, the north and east of the City, was an unpleasant place, quite different from the wealth and spaciousness he encountered when, at last, he emerged wearily from his train.

At the exit to the Friedrichstrasse Station, a policeman gave him a metal ticket with the number of a cab. He rode in his taxi down Friedrichstrasse itself, to where it joined the Unter der Linden about half way down. At least a mile long, with trees on either side, the Linden was the grandest, more controversially the most delightful boulevard in the world. At its north end, just by the Pariser Platz, were pleasure gardens and also the Arch of Triumph at the Brandenburg Gate. In the Sieges Allee in the Tiergarten themselves, splendid marble statues of German's Hohenzollern rulers were to be seen in dominant poses, permanently reigning over the mere mortals – Luther and Kant among them – who were their puny servants.

The Linden was nearly 200 feet wide, taking its name from the lime trees – interspersed with chestnuts – which lined it. Here were mansions, hotels, restaurants and – for nearly twenty years past – shops: the corner of Friedrichstrasse and Unter der Linden was Bond Street writ large.

As his taxi passed, the many soldiers could easily be distinguished from the rest of the crowd: stocky, muscle-bound Prussians, with jaws like granite and necks bursting out of their tight-fitting collars; prominent moustaches and short, bristle-rough hair; eyes without human warmth but hinting at malign intelligence; grey uniforms hugging close to the body, brass buttons on tunics and crimson stripes on trousers. He stared at them, involuntarily.

At No. 1, not more than seven years old, was the Hotel Adlon: the creation of Gause and Leibnitz. Built and decorated for not a pfennig less than twenty million marks, it had modern conveniences enough to make even American visitors gasp. Luxurious fittings both in the rooms and everywhere else in the hotel made a strange contrast with the threadbare grandeur of the Imperial Palace not far away. Indeed, here among the guests were often to be found those who had come to see the Kaiser – but who did not stay at the Palace at the other end of the Linden. The Kaiser himself had been present at its opening: *Es ist schöner als bei uns*, he had said.

Ransom had scarcely entered his room when the telephone rang. The voice at the other end was brusque and formal. 'Mr Ransom? This is Colonel Nicolai. A car will pick you up so that we may begin – shall we say late this evening at 10 o'clock?'

* * *

He had been advised not to question the arrangements and felt no desire to do so. He left his cases to be unpacked and made his way down to reception. Perhaps there would just be time to see one of those dreadful German tragedies by Hauptmann, Sudermann or one of the others at the theatre: anything to take his mind off what was to follow.

The hall porter gave him a long, apologetic account of the difficulties of getting theatre tickets at short notice in Berlin. You could try telegraphing; you could telephone; you could threaten; you could offer to pay twenty times over the fee for *Vorverkauf* – advance booking; you could queue, and discover that there was one box office for all nine classes from top gallery to boxes. Why, two hundred or more had queued for *Fledermaus* and the police had to be brought in to maintain order. Now, if Mr Ransom was looking for something simple, a nice young girl, sex in any form, that was available in a moment….

Instead, he wandered into the Unter der Linden. Past the offices of the *Berliner Lokal-Anzeiger*, where the latest telegrams and events of the day were exhibited. Past the Russian Embassy at No. 7, the former palace of Frederick the Great's sister, the Princess Amelia, which had been rebuilt in the 1840s. Here were the reading rooms of the *Chicago Daily News*; a choice of choicest cafés (Victoria or Bauer?); the depressing British Embassy, at the corner of the Linden and Wilhelmstrasse, which had been a purchase from a bankrupt railway entrepreneur nearly half a century before; Schulte's art shop, new in the past decade, next door to the sombrely grand Ministry of the Interior. And then, at the far end, he reached the great mid-nineteenth century monument of Frederick the Great: king on horseback, with an ermine-mantle and crutch-handled stick, set on a pedestal with its own reliefs.

Here he stopped, looking to the right at the Palace of the Emperor Wilhelm I, which the Kaiser had made his own residence. Would he perhaps see inside it?

From there he no longer had, or cared about, his bearings: he wanted to smell the city. If it seemed decadent, he smiled, it was certainly not the decadence of the tango or the turkey trot, the most serious of the apparent threats to the old values in England. Big apartment houses, left over from the last century and built round courtyards, were much in evidence, their overblown entrances hiding whatever might lie beyond. A heart of gold might lie under the abrasive, noisy rudeness that seemed to characterize the Berliners he observed, but it was as well hidden as their regimented dwellings.

He found, but did not enjoy, a plain white-walled restaurant in which boisterous good spirits seemed mandatory, his desire to examine Berlin weakening by the minute. 'We are a caring people,' he was told threateningly: 'We value our German sick, our injured, our aged. You British care only for war.' The curious thing was that, while the manner of the drunken speaker belied it, he was right: Germany, Haldane had told him, spent half as much again on social services as it did on its armed forces. Still, did the same benevolence extend to the Jews? Conspicuously absent from this restaurant, conspicuous elsewhere; successful, but not loved. As they ate, the overall atmosphere was to be enjoyed only by those fully admitted to it. Nor was there any reassurance in the fragmentary snatches of conversation overheard through the smoky room: 'The British army!…don't worry…when the time comes…soon…then we shall rejoice!' Such words were probably being repeated in a hundred places across the city.

He abandoned dinner without completing it. Two doors down the street was a barber's shop, which – when open – promised to produce upturned moustaches to match those of the Kaiser. At once he felt better, for he realized that he had wandered too far from the civilization he understood. It was not that this was Germany but that he could no more enjoy here the restaurant of the white-collar workers, or a landscape of working men's *Kneipe*, than he could in England.

Even so, he had not responded warmly to the atmosphere of Berlin. Mr Wells was doubtless right by his own definition when he said that the Germans had clambered above the British in the scale of civilization; but Wells's universe was alien to him, too: one didn't measure culture by a nation's education system, its scientific achievement, or its business prowess.

In the distance a band played music from *The Tales of Hoffmann*, while a solitary woman, squat and stout, harshly unfashionable in everything from her rigidly pinned hair to her heavy, square-toed boots, hurried past on the other side of the street. He hurried himself, in the opposite direction, seeking the way back as quickly as he could.

* * *

Back at the hotel, a car arrived for him uncomfortably quickly. The core of Imperial Berlin had its northern edge in the Unter der Linden. To the south, between the pleasure gardens and the Palace, the mansions of the plutocracy rubbed shoulders with those of the old noble families. His car took him in this direction, down the narrow Wilhelmstrasse, where embassies and government buildings were also to be seen. It slowed at No. 75, the Foreign Secretary's residence, passed No. 76 – the Foreign Office – and stopped at the next building, the home of the Chancellor.

The Foreign Office, identified by nothing more demonstrative than a number on a blue plaque, was still a rather gloomy reminder of Bismarck's dislike for modern gadgetry and austere distaste for extravagance. Inside it, three men had been deep in conversation for several hours.

The Chancellor of Germany did not usually leave his office next door; Bethmann-Hollweg had converted the billiard room that Bismarck had made his own office into the garden room, and both here and where he worked on his papers, he could relax. Now he seemed to have lost his customary calm. This tall and intelligent man, who played Beethoven, read Plato and studied Kant with facility, stood stiffly and awkwardly as his colleagues talked heatedly. Von Jagow, the Secretary of State for Foreign Affairs, sat at his desk casually drawing a succession of women on the notepad in front of him. A strong man, this, and one well aware of the problems of dealing with the military, represented here by their commander. The Chief of the Imperial General Staff, Helmuth von Moltke, always looked a powerful figure, though the power was waning and increasingly came from his inner determination in a battle against heart trouble. The nephew of the victor of the Franco-Prussian War, now in his sixties, was a troubled man, the victim of his own fears about his weaknesses. The Fatherland could always rely on the General Staff. Could the General Staff rely on its leader?

These were the officers who served the Kaiser Wilhelm II – talented certainly, but also with the neuroses of the unscrupulous and unprincipled.

The Chancellor had listened to the others. Now he spoke with conviction. 'At last we are ready for recognition as a *Weltmacht*: a presence on the world stage. We have the political strength, we have the military strength, we have the moral strength – and we have the economic strength. With Rathenau as head of the AEG we have the greatest electrical combine in Europe; with Von Gwinner at the Deutscher Bank we have the shrewdest financial brain in the world to further our interests. With these men, with all our talented industrialists, we can create a mighty economic unit in Central Europe with Germany at its head. When I was a boy we all looked to England for our sporting weapons; now the English sportsmen themselves pay extra for Krupp steel.

'But, gentlemen – as we continually remind ourselves – these plans are threatened. We are surrounded by hostile, calculating nations, mobilizing against us. We have never had our true natural frontiers: in the past, as now, we have been at the mercy of peoples ready to rush to attack us.

'It is vital that France is so controlled that never again will she be found among the powers. We must push Russia far from the frontiers of Germany and end her threatening influence over the Slav peoples for ever. If we do not – and I fear we shall not – I shall plant no trees in my garden for my children; for the Russians will come at us, intent on conquest. To preserve power, we must win power.'

Ransom's Cabinet colleague, Lord Haldane, would have been puzzled to hear these words. He had found in Bethmann, he told Ransom, the heart of a Liberal statesman, perhaps even an Abraham Lincoln for the times.

The Chancellor made it clear that he had not finished. He spoke, he himself fancied, in the tones of the single-minded statesman. 'Our fleet serves us well. It is right that it should be the favourite child of Germany: in it the onward-pressing energies of our nation are vividly illustrated. Technical skill, organization of an efficient kind – both are present in plenty.

'Politically, too, we can go forward. We have governed for two years now without the support of a substantial presence of the right in the Reichstag; but the voice of the *Wehrverein*, the Defence Association, will be heard outside Parliament and it will applaud our plans. We have made our position clear – I have myself declared in the Reichstag that we do not believe in anything so absurd as parliamentary government. Tirpitz was right: no one could imagine that the Reichstag that outlawed Frederick the Great, or the Frankfurt Parliament, or any other popular assemblies, would lead us. This nation is the product of individual men – individuals subordinated by duty to the State.'

Rhetoric was fine. Essential even. But Bethmann was wiser than that. 'None the less, our strength lies in unity. The Social Democrats can be wooed when the nation is threatened. Last week I talked to Deputy Südekum: when we march to the front they will be with us. They fight for us, and for our values, because they fight for Germany.'

'All of it can be managed,' Von Jagow commented, echoing the Chancellor's words: 'We are the greatest power ever known on the Continent of Europe. Who will deny it? Our industries breathe expansion, and our armies' – he glanced at Von Moltke – 'our armies are the mightiest guardians in the world.'

'In my opinion,' said Von Moltke, 'war is inevitable, and the sooner the better. I do not say that it will be easy. The struggle may be long and will push our people to the limits of exhaustion; but it is not to be avoided.' This time there would be no drawing back. There could not be: both the French and the Russians were strengthening their forces – and their alliance. And England? Ah, England. 'Nevertheless,' Von Moltke continued to his colleagues, 'it always comes back to England. It would take a vast army to launch a successful attack on her, and the British fleet would disrupt us. England can always wear us down.'

Bethmann looked thoughtful. Once he had seen England as a bulldog, not to be irritated. That dictated peace. Now he had come to realize what a house of cards he had been building all these years – an Anglo-German understanding that had no basis in facts, a mere diplomatic flirtation. Tirpitz was right again. England, the old pirate state, might once more succeed in letting Europe tear herself to pieces, and by throwing in her own power secure a victory for herself. *Germaniam esse delendam*. They would not say it but in their insidious, English way they would seek it.

'If we relied on Lichnowsky, we would not plan at all,' the Chancellor said with irritation: he had thought the appointment absurd – a man without even experience as an Ambassador. Thanks to Von Bode he had at least managed to cut from dispatches Lichnowsky's crass suggestion that policy should be guided only by the desire to avoid war at all costs.

'He keeps them amused,' said Von Moltke. 'If only we can keep them off-stage! The strategy, without them, is sound. The facts speak for themselves. Our frontier with France is a mere 150 miles in length. Where the Vosges do not act as a barrier, the French have their fortresses: Verdun, Belfort and the rest. We cannot afford the delays if we advance south into the Swiss mountains; but we can outflank the French to the north and west. Belgium gives us the answer, especially as we must respect Dutch sovereignty.' He paused. 'She must be the wind-pipe that enables us to breathe.'

Imagery of any kind comes unnaturally to him, Bethmann thought, though his expression did not change. Von Moltke lectured on – they were all lecturing each other this time, each conscious of it, each knowing that it was necessary. 'Publicly we continue to respect the neutrality of Belgium; but there, in Belgium, is the road to France.'

'It leaves the East weak,' said Von Jagow drily.

'Agreed,' Von Moltke responded crisply. 'But the Russians will be slow to mobilize and to some extent we can expect help from the Austrians in Poland. We have to knock out France first. Even now it is French loans that are giving Russia the railway network she will eventually use to threaten us. Everything suggests action now.

'France will not be so difficult: beer is a more dangerous enemy to Germany than all those armies of feeble Frenchmen.'

'Only England, I tell you again, can prevent us.'

'But that is why Ransom is here. You know the Kaiser's plan,' retorted Bethmann.

'Yes,' murmured Von Moltke, 'the Kaiser's plan. But I still don't understand why we need Ransom. We are risking a great deal anyway, and he makes it all the more dangerous.'

'You are forgetting the obvious,' said Bethmann. 'Think of the collapse in British morale if a respected Cabinet Minister is shown to be involved. They will feel totally betrayed. And we cannot lose: if the plan fails, the British still face a national crisis; if it succeeds, they will fall into hopeless confusion.'

* * *

Naturally, Ransom saw and heard nothing of these conversations. Simultaneously, he was ushered into the presence of the head of the Intelligence department in the adjoining building. In the next room was the newspaper and propaganda office, and above was another office sometimes used by the Kaiser when he was in Berlin.

Wilhelm had made a relatively hurried return from Austria,

where he had been visiting the Archduke Franz Ferdinand, the heir to the throne. Such a tragic family! The aged Emperor Franz Joseph had experienced one horror after another: the execution of his brother Maximilian in Mexico, the suicide of his son Rudolf at Mayerling, even the murder of his own lovely wife Elizabeth by an anarchist. A wonderful woman, the Empress Elizabeth, in the eyes of the Kaiser, who had first seen her – and fallen a little in love with her – as a child. Let them be spared more sorry, the Kaiser reflected, as he awaited the arrival of his English visitor.

Within what seemed a very short space of time, Ransom found himself facing this man: Frederic Wilhelm Victor Albert, ruler of Germany. The Kaiser wore the uniform of an officer in the Garde du Corps; beside him on the desk was a silver helmet with an eagle on the crest. In other circumstances he might have been confused with Lohengrin waiting to perform at the Opera and – whatever else – the physical impression he made was immediate and unforgettable.

He bowed as the Kaiser came towards him: a tall man, with a slightly ruddy complexion, brown hair and bluish-grey, icy, pene-trating eyes. His right hand seemed enormous as – with a studied informality – he took Ransom's in a vice-like grip.

His mother, the Princess Victoria, had fallen accidentally during pregnancy, and when the future Kaiser was being born his awkward position caused harm to his neck and a misshapen crippled left arm, while damage to his ear affected his sense of balance in later life.

On his left cheek lay a scar, frighteningly close to the eye, the result of a madman throwing an iron bar at him.

He seemed a caricature of the young man in his portraits, with a piercing, somewhat high-pitched voice that did not fit the image. Yet as they talked Ransom was not left with the impression of a man engaged in a sort of music-hall impersonation of greatness. The theatricality was there, certainly, but the reality of the power gave it added menace. Something, perhaps, of Frederick the Great seemed to linger in his spirit.

Wilhelm rocked restlessly from one foot to another, jerking his head up and down, this way and that, as he spoke. His face was pushed forward, his finger wagging, and then came a raucous laugh and a stamping of the foot, while he emphasized a point.

'In England you go to your office at eleven; you linger over luncheon; you leave at four; on Thursday you go to the country; you remain there until Tuesday morning – and you call it a weekend. The English fibre has been softened and it is rapidly disintegrating. Your poor show in the Boer War was a perfect example. Here in Germany everyone applauds obedience, discipline and industry; we teach it to our young people and it becomes their second nature.'

He stopped, but only for a moment. 'Not one of your ministers can tell how many ships of the line you have in your navy. I can tell them – they can't tell me. And your Minister of War cannot even ride: I offered him a mount and every opportunity to see manoeuvres. No horseman, unfortunately. A Minister of War! – and can't ride! Unthinkable!' He laughed, a strange, stilted laugh.

'Then, Sir, there can be nothing to fear on the part of such a great nation from one so enfeebled,' Ransom said.

The Kaiser's reaction was angry. 'You make an iron ring around us, an iron ring. England is embracing France. She makes friends with Russia. It is not that you all love each other: it is that you hate Germany. You never had a Napoleon to plunder your country houses in England. What would have become of your Gainsboroughs, your treasures then?'

'There is a lack of trust – on both sides. But that, surely, is all.'

'You English are like mad bulls, I tell you. You see red everywhere! What on earth has come over you, that you should heap on us such suspicion as is unworthy of a great nation? What can I do more? I have always stood forth as a friend of England…. Have I ever broken my word?…. You make it uncommonly difficult for a man to remain friendly.'

'It is this dreadful lack of trust,' Ransom said soberly, repeating himself.

Wilhelm softened. 'You are right, of course. Of England we must be wary, but it is the others that threaten us. Besides, you are divided. Is even your army wholly loyal? You are so absorbed by your Irish crisis….'

'The army knows its duty; and nothing could come of the Irish business while the two sides remained unarmed.'

'Yes, yes. So you expect me to be sorry that German arms are involved? Why should we discourage our businessmen? You must understand what worries me. While you are preoccupied at home you cannot be led, against your better judgment, into Continental entanglements. The problem is this: how to neutralize England while Germany faces her enemies. This is my reason for your being here: not any petty negotiations over a few thousand old rifles.'

'I still do not understand. And from what I hear Magnus of Hamburg will not be growing rich from these arms sales – the prices are too low for that.'

'Mr Ransom, you are not listening,' Wilhelm said impatiently. 'Germany's power grows daily, but I tell you frankly that there is no way in which the Reich may be made so strong that groupings of the great powers would not have the capacity to defeat it. Such a *Lebensaufgabe* might be attainable through war, but not if England is involved. On the other hand, if the English are not on Continental soil within the first five days of war, *they will never be on it.*'

The Kaiser put his arm round Ransom's shoulder. He smiled, revealing a set of good, strong white teeth. Then a staggering surprise: 'You are an honourable man, eh? You cannot be wholly cynical, for you are in love. While the rest of us bang our heads against the hopeless facts of history and can see in the future only an extension of the dreary difficulties of the present, you can find a haven in that love. I have watched you, Mr Ransom, and I know you; and presently you will see why your passion will lead you to help us.'

The temperature of the room itself seemed to drop in response to the icily threatening tone of the Kaiser's voice. Ransom stood rigidly immobile, his body no better able to cope than his mind, which seemed to have lost the capacity to process what was being said to him.

'You can see that the mass of your people will benefit if you leave the Continental nations to solve their own problems. You must lose the temptation to meddle – and I know how this can be achieved.

'One thing and one thing only could throw your nation into such confusion that it would not think of upsetting my plans. Mr Ransom' – the Kaiser now spoke in a whisper that nevertheless filled the room – 'Mr Ransom, it is perfectly simple. You see, we have to arrange, you and I, to assassinate my cousin. We have to kill the King of England.'

Ransom was left with little time to react. For a long split-second, Wilhelm fixed his gaze on him, then moved rapidly to his desk and rang a bell. Immediately, the door opened and he was ushered, almost – as he felt later – marched out, an attendant on either side.

* * *

The Kaiser picked up a telephone and instructed an aide to send for the Chancellor. He distrusted Bethmann a little, and was not persuaded that he had suppressed his obsessive desire to reach an understanding with England. How remote he was from realities, and yet how he enjoyed showing that he knew better than anyone else. The man was intolerable!

Nevertheless, he greeted Bethmann-Hollweg warmly, strode up to him, touched him lightly on the cheek. 'We have known each other a long time, old friend.' The Chancellor remained expressionless. 'There I was, on active service for the first time, a young lieutenant in the 6th Company of the First Infantry Grand Regiment, and where should we be quartered than at Hohenfinow, the home of the worthy Herr Von Bethmann and of your most admirable mother. It was the prelude to many such visits to see the old gentleman. And you would greet me, proud young head of the rural district administration. Were we the same people then?'

Still Bethmann did not move or speak. He knew what was expected, what was to follow. The Kaiser moved away, pacing up and down. His manner changed. 'The Englishman will help us. He will. But we must be careful. That mean crew of shopkeepers will do all they can to trick us. The famous encirclement of Germany has finally become a complete fact, and still there are those that believe she could be won over by this or that puny measure! England only waits for the desired pretext to annihilate us under the hypocritical cloak of justice: she will help France to keep the reported "balance of power" in Europe when in fact she is playing the card of all nations in her favour against us.'

The Chancellor decided it was time to make his own contribution. 'I am told that Northcliffe gives the editor of *The Times* unrestricted control unless he should, by some aberration, fail to be sufficiently anti-German. But the picture is not so black, according to Lichnowsky. Only the Northcliffe papers and the *Morning Post* talk of joining a European mobilization.'

'Lichnowsky! Lichnowsky!' Wilhelm exploded. 'The idiot! Look what he writes to me here.' He waved a letter and read from it. '"Sir Edward Grey has a very definite wish to render political relations between our two countries as cordial as possible." "Sir Edward Grey has a straightforward and frank character that makes him abhor any double-talk, so that one can see very quickly what one can expect from him. He wants, as do the great majority of politicians here, to live in peace and friendship with us, *without of course thereby wanting to relinquish his connections with France and Russia.*" The man's a fool!'

One can't censor *all* the dispatches from one's own Ambassador, Bethmann thought. Most, but not all. 'Grey is a false dog who is afraid of his own meanness and false policy' – Wilhelm's tirade continued. 'Mean and Mephistophelian.' He stamped on the floor.

'Need we fear sheep?' Bethmann asked. He judged that it was better to fuel the fire than to let it out: the Kaiser's worst moments were his moments of doubt. If, as Bismarck had said, he lacked a sense of proportion, everyone was advised to take account of that.

'No one could trust an Englishman,' the Kaiser said more thoughtfully. 'We Germans express our approval, and our aversion, openly. Lichnowsky only has to see London behaving politely to him in Society, and he assumes that there is a politically friendly message intended. No one who knows the English well could ever confuse the form with the substance.'

Calmer now, he picked up his pipe, which had set into its bowl a large silver 'W' surmounted by some fabulous beast. He began to puff, enjoying the tobacco he had had specially blended for his own taste. He wanted to be free of these worries, to return to his own apartments in the Palace where he could find at least fitful sleep – as the official word would have it, 'His Majesty works alone.'

How often they had rehearsed the ground, and come always to the same conclusion. The people would be with them, a few traitorous Social Democrats excepted. The thought prompted, his anger mounted again that there should be a single man disloyal to the nation. He said to Bethmann: 'There is only one master in this country. I am he, and I will not tolerate another. We cannot allow these Socialist anti-military demonstrations. Our streets must be free. If necessary I shall proclaim martial law and have the leaders one and all, *tutti quanti*, locked up. We will have not Socialist propaganda now!'

The Chancellor ventured: 'The majority are with us. Deputy Hecksher warmly applauded the creation of our fleet in the Reichstag only the other day.'

Wilhelm looked wistful: 'When I was a little boy I was allowed to visit Plymouth and Portsmouth with kind aunts and friendly admirals. I admired the proud English ships in those harbours. They awoke in me the desire to build ships of my own like them.'

The wistfulness went: 'Nations rise and fall. Boundaries can be shifted. Ask Mr Bartholomew whether there is any end to map-making. Britain has herself repainted in red the greater part of the world in less than twenty years. Now we should do a little painting of our own. Do they expect us to have our fleet locked up in the Baltic for ever? With our trading strength, do they still hope to satisfy us with Hamburg, Bremen and a mere few miles of shallow coast? Economically, the Low Countries are already part of greater Germany.'

'But will there be more than one fleet to face? Only last week Sir Edward Grey denied to the House of Commons the existence of an Anglo-Russian naval agreement. Can this be true?' The Chancellor was voicing his own doubts, reinforced by the knowledge gained from German secret intelligence, but the Kaiser's memories gave him the clear answer. In Berlin itself, just a year before at the wedding celebrations of the Princess Victoria Louise and the Duke of Brunswick, he had surprised his cousins, George V and Tsar Nicholas, plotting in their apartments. Was there ever a greater treachery? Had not the Tsar previously, and without prompting, clasped his hand and embraced him, giving his word of honour as a sovereign that he would never draw his sword against the German Empire, least of all as an ally of England?

'I tell you clearly,' Wilhelm said, 'that no nation has the right to dispute the place in the sun to which we are entitled.' Bethmann-Hollweg betrayed none of his inner reaction to the fanaticism etched into his monarch's face, the blazing madness of his eyes. In all essentials the Kaiser was right; he could be safely followed. But quietly, for God's sake. One source of cacophony in a disordered universe was sufficient. The Chancellor nodded silent assent as Wilhelm, now staring unfocusedly into the far distance, into the future, spoke softly: 'Germany, Germany, over everything in the world, the first power on earth, both in peace and war. That is the place which I have been ordered by God to conquer for her, and which I will conquer for her, with the help of the Almighty.' He clutched the top of the chair behind his desk until his knuckles shone white in the darkness. 'Whatever experiences are in store for the Fatherland, we will emerge from them – we will emerge triumphant because we Germans fear God and nothing else in the world.'

The Chancellor, calmly, quietly, withdrew. If Wilhelm heard him leave, he gave no sign of it. Now he sat in his chair, his memories crowding forward. There he was once more, addressing his troops at Bremerhaven before their departure to quell the Boxers. No quarter. No prisoners. Wield your weapons so that for a thousand years to come no Chinaman will dare to look askance at a German. Pave the way once and for all for civilization – our civilization.

Ever since he had been commissioned into the first infantry regiment of Guards on his tenth birthday, his military destiny had been clear. It was in the blood. Just as his grandfather had been able to rely on the army of Coblenz, just as the army had welded the German Empire, so he too could rely on it and his new navy – *his* creation – to go on to greater glory. No parliamentary majority ever achieved anything. The weak fools....

Wilhelm suddenly scowled. Only one real problem. Only one. The King must die. He must.

CHAPTER NINE

Time for fear

RANSOM'S reactions that night were varied: a refusal to believe that the discussion had been real; the idea that some elaborate joke was being played on him; the possibility that the Kaiser was mad. The speed with which everything had happened made it so difficult to absorb. In no time, it seemed, he had been wrenched from his comfortable daily life to go on a special mission, the success of which would be bound to give the middle-aged lack of steam in his career a new impetus, only to be thrust squarely into the middle of the nightmare plans of the most powerful warlord in Europe.

What was to be done? Call the British Ambassador? That would have been the proper and responsible action for someone in his position. But had the Prime Minister alerted the Embassy to his presence? Probably not – the whole purpose of his visit would be destroyed if the professionals were allowed to interfere. He wished he understood more about behind-the-scenes diplomacy, but there was no way he could have known what to ask.

And there was Anna…the one concession to excitement in his

life, or so he had thought. Mistresses were commonplace, but if they were anarchists, it seemed that they made dangerous companions. Could she really be party to murder – the murder of a king?

A single step off the highroad of success and convention and he had been hurtled into a wholly unfamiliar world.

There was another thing, too – an equally new experience. Fear. He had been escorted back to his hotel by four sour but efficient men in uniform: what he saw in their eyes and felt in their manner towards him convinced him that now was not the right time to do anything precipitate. Best to hang on, find out more, go from there....

His fists were clenched as he lay on his hotel bed, and such thoughts as these were his unwelcome companions until the early morning.

* * *

There was little time to take stock when morning came. Bizarrely, Wilhelm had invited him to breakfast and, in a gesture of somewhat meaningless independence, Ransom insisted to the aides assigned to him for his 'protection' that he should walk to the palace.

The air seemed chill despite the season as he made his way briskly to the other end of the Linden, then along its continuation to the Schloss-Brücke. He crossed into the Lustgarten – originally a garden belonging to the Palace, which had later been turned into a drill-ground by Frederick William I. Here he took stock of his surroundings.

His sombre companions were some twenty paces behind. To the north lay the Altesmuseum, to the east the Cathedral. And there, to the south, was the Palace itself: a huge rectangle enclosing, as he was soon to discover, two large courts. Facing him he could see the great wrought-iron gates in their portals, while on the balustrade statues of the Emperor Wilhelm I as Jupiter, the Empress Augusta as Juno, the Emperor Frederick III as Mars and the Empress Victoria as Minerva surveyed the scene in magisterial fashion.

Here the Kaiser had made his home. Through the window of the Picture Gallery used as a banqueting hall for up to 400 guests, he looked out on the Linden and the Lustgarten. On either side of him, scenes of triumph in battle by Röchling and others recorded the progress of the Kaiser's ancestors, while he himself looked on in approval, dressed in the white uniform and silver breastplate of Laszló's romanticized state portrait.

Presently, Wilhelm emerged from the next room, the throne room, Ransom imagined, in this palace with more than 700 apartments. Ransom walked towards him and bowed, at their backs a serene Van Dyck of Charles I of England and his Queen: how close in blood were the royal houses of Europe that had fought each other so bitterly for so many centuries. Not for the first time, the thought struck Ransom in the presence of this man, that there was nothing to match the cruelty and single-mindedness of family conflicts. He said little. 'Good morning, Mr Ransom. I have a surprise for you. You will follow me, eh?'

Dressed in the uniform of the Death's Head Hussars, he led the way through the door. 'I am going to show you the invention of the greatest German of the twentieth century.' It was some time before Ransom understood what he meant, for they walked along endless corridors, through a multitude of rooms of great splendour, past the royal apartments themselves on the side of the Palace overlooking the Schlossplatz – a journey punctuated by occasional staccato bursts of information on the significance of what they encountered. At last, outside again and while he was still trying to recover his sense of direction, they came upon their goal: a Zeppelin, Count Zeppelin's giant flying invention.

He was still perplexed as to how so large a beast could have landed in so relatively small a space when they became airborne: a terrifying experience at first for the uninitiated, but – despite the luxury of the saloon – one that became merely discomfort from the extreme cold. The Kaiser's enthusiasm was unstoppable. 'No known defence will serve against these machines. 700 feet long. The capacity to ascend to 8,000 feet. Travelling at up to 60 miles an hour over long distances….' He laughed. 'And if the bombs aimed at the Houses of Parliament miss, you can be sure that they will hit Buckingham Palace!' Ransom was unsmiling, in huddled indignity. The Kaiser laughed again. 'I joke, of course! But make no mistake. Already, two years or more ago, Count Zeppelin carried twenty-five men and more than five tons nearly a thousand miles. A thousand miles! And in winter weather. We Germans could be in Paris, and back, with hundreds of miles to spare. We have the weapon of the future today!'

They shared a drink from his flask. 'But now we are at peace,' he said abruptly. 'We go to see the Empress at Potsdam, where we can enjoy quiet. Long ago, I gave instructions that the wretched telephone was never to be used while I was there: anything of sufficient importance is brought by hand.'

'"It is not necessary that I should live, but it is that I should do my duty",' Ransom ventured, quoting Frederick the Great.

'Ah, yes,' the Kaiser affirmed vigorously. 'I like you, Englishman. I like your puritanism. But Frederick built the Neues Palace: that was part of his duty. In the library you will see his own portrait by Voltaire. We are not, you know, a barbarian people.'

And there below them was the summer residence of Frederick the Great: 700 feet in length, three stories high, with a large dome in the centre. As soon as they had landed, the Kaiser gave an enthusiastic account, with much pointing and gesturing, of his own restoration work: the improvements to the chief façade, overlooking the park, the addition of a large terrace. Past the armed sentries at the gates, past the liveried servants at the entrance from the gardens, through the Shell Room with its magnificent shells and minerals and stones, to the private rooms of the Kaiser in the north wing. Thence – at last – to an ornate breakfast room, cluttered with paintings and family photographs.

The scene was otherwise strangely domestic. The Kaiser's wife, Dona, the Empress Augusta Victoria, smiled and spoke in a way that would have deflated the most hostile and warmed the tensest of encounters. Bismarck had said that the 'Holstein cow' would at least introduce a new strain into the Hohenzollern family, but he had been proved right in a way he could not have predicted. For his part, Wilhelm had no consuming desire for his Empress; he was never uncontrollably in love with anyone, certainly not with this cheerful, white-haired *Hausfrau* without beauty or brains or even money. She was tolerable, except when she kept him awake with her endless prattle on family matters. His idea of the good family man, a very German one, was he who found a wife early, gave her lots of children, provided for her, protected – and forgot about – her.

She seemed to Ransom a warm and modest woman, at home in kitchen or nursery, and she talked earnestly of her work in hospital administration, of her attempts to stamp out vice and to raise money for the church. Disarming in manner: the antidote to all those sharp-tongued, sarcastic, cutting Berliners, he decided.

'How I hate this heat, don't you Mr Ransom?' she said in a moment of silence. He smiled politely, suppressing a shiver at the memory of his early morning Zeppelin ride. 'And how I enjoy the long winter evenings,' she went on, with a naïve enthusiasm. 'Here in Potsdam, you know. We sit with our needlework at a big round table, my ladies-in-waiting and I. The Emperor might read aloud, or look at the English papers. *Punch*, you know. They are a little rude, you know. They show him as a sea-serpent or an or-gan-grinder. But,' she added hastily, with a glance at her husband, 'he is very good-humoured and does not mind. Then early to bed, so as to be fresh for riding in the morning. I love that, you know!'

They ate without servants, the Empress waiting on her husband, preparing his food, clearing his plates. She did not actually seem to eat anything herself, though there was much from which to choose: eggs, bacon, steak, chicken au paprika, macaroni….

'Your women are very troublesome, Mr Ransom,' the Kaiser said. He wondered what he could mean for a moment. 'What in heaven do women want with a vote! There is no movement here, and if you begin burning houses and horsewhipping people in Germany, what do you think the police will do? No flowers and newspapers. No freedom two days afterwards. We deal with people differently here, I may tell you.'

Ransom was beginning to learn a technique for dealing with all this and modestly commented: 'I believe it was Prince Bismarck who understood the question best when he put women in politics on a par with professors engaged in the same. *Die Professoren und die Frauenzimmer in der Politik!*'

He had said the right thing. Wilhelm grunted contentedly. 'Women should stay at home and look after their children. I attribute the foundations of our greatness to three things: to our beef, to our beer – and to our Bismarck!'

The Kaiser ate with astonishing rapidity. Restored to geniality, he spoke effusively of his English experiences. 'I was the only one of the grandchildren who could remember Prince Albert. Queen Victoria approved of me for that reason, I'm sure. At Windsor we would go and drink tea and make butter and cream cheese in the little kitchen fitted out for us at Frogmore in the Park. I showed great fortitude when the dentist assaulted my teeth: the Queen gave me a freshly minted gold pound and I have it to this day.'

He stopped, while the Empress gave aid to his one good arm by cutting up the food on the plate before him. The Kaiser, it seemed, was the mirror image of his country: noisy, aggressive, moody, sometimes dejected, sometimes exuberant, never at peace.

'My uncle told me that he always had the pleasure of his favourite pie when he visited the Queen – there was a turkey, which was stuffed with a chicken, then a pheasant in the chicken, then a woodcock inside the pheasant. What a splendid lady! Never in my life shall I forget the solemn hours in Osborne at her deathbed when she breathed her last into my arms. I shall always remember how kindly this great Queen was to me, and the relations she kept up with me, though I was so far her junior, she having carried *me* about in *her* arms. My very last time in your country, four years ago now, was at the unveiling of the Memorial in the Mall.'

In his mind's eye, Ransom remembered his own last, rather drunken sight of the Memorial, on leaving the Buckingham Palace Ball those few weeks back. Perhaps the Kaiser really did see European affairs as an extension of family politics, with him cast as the good prince, surrounded by his (mostly) wicked relations. His mother, after all, had been English, 'the English Woman' her nickname to the acerbic Berliners. According to Margot, though, she was the source of the Kaiser's annoyance with England: he grew tired of her criticisms of German intolerance and her staunch belief in the superiority of everything English. When he later reflected on all that he had seen and heard, he could begin to understand why the Kaiser seemed to have so little regret that the only means of ensuring British neutrality was to kill his cousin, George V.

After breakfast. the Kaiser enjoined Ransom to go riding in the park, though not before one of his valets, Schulz, had pressed on him an urgent telegram from his aide-de-camp. He seemed eager to show how well informed he was. 'Already this morning, before our meeting, I have been through newspapers, important magazines, all influential sources of news. We must watch what is being said about us, and who is saying it!'

They stood on the terrace. 'They said it would be impossible to build a palace on such a marshy spot as this, and Frederick set out to prove that it was not,' the Kaiser said. 'Besides, he was able to show that he still had some money left after the Silesian wars! Very important to a monarch, you know: money.' Above them, misshapen cherubs' heads and wreaths of flowers decorated the upper windows; on the roof, and again on the terrace in front of them, was a multitude of Neo-classical statuary. To the left was the gravelled courtyard, the Sandhof, where Frederick the Great had drilled his soldiers; to the right, beyond the kitchens, the chapel and the quarters of the Palace guard – handpicked from all the regiments of Prussia – were the royal stables.

As they cantered, the band which was permanently stationed in the gallery of the stables, played military music. Wilhelm talked incessantly, butterflying from one subject to another, mostly his dislikes: how he hated to encounter the fat Jewesses while riding in the park (whether it was more because they were fat, or more because they were Jews, was not clear); how his own generals disapproved of his wonderful, impossible cavalry charges on manoeuvres ('the imbeciles!'); how the delights of Homer ('that glorious man'), of Horace and of Demosthenes, had been ruined for him under the scalpel of his fanatical tutor (each clause 'dissected and split up, till to his delight he had found the bare skeleton, and then exhibited it for the admiration of all. It was enough to make one weep'); how he could still remember the exact spot in Buckingham Palace where he was frightfully sick from eating too much plum pudding....

Madness! Yet sometimes moving: 'The Rhine, the river where we grow our vines, the name of which is endeared to us by our legends, the river where every castle, every town, speaks to us of our past.' In Westminster Hall for Edward VII's funeral: 'The old, grey hall, covered by its great Gothic wooden ceiling, towered imposingly over the catafalque, lit by a few rays of the sun filtering through the narrow windows. One ray flooded the magnificent coffin of the King, surmounted by the English crown, and made marvellous play with the columns of the precious stones adorning it…. I went up to the catafalque with King George, placed a cross upon it, and offered a silent prayer, after which my right hand and that of my royal cousin found each other quite unconsciously on our part, and met in a firm clasp.'

The irony was not a gentle one, but the expression changed too rapidly for anything to be made of it: 'You democratic countries,' he observed sharply, 'seem to need these medieval pageants. We order these things better in our young German Empire.'

Icily serious now: 'It was the soldier and the army, not parliamentary majorities and decisions, that welded our Empire. It was here in Potsdam as a boy that I flung myself into my father's arms and saw my grandfather on his victorious return from France for the first time as German Emperor,'

'See here. See, these are the spurs of Charles XII of Sweden. Picked up at the Battle of Poltava.'

This was excitement, wasn't it?

* * *

The tranquil beauty of the gardens at Potsdam, hidden away behind big beech hedges, would always be – for Ransom – modified by the nightmares of his visit to Germany. Before lunch they made the twenty-mile return journey to Berlin, and in the early afternoon he was taken to an address in Koenigergratzerstrasse which turned out to be the headquarters of German naval intelligence. Like all Prussian government offices, it was impressive in its lack of ostentation, with an organization which was obtrusive but none the less efficient. He passed through three anterooms, accompanied by an orderly, to find Colonel Nicolai, who had left his usual office in

Wilhelmstrasse for the meeting. This imposing Prussian member of the General Staff was fluent in Russian, French and Japanese, as well as English. He took some time to get to the point, seeming to want to explain what his motives might be.

'Spying, Mr Ransom, is an occupation for gentlemen. When I took over here last year, I found to my pleasant surprise that I had a group of cultured, cultivated patriots working for me. Of course, we have to rely on many kinds of informers, but it is vital – for that reason – that the men in command should provoke respect.'

Ransom was not very friendly in his response, since he did not care for this meandering around the issue. 'I should like you to tell me how it can be that Anna Kinsky comes, in some way that I certainly do not understand, to be connected with your operations.'

'I understand your concern,' was Nicolai's polite rejoinder 'but I think you must ask her that question yourself. It is not for me to comment. What I would wish you to understand is how we in Germany are threatened. I have more and more evidence that the Russians have all the information they need on our policies and plans; and if the Russians have it, the French will have it too. In these circumstances, we have to fight back.'

Privately, Nicolai was reassured by the thought that the French were unlikely to take seriously any information fed to them by the Russians, but he did not say so. Besides, he believed he had an accurate knowledge of the location, numbers and armaments of the opposing forces: if it wasn't for the Kaiser's plans in England, he would be preparing to take his family on holiday into the Hartz Mountains. Did England matter so much? The Kaiser himself had passed on to him a letter from the English Admiral, Montagu, complaining about his own First Lord, Winston Churchill. He had it on the desk now – 'We are in an awful mess…. No constitution. Territorials failing fast. The people only think of football or strikes.'

None of this did he betray to Ransom at the time. None of it would influence his totally professional attitude to the job in hand. He had given his promise, and he would keep to it – 'I swear by God, the almighty and omniscient, a solemn oath that I shall serve my Lord, his Majesty, the King of Prussia, Wilhelm II, my most gracious Sovereign, truly and loyally in each and any situation on land or sea, in time of war or time of peace. I swear to work for the good of his Majesty and to prevent all harm from touching him.' A good, an excellent creed.

As ever since Ransom's arrival in Germany, he was left with a confused and possibly contradictory picture of a nation which thought itself beleaguered and expected doom, and yet also showed abundant evidence of its own aggressive and expansionist aims.

'The main part of what I want to tell you is strictly practical information,' Nicolai continued.

'You seem to have taken my participation for granted,' Ransom said coldly. Von Bode had been the same in London.

'You will make up your own mind. There is time. That is not my concern, except to remind you that a British Cabinet Minister who consorts with an anarchist is in a dangerous position.'

'Blackmail?'

'The facts are what is important. A few telephone calls and your career could be in ruins. More than that, you stand to lose the love of Anna Kinsky if you do not help.'

'We shall see,' Ransom said, angry and bewildered at the same time.

'Mr Ransom, I have no reason to care anything for you.' Nicolai looked at him with something close to contempt. 'I do not like the way you and your dilettante fellow-countrymen play at life. But that is irrelevant – now you should listen.'

He sat down behind the desk. 'We only make use of the weapons that are used against us. If we allowed ourselves a little moral squeamishness, we would only suffer the consequences. As it is, we are surrounded by enemies, but we are not unprepared. I can afford to be indiscreet with you because I speak from strength. In England you are watched. I mean you personally. Our men carry no identifying documents; they are professionals, totally loyal and utterly single-minded. In some countries it is easy. In France, the honour of the Republic pulls no heartstrings like the love of the Fatherland embodied in its King or its Emperor or its Tsar. Even in Russia there are ways: every country has its quota of cutthroats, the universal riff-raff who will owe loyalty to anyone who will pay to give them danger. You would be right to be warned.'

It was a sombre speech and he could see the effect it had on Ransom, who lapsed into silence as Nicolai explained the guidelines under which the operation was to be planned. Ransom was to report back to Asquith that the German government was perfectly willing to curb the exuberance of its arms salesmen, if only it could be convinced of the good will of the British. The Irish were no concern of Germany and some concrete agreement might be negotiated. Otherwise, he was to do nothing, until he was contacted anonymously or through Von Bode. On no account must he himself approach anyone at the German Embassy. The occasion of the assassination attempt was still to be decided: it was to be disguised as an offshoot of the Irish troubles and all links with Germany were to be hidden. Even if it failed, all roads were to lead either to the Irish or to the anarchists....

As Ransom was leaving the building, he glimpsed a figure disappearing into a room down one of the dimly lit corridors. It was someone he had seen before, he was sure, but he could not think where. Nor could he explain his sense of unease at seeing the man now.

That such apparently chance events sometimes change lives, he was eventually to discover.

CHAPTER TEN

Ascot and its aftermath

O N the day that Ransom arrived back from Germany, Wednesday the 17th of June, Colonel House – President Woodrow Wilson's special emissary in Europe – wrote to the White House: 'I find everything here cluttered up with social affairs, and it is impossible to work quickly. Here they have their thoughts on Ascot, garden parties, etc., etc. In Germany,' he added, 'their one thought is to advance industrially and glorify war.'

The Kaiser, engaged that day in opening the Hohenzollern canal, connecting Berlin by water to Stettin, was actively supporting this analysis.

At about the same time, Ransom himself penned a short note. 'Dearest Anna – I feel betrayed: but in a puzzled sort of way. You have been using me, haven't you? How can that be, my love? You *must* explain. Your loyal one – W.'

Perhaps all the other members of Society who rushed off to Royal Ascot had similarly deep preoccupations behind their apparent concentration on this vital event in the social calendar. If so, it was hard to tell. The only major drama so far had been the Royal Hunt Cup, in which there had been a mix-up at the start. Braxted, who was in the end to finish second, pulled and jostled at the gate, firing some of his excited fellows to join him and face the whip. It was a very cool customer, Lie-a-Bed, who eventually came out winner.

The usual Ascot thunderstorm had sensibly decided to take place on Sunday before the meeting (the torrential rain in which Ransom had departed for Germany), and the weather was reasonably warm, if – to begin with – a little fresh for the predominant style of costume. Only the Queen and one or two dowagers who had given up the hope of persuading anyone that there was an ounce of youth still left in them wore ruffles round their necks. One couldn't help thinking, he decided, that – despite everything – Rosalind looked rather glamorous in gown of lime-green charmeuse, black over it, and stockings and shoes of the same colour. She did not need to be as daring as some, who wore frocks of such fragility that – as Margot observed – an angel would have caught a cold in them.

The Grandstand had not been repainted since 1905, when the fresh paint had caused more than a little hurt to many expensive and specially designed outfits. From here, Rosalind and Walter watched the Royal procession in open landaus, each pulled by four horses. The postilions in Ascot livery of red jackets, black velvet hunting caps, white buckskin breeches and top boots could be espied at a distance, and soon the crimson and gold of the Royal carriages came into clearer focus. Dark beech and darker pine framed the familiar heath, while limes shaded the lawns of the enclosure and paddock. Rhododendrons bloomed at appointed places. The police had cleared everyone from the course itself for fear of Suffragettes and at least one protesting lady was kept outside the iron gates at the bottom of the Straight Mile.

The Queen, in pale mauve with hat of ostrich feathers, still contrived to look plain. She smiled permanently, a weaker expression than the similar one on the face of the Queen Mother, accompanied by her sister the Tsarina, and making her first visit to Ascot since the death of Edward VII.

The Royal cavalcade also included Prince Arthur of Connaught and Prince Henry of Battenberg. Suddenly Ransom saw them both jump (his own reactions always being very slow) when a sound something like a pistol shot rang out as the procession approached the Grandstand. All eyes turned to the Royal Pavilion, where an embarrassed Marine had banged the big drum in order to bring the band to attention to play the National Anthem.

From the upper part of the Stand, the hundreds of parasols in pink and blue and scarlet and yellow made the scene seem like a gigantic, colourful garden. Many of the parasols were in the shape of a pagoda, but there was still room for the brave spirit who did not want to follow the crowd and had the style to bring it off – like Margot with her butterfly parasol in black lace over white. As they watched, ladies of all descriptions paraded with unquestionable elegance in dainty white embroidered muslins and crepes, or taffetas shot with two or more rich tones and satins of a wonderfully soft pliable variety. Diaphanous drapings, in the form of tunics or flouncings, contributed to a spectacle of ethereal beauty.

Amongst the men, white top hats everywhere, a few of the flamboyant in check trousers and, for those concerned with the finer points, a noticeable absence of button holes and the white spats that were once *de rigueur*. It felt good to be back with reality, on home ground.

It has been said often enough that the English cannot enjoy pleasure except in sadness, that they distrust gaiety. If it is so, Ransom thought, then it is more relevant, and more true, that in England sport and society are inextricably intertwined. Indivisible, indeed. When they say that foreign race meetings are 'fashionable', they cannot have experienced the huge, disorderly, brilliant garden party that is Ascot. The Duc de Morny, with the help of Napoleon III, did much for Deauville, but no one could pretend that it was anything more than, at best, a French Goodwood.

After the first race, at about 1.30, there was a break for lunch. The paddock luncheon room had been enlarged, but with the exception of Rosalind's unmarried, and rapidly aging brother Rupert, who went off to revel in the Lucullan and all-male delights of the Bachelors' marquee, their party – the Churchills, the Asquiths, Rosalind and Walter – came by invitation to the Automobile Club repast. Somewhat ironically, in the circumstances, since the cramped run down from London (Rosalind even more disapproving than Walter) in Rupert's Met – a 40-horsepower open sports model, the Métallurgique, capable of doing up to 80 miles an hour – had not been for the faint-hearted: cyclists, traps, charabancs and mere pedestrians hooted out of the way without previous provocation. The Churchills, wisely, had come by train: a mere 50 minutes in the comfort of a non-stop London and South-Western express, with a covered walk as one crossed from the station to the course.

Ransom opened his folded newspaper. An advertisement advised: 'Charles Villiers Chapman, Turf Commissioner, Member of the leading London Sporting Clubs, Best Market Prices Guaranteed, No Limit, A Turf Accountant of Note, Payments of Winnings made by Bank Notes, Postal Orders, or Cheques at Clients' Opinions, Telegrams: "Repayable, Reg., London", Mayfair 890, 24-26 Maddox Street, London W.1, No Representatives on any Race Course.' Now why should that be an advantage, he murmured.

'What?' asked Winston.

'To make your money from betting, but steer clear of race tracks.'

'I can see that *you* will not go far in Society,' he noted, as if Ransom were just a child. 'Or doubtless, in making your fortune in gambling either. How was Germany?'

He surprised himself by not showing surprise. Officially, he had been ill with a mild form of influenza, which had kept him in bed the previous weekend and during the early part of the week. How much did Churchill know, and who had told him? Ransom said, in a relaxed tone: 'The Berliners eat like pigs, all day: when breakfast is over, it's time for a heavy mid-morning snack; then lunch, followed by coffee and cakes mid-afternoon, tea, dinner and supper for those who last the course. It does the women no good, in fact I don't suppose it does anyone any good. But you know how it is: plenty of meat, plenty of beer – staples for a conquering nation.'

Churchill nodded, as if satisfied by the answer, and – to Ransom's great relief – showed no immediate desire to probe further.

'I hear that Gunter's are doing the catering at the Bachelor's,' said Rosalind. 'Just for them and for the Ascot management, I believe.'

'I don't think we need envy Rupert,' observed the Prime Minister, eyeing the plentiful fare before them. He must have heard Winston's question, Ransom thought, but they all seemed to be good at this particular game of poker – there had been no taking of him aside, no request for an immediate report.

On the table, in front of each place, was a strawberry plant resting in a silver pot and bearing the ripe fruit, beside it a silver dish with cream and sugar. Asquith drank from his champagne glass. 'There will be an end to this one day, you know,' he observed. 'All this effort for just four days' racing a year. I wonder that it even survived Queen Victoria – that wonderful lady was sometimes a great trial.' He mopped his brow. 'She created what you might call a hugger-mugger of a most exceptional kind by refusing to allow any changes in the management of the course. After Albert's death, the

Royal Enclosure became the private preserve of the Master of the Buckhounds. The squabbles between the Master and the trustees of the Grandstand make one feel quite weak.'

'We are free, at least, of the presence of certain Conservative gentlemen,' said Winston genially. 'This very afternoon the Duchess of Wellington breaks custom with a party in the pleasure gardens between Apsley House and the Hamilton Gardens. For myself,' he said, joining the company in a spontaneous raising of glasses, 'I do not think the band of the Grenadier Guards and afternoon tea is a sufficient attraction.'

'You are staying for the weekend?' enquired Rosalind.

'Oh, I would not want to go that far: Boulter's Lock on Ascot Sunday reminds one of nothing so much as Clapham Junction railway station.'

'You dislike pretty girls in rather nice white frocks and rather nice pink hats?' Ransom asked in mock scorn. Everyone understood his reference. They all knew inside that Henley Regatta was a middle-class affair, a jamboree for the upper middle class, just as Ascot was really for the upper class. What scorn Anna would have shown for such nonsense – the nonsense by which they held their lives together. God! Anna!

'You are all welcome to join us at the Wharf,' said the Prime Minister. 'I must be in London tomorrow, but we shall go down in the evening for the weekend, I expect.'

'Yes, do come,' added Margot, her low-pitched voice cutting through the raucous noise from the tables around us. Ransom shook his head politely, as did Winston. 'Let the women leave us in peace,' he said. 'Clemmie and Rosalind: excellent company for a Prime Minister. Walter and I have other matters of moment to consider, eh Walter?' Ransom shrugged. Churchill was being playfully opaque. But so it was agreed.

'Now, to business,' Churchill said. 'The races are unusually open this year. A challenge. We can certainly do without another experience like the first race. The St James's Palace Stakes, indeed: they should call it the Bookmakers' Delight Handicap.'

'I thought Jack Joel's jockey put up a rather poor show,' agreed the Prime Minister. 'The fellow seemed to have no strength. Don't you agree, Walter?'

'The much respected First Lord has already put me in my place once on such matters,' Ransom managed. 'I can only tell you that I was resolved to put £2 on Mr Joel's Happy Warrior and when I came to the ring, the fellow cried "7-4 on", as if the colt was the finest ever fowled. I declined, and consequently am almost as happy as Colonel Hall-Walker, the owner (I believe) of the remarkable beast that won. Nothing ventured, everything retained: a sound philosophy at the racecourse, as everywhere else.'

Rosalind's face showed something close to a scowl. She would only ever feel at ease herself with a cautious approach to life and yet she had always seen her husband's caution as a form of pomposity. Probably she hated herself for suppressing so deeply the recklessness which might once have been there, which – in some measure – was in all of us. It was sad to see so clearly why she would always be unhappy, Ransom thought.

'Horses!' said Margot, feigning a lack of interest that was unconvincing in someone whose bony hands had lost control of the reins of more hunters than most people experienced in a lifetime. A reckless rider, living a reckless life. 'Horses,' she repeated. 'As if that was why we were here. The capes. The capes. Lady Chesterfield's purple-collared one, Lady Mond's black satin revival. Who else have we seen?' she asked, addressing Rosalind and Clementine Churchill.

'Why it should be thought desirable to disguise womanly curves, I cannot imagine,' Winston interjected. 'I accompanied Clemmie to Léonie's and said to her, wisely, "It looks to me all wrong." She merely replied that she knew it was quite fearfully right.'

'At least you are saved the expense of a bag: not gold or platinum or diamond, or a combination of the three,' his wife replied. 'It is not at all clear to me where one is supposed to put one's things with this new fashion....'

The tittle-tattle continued, but by now the champagne had gone to Ransom's head. Was there ever such a drink to give oblivion to fears and make all seem brilliant?

* * *

At the end of lunch, he arranged to rejoin Rosalind in the paddock for the Gold Cup. 'I'll meet you at Vesta Tilley's hat,' she said in a rare and successful attempt at humour. The hat concerned, with the tallest black feathers ever seen at Ascot, towered above its rivals. Fortified by the alcohol, Ransom allowed himself a smile at Min Starkie, dressed in a gown of black and white stripes, with hat of black and white plumes, hose visible from the knee downwards with the same combination: she might have been taken for a zebra.

The Royal party had come from Windsor, where the presence of the Russian and Austrian Ambassadors suggested that the King might be engaging in a little unofficial diplomacy. Ransom had spent one Ascot there himself with Rosalind – at a time when pageantry and dining off silver plate had more appeal for him. Anna, who always dressed simply, often in black, had been astonished by the account for Rosalind's clothes during this single week, which had fallen out of his pocket in their haste to find each other's bodies: 2 new dresses for the mornings, 4 complete outfits for the races, 5 new evening gowns. That had been in the early days, when the slogans of disrespect, perhaps disguising shock, had come passionately from her: now the judgments would be more subtle, or more plaintive, unforgiving save when swept away by the desire they still held for each other's souls, expressed in their lovemaking.

The Queen was known not to enjoy racing. She may have enjoyed the spectacle; she certainly laughed frequently, and heartily. Ransom had become used to identifying her at a distance. She never changed the cut and style of what she wore – wide in the skirts, close in the bodice. Always the same kind of hat: high-crowned, narrow-brimmed, smothered in flowers or – as he had already noticed today – in feathers. Next to her, the King, joining – leading – the fashion for white top hats. (Fortuitously, old Mr Sykes in Jermyn Street had told him to discard his favourite silk hat when he had dropped in to have it ironed. No one else seemed to have needed to be helped to avoid a social gaffe: a sign of his preoccupation during these last weeks.)

At least four Americans in the Royal Enclosure, he noted – the American Ambassador and Mrs Page, Edward Bell and Whitney Carpenter. There was Lady Elizabeth Keppel: a version of Margot, without her fire, packaged in champagne crêpe. And the Marchioness of Bute, in cinnamon, orange and white, her temper apparently matching the bright colours of her clothes as a fearful detective tried to ensure that the wrap she had wanted for the cold was not concealing some Suffragette agent of destruction. The suspicion was misguided in this case, but not wholly misplaced: in this strange era, if the ladies were not destroying people and property, they could even be found steeplechasing, like Lady Nelson on her Ally Sloper. *O tempora, O mores!* the Tories cried.

He had passed the Marlborough, the Bachelor's, the Guards Club marquees, and those of the Greenjackets and Artillerymen, amidst a throng of people now flushed by lunchtime wines. A nod here, a nod there, smiles of recognition helped by mutual inebriation. Then a last glance at the Royal Enclosure, and back in the direction of the paddock for the afternoon's racing.

If the women were more astonishingly attractive – eye-catchingly so – year by year, the horses were uncommonly poor. The

Gold Cup was the only classic race during the week and the entry was lacking in class, leaving aside the French pair, Brûleur and Nimbus – perhaps the best racehorses in Europe. Among the forty or so English entrants were Louvois and Night Hawk, winners of the Two Thousand Guineas and of the St Leger, respectively; but much better 4-year-olds had been known. Brûleur was suffering from a bad passage across the Channel and was well beaten by the turn for home coming into the straight. It looked as if Will Brook was going to spring a surprise until a hundred yards out, when the 5-year-old, Aleppo, got up and outstayed him, emerging as victor by three-quarters of a length.

In the midst of the excitement in the closing stages, someone Ransom did not immediately recognize jostled past him. It was Kell – his hair had been greyed and he was unshaven, sufficient in an unfamiliar situation to create a disguise without going into a more detailed charade. 'Excuse me a moment, darling,' he said to Rosalind, acting out his own charade. He followed Kell to where they could still be seen to be part of the general gathering excitedly discussing the results of the race, but just out of earshot of anyone else.

'I've been anxious for news,' said the Captain, with no trace of anxiety in his voice.

'Yes, I'm sorry, but – as you see – life doesn't leave one much time for skulduggery.' This, at least, was true: if there was one thing indisputable about the social life of the English upper classes in June 1914, it was that full attention was demanded. Besides, a rushed preparation for Ascot was an excellent excuse for suppressing the extraordinary experience he had just had. 'Look, I think you can forget the whole arms business. It is happening, but I'm on to something much bigger – so big in fact that it puts the whole Irish business in the shade.'

'I'm listening.'

'I think there's going to be some sort of plot to kill the King.'

Kell grunted. He didn't look surprised, though in actuality this was the last thing he had been expecting. 'You have been busy. What's the story?'

'Well, that's the trouble. There isn't much of one. All the Germans I saw, one by one, including the Kaiser himself, gave the same account: Germany was threatened, beleaguered by her enemies; Britain must not be tempted to join them, and if she felt tempted, the Germans would be forced to keep her occupied by doing all they could to encourage the Irish dissidents – from either side. Convincing, perhaps, but all said with the sort of friendliness that makes one feel frightened.'

'Yes, but the plot?'

'Explicit, but not proven, I'm afraid. You won't believe this, but in my hotel room – just after I had seen the Kaiser, as it happens – I found a brief but very pointed note to the effect that I should believe nothing I was told and that the Kaiser himself had sanctioned a plan to assassinate King George V before the end of the summer.'

Ransom was right: Kell did not believe him. But he did not say so. 'A hoax?'

'Perhaps. It didn't feel like it.'

'You have the letter?'

'No, I destroyed it.'

'That was a mistake.'

'What would you have done in my position?' he asked angrily. 'I am not in the least ashamed to say that I was frightened.'

Kell, who was too experienced to forget where he was, merely grunted again, smiled and put his arm round Ransom's shoulder.' 'All right, we have to pursue this – but properly. If it is going to be dangerous, there are things I have to tell you, as well as vice-versa. We must meet soon.' With this he nodded and quickly disappeared into the crowds.

CHAPTER ELEVEN

The King is annoyed

A S it happened, they might have met again more quickly than either of them had anticipated. Ransom had promised to drop in on Lloyd George to discuss the Chancellor's Budget problems at about half-past seven that evening, while Kell made his way in and out of the front door of No. 10 Downing Street, which adjoined the Chancellor's residence, in the space of fifteen minutes not long before.

Asquith had much on his mind. On his return from Ascot he had received the news that the railway workers, in conference at Swansea, had approved in principle the projected alliance with the miners and the transport workers. The possibility of industrial action combined with Ulster strife and God-knows-what on the Continent was not a pleasant one. He listened silently as Kell quickly reported his conversation with Ransom.

'I'm inclined to take the assassination story seriously,' Kell went on. 'Ransom doesn't have the sort of mind that could invent it; besides, what would be his motive? Nor do I see him as a dishonourable man....'

'I trust not,' Asquith interjected.

'...but,' Kell continued, 'I can see that he might quickly get out of his depth and play for time by telling half-truths.'

'Why should he?' asked Asquith, not at all ready – Ransom subsequently discovered – to abandon a colleague whose whole demeanour and way of life seemed so much a part of his settled universe.

'The girl. Anna Kinsky. There's much more to be found out there.'

'Um,' said Asquith, but – allowing his political instincts to prevail – added not unsympathetically 'then you must find it out. But now you must excuse me, since I have to wade through some rather muddy Irish water with the King.'

* * *

Like Kell, Ransom was also preoccupied with Anna. Where was she? How did she fit into all this? He loved, God in one sense he loved her, but it was not a love that he could express properly within the constraints of the life he lived. And how could he be sure of that love? Or hers?

None of these questions had seemed pressing before – she had become, almost, a part of his ostensibly well-ordered life; but now he had been given a sense of deep insecurity that had rocked his existence to its foundations.

Even so, as he had found at Ascot, it was comfortingly difficult to forget all that environment, breeding, experience had taught. As he walked with the Chancellor in the walled-in enclosure called a garden, which backs onto No. 10 and No. 11 Downing Street, it was not that difficult to slip back into at least a superficial concern with everyday matters. He had buried his private preoccupations more deeply, though not more successfully, than his ambitious colleague, who – for all his romanticism – understood and enjoyed the world as it was.

When Ransom arrived, he found Lloyd George with Lord Riddell. L.G. was lying on his back on the sofa reading Bagehot's economic essays. Even now, this might have been thought a somewhat unusual exercise for a Chancellor. Things had not changed that much from the days when Lord Randolph Churchill confessed that he had often wondered, when decimal points were explained to him, 'what those d----d dots meant!' It soon became clear, however, that Lloyd George was seeking self-justification rather than a new economic theory.

He read an extract on Gladstone's economic policy and remarked: 'You see, they have always been talking in the same way. They spoke of Mr Gladstone as they now speak of me.'

'The opposition to his budgets never reached the same degree,' Riddell said, as they both helped themselves to the whisky decanter.

'I had no desire for a taxing budget this year. It was not the time for it. Winston forced us into it with the increased naval expenditure. For months, as you know, I fought against that: to ask for too much – not twice but two-and-a-half times the last naval budget – was madness.'

'It's a long time since the Tories were in power,' Ransom said drily, 'though I suppose you helped your status with the anti-war crowd amongst our own lot.'

'And do you say *they* are wrong? The Germans are behaving with sweet reason, as you should know. I wondered if the timing of your little disappearing act could have had anything to do with the signing of the agreement for the extension of the Berlin-Baghdad railway,' said the smiling Chancellor.

It hadn't. But – with renewed alarm that his excursion to Germany seemed to have become semi-public – Ransom refused to rise to the bait. He said: 'But the Navy has nothing to do with all these other changes.'

'No, yet while we were about it there was no reason why we should not have provided for other things besides the Navy. I'm disgusted by these rich men. They say to me, "You are a thief! You are worse, you are an attorney! Worst of all you are a Welshman!" That is always the crowning epithet … I tell you, Walter, I am proud of the little land among the hills.' He raised himself from the sofa and walked a little unsteadily over to the whisky. Calmer, but almost menacing, he continued: 'You should look on the fall of the Ribot Ministry in France and learn from it: the people will no longer accept a government which represents the contented and well-to-do.'

Riddell smiled and took the opportunity to make his departure. Ransom snorted, but made no comment on what L.G. had said. He did not see it like that. It was like 1909 again: with a large deficit, tax increases were unavoidable. It was easy to rationalize the need by getting at the rich. When Lloyd George introduced his Budget into the House in early May, income tax was up 2d, graduated surtax was to start at £3,000, and death duties were also up. The Chancellor had proposed allocating more funds to education, to poor relief, roads and public health. There had been opposition from affluent Liberals and a deputation had been to Asquith while Ransom was in Germany.

'At the end of the day we can control our own people; it's these damned technicalities that get me down,' said Lloyd George wearily. The Conservative Opposition had asked the Speaker whether the Finance Bill was a genuine 'money bill' as defined by the Parliament Act. Mr Speaker confessed that he did find it somewhat irregular and the Lords would use that excuse to throw it out.

'The Parliamentary draughtsmen let me down badly. They should have found out beforehand what the Speaker's decision would be.'

'We shall have to amend the measure.'

'Yes, we shall have to amend – truncate more like. And there will be derision. It doesn't help a man's popularity.'

'Or his ambitions.'

'All of us have those, don't we? That's why we're in the game.'

'Provided our ambitions coincide with the public good.'

'I've never doubted it. Do you?'

Ransom did doubt it, but shrugged. In the beginning he had wanted to use political measures to ameliorate social conditions and, he supposed, he needed the applause – and the power – that went with that. But now the question was irrelevant; he had lost the skill of self-deception because he could not match the stamina and single-mindedness of some of his colleagues – Lloyd George especially.

Lloyd George swallowed a considerable amount of whisky at one go from a large glass of the liquid. 'You know, Walter, I sometimes think that we political animals can only ever be truly frank to our lovers. They'll take anything. You can tell them that you are prepared to thrust all love aside if it gets in the way of your mission....'

'Ambition....'

'Mission, ambition: it is the same I tell you. And they love you for it. Your love for them is stronger, sincerer, the more you say you may have to sacrifice it. Women are like that.'

Not Anna, he thought. But perhaps L.G. was just the greater man, in this respect as all others. At least he felt no need to cultivate him. He was deliberately argumentative: 'The whole affair has been a shocking muddle. You know that the Budget Committee only became aware of your proposals at the meeting shortly before you introduced the thing itself.'

'I do know it. It was precisely to forestall discussions that I spoke for three hours,' said Lloyd George with some satisfaction.

'Only the results matter. Here was a complicated, tedious Bill – and you talked of passing it in a week.'

'Tush. It would still have worked if the Treasury men had been awake.'

'You overwhelm them with a torrent of reasoning; and then they can see only the plausibility.'

'Then so should the Opposition. The country will, I'm sure of it. It all sounds convincing, doesn't it? We are carrying on our proven policies of strengthening national defences against possible enemies abroad and against actual enemies at home: poverty, disease, unhealthy homes, suffering from poor conditions…. There must, as a consequence, be a fair contribution to be levied on wealth.'

Quickly, as ever with Lloyd George, conversation turned into speech-making: the rhythms of his sentences made it so, but the rhetoric was also imbedded in the soul of the man. 'The plutocrats talk of "the false humanitarianism" of our legislation; they say it will destroy wealth. Walter, Walter, the Power that governs this world does not punish with bankruptcy nations that do kindnesses to the old, the feeble, the broken and the sick. We shall beat the rich men back to the gates of their mansions and beyond.'

He stopped, suddenly tired and saddened. 'But people are so unreasonable. It would be a deal easier if one could rule oneself, free of the plots of one's own Prime Minister – and of monarchs, for that matter: I shudder to think what Asquith and the King are up to at this very moment.'

* * *

It was true that, about half an hour before, the Prime Minister had gone to the Palace for his audience with the King. As he waited, he talked to George V's Private Secretary of his difficulties. 'Yes, there is the indignity of the thing,' he said. 'Mr Lloyd George never seems at a loss for expedients to humiliate the Government of which he is a member.' Asquith did not know that his Chancellor had once toyed with the idea of a 'Government of Businessmen': under his own control, of course, a control that would have been simple compare with the initial need to shoulder aside Asquith & Co.

Stamfordham, who had been Principal Private Secretary to Queen Victoria in the last six years of her life, had his own problems: he had begun to notice in the eyes of her grandson, George V, the same rigidity that had revealed so clearly vexation in her. Arthur Bigge, as he had once been, was one of the twelve children of a Northumberland clergyman – the Vicar of Stamfordham; his elevation to the peerage had coincided with the King's accession to the throne. He had long experience of monarchy, for he had met the Empress Eugénie – who introduced him to Queen Victoria – when she lost her son in an ambush in the Zulu War of the late 1870s. Asquith did not like him much and made himself a renewed mental note that the man's wings needed clipping.

'I don't think you will find that His Majesty is over-concerned with the obscure details of financial policy,' Stamfordham said. 'He has become, as you know, more than a little anxious to find a successful conclusion to the Irish difficulties.'

This was true. And one source of the King's irritation was the Prime Minister's great reluctance to act decisively. Asquith hated to try to anticipate events. For some months now, he had been reassuring the King, who had clearly failed to be reassured.

'You surely understand, Prime Minister, that I cannot let a Civil War be started. Nor, as a matter of fact, have I some of the power which some of the Conservatives blame me for not using. They reproach me for letting your Government do just what it likes and hint that it was different when my father or grandmother were alive.'

'It is indeed difficult, Sir,' said Asquith soothingly.

'And then, on the other side, we have Labour Members openly accusing me of encouraging military officers to send in their papers so as not to have to carry out their legal orders when the crisis comes to a head. I should like to know, Prime Minister, whether it is seriously thought by the people of this country that I may constitutionally use a Royal veto to Home Rule? With the veto of the House of Lords now so restricted, it seems to be suggested that it is up to me to give or to withhold it.'

Asquith came as near to laughing as a Prime Minister can before his king. 'The idea is fantastic. The veto has not been used for two centuries; it must be seen as a nominal prerogative.'

The King nodded. 'But the man in the street?'

'I take an optimistic view, Sir. Things will settle down. They would have done so already, were it not for Carson.'

'But what if the Bill should result in Civil War? What if we have the army shooting our fellow-countrymen?'

'We can compromise. Carson may accept a scheme that excludes Ulster from Home Rule for, say, five years. *The Times* does not help by encouraging him to hold out for the "clear cut" – that is, omission of Ulster from the Bill altogether.'

'Should we have a Conference to discuss the whole matter?'

'I think, Sir, that there is no need for the present.'

'I'm not so sure. It might break the deadlock. I shall, perhaps, have a word with Lansdowne.'

Asquith's annoyance began to show. He spoke with distinct coldness, 'Of course, Sir, I can have no objection if you with to seek the opinion of an Opposition leader. It would be better, I suspect, if I were to submit a detailed memorandum to you on the subject.' God! The man was so obstinate.

The King, just perceptibly, sighed. He nodded his assent to the Prime Minister, who quickly made ready to leave.

'I hope that all is in order for the announcement of my Birthday Honours tomorrow,' the King asked sharply, as if this Prime Minister might have managed to upset his wishes even on this simple matter.

Asquith, who knew perfectly well that King George knew perfectly well that there were no problems, decided on tact and politeness. 'Indeed, Sir. Lord Kitchener's Earldom will be well received and such is the popularity of the Russian season at Drury Lane that Sir Joseph Beecham's baronetcy will be positively acclaimed.' But then he continued: 'Perhaps we should suggest to Dr Fraser, having won his knighthood, that he should devote a new volume of *The Golden Bough* to the prehistoric origins of such honours!'

The joke was a mistake. The King grunted, and Asquith respectfully withdrew. 'I shall look forward to seeing Your Majesty at the Birthday dinner on Monday. The House will, of course, be adjourning early.' There was only one thing the Prime Minister really cared about in connection with the Honours List – that it did not involve a by-election.

* * *

When Asquith was gone, the King let out a groan. The Prime Minister was maddening, but it wasn't just him: the Conservative leader, Bonar Law, had given him a terrible, an unforgiveable time at their last audience. He had spent a sleepless night with the conversation repeated over and over again in his head.

'I trust there is not going to be any violence in the House of Commons this session?'

'Well, Sir, I do not think that Your Majesty can suggest that the Opposition has forgotten its duty to the country or the Throne in the midst of our sharp party fights.'

'Certainly not.'

'But you must remember, Sir, that we not only very strongly

object to what the Government is doing but that we think that they have pursued their objectives by trickery and fraud.'

He hadn't known how to reply to that.

'May I talk quite freely to Your Majesty?'

'Please do. I would wish you to.'

'Then, I think, Sir, that the situation is a grave one not only for the House but also for the Throne. Our desire has been to keep the Crown out of our struggle, but the Government has brought it in. If it will not resign, then you must either accept the Home Rule Bill or dismiss your Ministers and choose others who will support you in vetoing it – and in either case half your subjects will think you have acted against them.'

He had reddened, again unable to decide how to reply.

'Have you never considered that, Sir?'

'No. No, it is the first time it has been suggested to me.'

Didn't he have the right to expect the same faith and trust from the politicians as he gave them? Shouldn't they seek to avoid unnecessary conflict, to encourage conciliation, as he did? Never in his life had he done anything he was ashamed to confess, never had he deliberately concealed things, or manipulated others for his own purposes. What had happened to the Tories that they should choose a Glasgow iron merchant to lead them? Derby had tried to reassure him: a good sense of humour and a good head for figures, he had said; all the qualities of a great leader except one – no personal magnetism. Hum. No magnetism at all, as far as *this* King was concerned.

As George V turned to look at the mirror above the fireplace, he saw through the half light an imaginary picture of himself, long removed from the endless studying and signing of incomprehensible pieces of paper, freed from the need to understand the affairs of state, the boredom of repeated receptions and the irritation of stubborn Prime Ministers.

He saw instead a figure in a suit of light brown tweeds, with Homburg hat – slightly more rolled than most, wasn't it? Boots and shooting spats. Two grave but friendly old spaniels by his side. Then off to the wild and exposed stubbles on the Sandringham estate. A moment's silence as he watched a high flight of gulls coming in from the Wash. An eerie, distant whistle pierces the air as the beaters advance. Soon the first covey is up and on the wing. His left arm – a nice, idiosyncratic touch, he decides – is extended straight along the barrel; both his eyes are open. All guns rise to fire….

Damnation. It was not that he disliked or distrusted Asquith. He had been quite angry when Salisbury suggested that one could not believe a word the Ministers said. What he could not face was the odious and impossible position of having to sign the Home Rule Bill without a simultaneous Amending Bill which would be palatable to Carson and all the Protestants. The Government must act quickly to introduce the Amendment – perhaps allowing the Ulster counties to vote themselves out of Home Rule for a period: it should be done within a week. But would the Lords accept it? Would it satisfy Carson, or even Bonar Law?

There were only problems, no answers.

CHAPTER TWELVE

Frustration on all sides

THE Amending Bill was duly introduced into the House of Lords by the Government leader there, Lord Crewe, on Tuesday, the 23rd of June. He spoke with little regard to the emotions of his subject, but accurately enough in his summary of the primary reasons for the changes: to meet the religious forebodings of Ulster and its fears regarding the business capacity of the men of the rest of Ireland. Almost in passing, he acknowledged that the Government would not be unwilling to give their consideration to further amendments. In allowing six of the Ulster counties exclusion for half a dozen years, the Bill was the equivalent of what Carson had once called a sentence of death with a stay of execution.

The Opposition in the Lords amended the amendment to exclude all nine Ulster counties – a controversial scheme because some of them contained a very mixed Catholic and Protestant population – without option or time limit. The Bill in this form would go back to the Commons on 14 July, when Redmond and disaffected Labour and Liberal Members would vote against it, threatening to bring the Government down.

The Irish debate in the Commons itself had been very rough. As the House was assembling, above the Chamber in the Ladies' Gallery, there had already been a continuation of the quarrel. Speaker Lowther struggled hard to keep his good humour when he wrote despairingly to Margot – whose daughter had figured prominently in the altercations – afterwards: 'I have as much as I can manage in keeping order amongst the devils below, without having to control the angels above.' The episode later figured in a novel by Mrs Humphry Ward, but – removed from fiction – it was no subject for humour at all. Bonar Law was implacable:

'How can the Government pretend to force a scheme such as this upon the whole of a great community who were born to exactly the same rights as the citizens of Lancashire or of Middlesex and whose sole prayer is to be left to hand down these rights undiminished to their children? Does anyone suppose that any Prime Minister can give orders to shoot down men whose only crime is that they refuse to be driven out of our community? Were any Government to force bloodshed in such circumstances it would succeed only in lighting the fires of civil war which would shatter the Empire to its foundations.'

Asquith was firm in reply. What the Opposition leader had said had no parallel in the language of any responsible statesman in British history. He shuddered to think what might happen if Bonar Law and his friends became responsible for the Government of the country.

'We shall have gained power by clearly stating what our intentions were – which the Prime Minister has not done': Bonar Law was coldly furious.

'It is a declaration of war against constitutional government,' Asquith insisted.

'These people in the North and East of Ireland, from the whole of their past history, would prefer to accept the government of a foreign country rather than submit to be governed by the honourable gentlemen below the gangway.'

Uproar. Anguish. Meanwhile, outside Parliament, Viscount Milner, who had close family connections with Germany, had continued to collect money behind the scenes so as to purchase more German arms for the Ulster Volunteers and to back the Protestant Provisional Government. Both he and Bonar Law were well informed of the confused intentions over the Irish situation for one very good reason: the man George Dangerfield described as the tallest, ugliest, cleverest officer in the British army, Major-General Henry Wilson, gave them verbatim accounts of the meetings of the relevant Cabinet committee. A Protestant from County Longford, Wilson now enjoyed the role of Director of Military Operations at the War Office.

No one could be certain what might happen next, for it was not at all clear – outside the rhetoric of the House of Commons – how far Bonar Law was prepared to go: in his inscrutability, he was, as Max Aitken said, 'the sombre raven among the glittering birds of paradise'.

Nor was there much comfort for Asquith and the rest – it was, after all, Ransom's Government too – in the reaction from the moulders of public opinion. As the Prime Minister read the first edition of *The Times* in bed the morning after the debate he cursed the Irishmen of both sides as vehemently as he could without upsetting the good order of his breakfast tray. 'The Amending Bill is so manifestly a frivolous pretence at dealing with an exceedingly grave situation that we cannot help feeling that the Government have only introduced it to gain more time.' Careless drafting… gaps…absurdly inadequate after three months of simulated cogitation…based on the assumption that procrastination will result in the disintegration of the Ulster forces: the analysis was much too close to the truth to be palatable.

* * *

Most member of the upper classes, however, were far too busy displaying a different sort of earnestness during these weeks to worry over much about the complications of the Home Rule affair. They were following with some devotion the daily social round. Even Ransom had enjoyed a relaxing weekend before the turmoils over the Amending Bill, for he had decided that Henley was, after all, worthy of them. Sunday morning had begun with heavy rain, but by midday the sun was shining along the river from Richmond, by Molesey and Staines, to Windsor, and on to Oxford and the joys of Cliveden and Cookham and Pangbourne. Three hundred boats or more had gone over the mechanical conveyor in the backwater at Boulter's Lock by mid-afternoon: steam launches, electric canoes, punts in profusion, providing a spectacle for the crowd jostling on the towpath.

These mid-summer days had a character of their own, which – even in the peculiar circumstances in which Ransom found himself – could not wholly be obscured from view. Silver teapots surrounded dainty cups as, in the silvery babble of women's voices, the great issues of the day were debated. In the match between Brookes and Froitzheim at Wimbledon, the German recovered gallantly and came close to winning; it had been clear that the crowd was on his side. The Suffragettes, it was said with polite titters, were preparing to blow up the whole of Ireland – the wretched Emerald Isle was distracting public attention from their cause.

Also on the social circuit, as the bright young things took to smoking in the cinema, Mr Bernard Shaw was heard to remark: 'Had I ever smoked, I should not now be the first intellectual of Europe.' His new play *Pygmalion* had opened at Her Majesty's with Mrs Patrick Campbell – newly married in real life to George Cornwallis-West – as Eliza Doolittle. The original Pygmalion, Ransom reflected, had taken a block of dead ivory and made of it so fair a figure of a woman that he fell in love with his own creation. Aphrodite, obligingly, brought it to life at his request: would that real life were so simple.

His own, despite these pleasantries, was in at least one sense in considerable turmoil. The worst thing was the uncertainty: he had not seen Anna now for more than two weeks and all his questions were left unanswered. There was no sign of her at Clarges Street, no sign of her in the other, rather few, places, he could think of trying. He realized how little of each other's lives they had been sharing and – while this had never seemed a problem before – it now seemed a further sign that matter were out of control. What good was a relationship that amounted to an occasional indulgence, when it could threaten his career, his country, perhaps his life? And yet…to see her, to hear her, to be with her: happiness was the mother of courage and she was the provider.

* * *

At last, on the same day as the introduction of the Amending Bill into the House of Lords, a note arrived from her: trust her, be patient, she would explain. Nothing more. Then came a frustrating surprise, after several days of one of the most frustrating weeks he could remember.

First he had talked with feigned enthusiasm to the delegation of German manufacturers who were entertained at the Guildhall. It was, perhaps, no more bizarre for them to visit a country with which they might soon be at war than it was for their fellow-countrymen to open in Munich, on the same day, the Congress of German Trade Unions – an organization on which the Kaiser might also be expected to make war.

Then he had talked politely to the Portuguese Ambassador,

whose Cabinet had just resigned, at the King's Birthday Banquet. He listened intently to homilies on Portuguese politics – while his mind wandered in search of Anna.

He had also talked endlessly to a group of well-meaning ladies assembled by his wife to sell artificial roses for Alexandra Day, in aid of the charities patronized by the Queen Mother.

And he had to write, with fulsome sincerity, to the Master of Exeter College, Oxford – where he was an Honorary Fellow – to express his deep regret at being unable to attend the sexcentenary celebrations of the College.

So it went from Monday, through Tuesday's formal progress of the Amending Bill, to Wednesday, the day after he received Anna's note.

Lloyd George, whom he met after lunch, was agitated – not about Ireland, but about his Budget. As they walked into the House of Commons, the Chancellor said: 'Whatever they say about Ulster being the one question before the country, there still seems time to accuse me of robbing the purses of the wealthy.'

'I thought that was what you wanted?'

'I'm proud of it. But I'm weary of it too.'

'In the days of Peel and Gladstone the House devoted even more time to financial questions.'

'This is no devotion: this is obstruction, deliberate obstruction. It must end.'

'We need to carry our own people,' Ransom observed.

'We must. The Tories mean first to defeat this Liberal Ministry, put an end to it. They want to defeat Home Rule, they want to destroy the Parliament Act. That is going to be their purpose, and we can only thwart it by absolute unity among *all* the progressive forces inside the House of Commons.'

They passed into the Chamber. The Chancellor would not have been pleased to have heard the mutterings on the Opposition back bench, which were none the less loud and well prepared enough for an eager journalist's ears to catch and record.

'Take my word for it – the Welsh wizard's gasping for breath. He's dazed I tell you, furiously angry at everyone and without any idea of what to do next. Habit suggests going for the Dukes – if his loving colleagues will let him....' The humour was tinged with malevolence. 'George is a pigmy on the stage of history, a glib, emotional little ranter who has only the haziest idea of what he wants.'

The Prime Minster made his entrance. More noisy mutterings. 'Now, here comes a statesman. A statesman, you know, is a politician who hasn't the courage to say no.'

'But let's be serious. The rich Liberals, the quiet ones who pull the strings, have turned against George. They won't pay these new taxes – and they won't subscribe to party funds.'

'Ah, well.' The anonymous but not untypical Tory backbencher gestured in the direction of his own leader and said to his companion and anyone else who would listen: 'If Bonar Law's experience has grown as fast as that bald spot on his head, he won't let the Government escape.'

The Chancellor had already had more than a few awkward moments in the House of Commons. At times he would be seen to crack jokes with Asquith; more often he would hastily consult his private secretary and guardian angel, Howard Whitehouse, or seek succour from the Treasury watchdogs under the gallery. The Opposition had a strong card in Felix Cassel, the former lawyer who now delighted in the intricacies of public finance: he supplied what the satirical magazine *Truth* called 'the counterpart to Lloyd George's Celtic melodies'. The gossip in political circles was relentless: how could the Chancellor expect to get his Bills through, unless the House was ready to meet again in November?

There was a simple answer – the guillotine to circumscribe the amount of time spent on discussing the proposals – but it was not simply applied. Some attempt must be made to persuade – persuade the faithful especially. In a noisy and crowded House, Asquith made a defensive speech. Predictions of financial disaster from increased Government expenditure and so-called confiscatory taxation had been made nearly seventy years before when the Corn Laws were repealed. They were made again when succession duties were introduced in 1853, when Harcourt introduced his Budget in 1894, and Lloyd George his in 1909. 'And yet,' the Prime Minister insisted, 'the last twenty years have seen the largest investment of capital in British history. I do not, I tell you I do not, disregard the need for economy, but expenditure on the Navy cannot, must not be reduced, and that on social reform is bound to increase.'

The House was not convinced. Still less by Winston Churchill, who spoke next. Ransom later recorded in his diary that he dwelled on such details because he wanted clearly to convey the matters that seemed of the greatest concern to them all during these days, though this particular debate had its own particular climax – of a personal kind – for him. History is written around hindsight and in the light of all that happened afterwards the real significance of these Budget squabbles, and Churchill's contribution, has long since been lost. Certainly the First Lord was listened to: the majority may have been right to distrust his motives and remain unconvinced by his arguments, but he held their attention.

'There have been three great Budgets with which my right hon. friend has been intimately associated [he said]. I am not now talking of the finer points. I am talking of the great purposes of these Budgets. My right hon. friend divided with the Prime Minister the honours of the Budget which gave us Old Age Pensions. That was for the aged – for the past generation. Then there was the great reform which was his own and no other man's – the change that gave us national insurance. Now we have come to the greatest reform of all – today we are concerned with the coming generation.

'On the coming generation, on those who are children today, depends the prosperity of our race. If we can help that generation, we shall have dealt with a problem which will go far to ensure the maintenance of that great position which this country holds.

'It has been said that the Budget is costly – so it is; but it is productive expenditure. There has been a great deal of social reform in the last nine years and a great increase in the productive capacity of the nation. The national income, according to the best experts, has been going up and up. We are spending no more in proportion to the national resources even under the "extravagant" proposals of my right hon. friend. And we are spending it in quite different ways.

'All over the world we are face to face with a demand by the democracy for a greater share in what is produced. You cannot ignore that. It is no use being like our critics on the other side of the House – full of criticism, but with no constructive proposals. The one thing to be done is to face the facts, and we have been facing them: instead of direct and indirect taxation being about equal, as they were when we first came in, and the burden falling most heavily on the labouring classes, today direct taxation is to indirect taxation as three is to two. That is a great change.

'If you wish to get stability in your Constitution, if you wish for a restraining effect on the great democratic movement, you must have an effective restraining party.

'The only effective conservative party that I know in this country is the conservative party to which I belong.'

Ransom had to admit that Bonar Law was fiercely effective in reply. The Chancellor of the Exchequer had failed to control expenditure. He had imposed taxes which were excessively costly to collect. He was promising not retrenchment but extravagance. He had turned extravagance into a principle and was trying to use his Budgets to correct inequalities of wealth. He seemed to be suggesting that it was mere luck if one was industrious and thrifty or a wastrel. The idea was preposterous.

Suddenly, in the midst of the familiar uproar in the House, Ransom found himself staring into the eyes, the beautiful eyes, of Anna – attentively listening in the Strangers' Gallery. As he pushed his way past his front bench colleagues out of the Chamber, confusion spread.

Disjointed snatches of conversation and loud shouts filled the air. 'What a muddle!' cried one Unionist. 'Tax the rich and you take away employment,' said another in more stately fashion: 'Luxuries mean WORK for the lower classes. WORK!' 'EVIL! An evil idea: to squander the wealth of the country on social misfits,' declared his neighbour, to add to the general noise.

All these words swam round in his head incoherently. He knew he would be too late, and he was. She was gone.

He took a deep breath, then several more. Self-control must reassert itself, and to a limited extent it did: if the world seemed to be going mad, he was not going to accept the situation without a fight.

If only he could get to grips with some of the uncertainties. Had he misunderstood what he had heard in Germany? Had he been hoaxed? Drowning men are vigorous in clutching straws.

* * *

The Midnight Ball at the Savoy that evening was not calculated to restore a sense of reality. The intention was to look as medieval as possible, while Cecil Macklin's new ragtime 'Caper Sauce' kidded the middle-aged that they were still youthful. It was in these circumstances that an unwelcome guest, Von Bode, took him aside and whispered that the assassin was in the country. The right moment would come soon, and his help would be needed.

It was as well that Kell at least had tried to be thorough: he had employed what limited resources he had in trying to find out more about the German plans, and the very fact that no one had come up with anything seemed to indicated what he already knew – that the operation was being handled from the highest level, with few let into the secret. Someone may have been indiscreet to Ransom, but the reasoning must have been that the worst risk the Germans were taking was to make the far from well-developed British intelligence jumpy. And yet Ransom surmised that he also saw in him a trump card of a kind – whatever his feelings for Anna, and however she was involved, Ransom was no traitor, was he? Kell assessed the risk, and took it: Ransom was given an intensive course in self-defence and the use of firearms.

His efficient teacher forgot nothing as he took Ransom step-by-step through Hugh Pollard's standard manual. There were no good revolvers for long-range work, he learned. Some, like the Mauser, were sighted for extreme ranges, but even used as carbines their accuracy over 400 yards was very variable. The Maxim silencer, employed on rifles, could be applied to revolvers, but the techniques were tricky and private adaptation was necessary. Pocket automatics had the advantages of being rapid-firing, flat and concealable, but they had a tendency to jam. Besides, the idea that you could shoot through the pocket was largely a myth; it might work at three or four yards range, but there would probably be one shot only, since the pocket prevented the empty case from ejecting and again jammed the weapon. Best use could be made of a holster which would not be noticed but which could be easily reached: suspended from a loop of leather, fitting over the left shoulder, it was further secured by a light strap passing round the back and over the breast under the waistcoat.

Look straight at the target – act automatically, suppressing any need for a separate brain message for each shot – bring the weapon back to the point of aim after each discharge….

In Berlin he had been struck by the number of rifle galleries he had seen, partly because of the crowds surrounding them, each man impatiently waiting his turn as if the whole city was vitally concerned to improve its shooting skills. He thought of this when, a few days later, he went to the King's Gallery, off Panton Street, Haymarket: a revolver range incongruously next door to the Prince of Wales theatre, where he could experiment with the variety of weapons. Despite Kell's conscientious instruction, it was clear that he had much to learn: his hand shook slightly while the man at his side casually fired six shots out of a Webley Target revolver into a 12-inch-square card at 12 yards in less than two seconds. This marksman, Gerry Buckton-Smith, turned out to have useful answers to all his questions (only later did he learn that he was one of Kell's men).

Buckton-Smith was full of anecdotes. He spoke rapidly, but calmly, and Ransom did not think at the time to question him too closely – he was too busy listening. His experience took in duelling, for – somehow – Buckton-Smith had been admitted to the French society, 'L'Assaut au Pistolet', which employed breech-loading duelling pistols of .44 calibre in an elaborate ritual. He even gave Ransom the card of their official armourers – Piot-Lepage, 12 Rue Martel, Paris – as if he were already part of the fraternity.

Much more to the point was some down-to-earth advice on gun care. He seemed to think that this was as important as the skill itself and not to be left to anyone else: clean the barrel with a bristle brush dipped in cordite cleanser, then again with flannel pieces wrapped round the brush. 'See here,' he said, holding out his own revolver: 'You could draw a white silk handkerchief through there without dirtying it.'

Assassination: gradually it acquired greater reality for Ransom. If – as had happened that week – Francis Prudhon could shoot Henri de Rothschild in a Paris street because his dairy business had been ruined by Rothschild's charitable enterprise for supplying milk to mothers, surely such violence was possible when war between nations was at stake?

CHAPTER THIRTEEN

Assassination in Bosnia

THERE was an immediate irony ahead. The heir to the Habsburg Empire, the Archduke Franz Ferdinand, had left Vienna on Tuesday, the 23rd of June for a tour of inspection of his Bosnian garrisons, while the armed forces engaged in manoeuvres. On the following Sunday morning – the anniversary of the extinction of the medieval Serbian kingdom by Sultan Murad I more than six centuries before – he made his official entry into the Bosnian town of Sarajevo.

The Serbs, who had gained their independence from the Turks some decades before, were for ever plotting in Bosnia, whose recent annexation by the Habsburgs had produced more than one international incident.

There was no mistaking the Archduke – dressed splendidly in his white tunic, adorned with decorations, and a plumed hat. With him was his wife, the Duchess of Hohenberg, herself in a sparkling white dress, and white hat with ostrich feathers. Suddenly, and without warning, a bomb was thrown at their car: it failed to

explode immediately, but caught the following vehicle, injuring several people in the process. 'So they greet us in your town with bombs,' said the Archduke, apparently unshaken. Herr Potiorek, Bosnia's Governor, was reassuring. 'Sire, there will be no more bombs. There is no danger.'

Ransom was told that the Archduke merely grunted. Franz Ferdinand had always been convinced that the Balkan territories were no great asset. Everyone knew that Serbia was the home of a pack of thieves, ruffians and murderers, living in an unfriendly landscape punctuated only by a few struggling plum trees. Best, nevertheless, to be careful. The decision was taken to avoid the centre of the town.

Alas, in his excitement, the confused driver forgot these instructions and turned into Franz Joseph Strasse. Potiorek shouted to him to stop. There were just two shots. Franz Ferdinand and his wife died.

Except for Foreign Office officials, members of the Cabinet and those alert enough in the London Clubs (where telegrams were posted), the news from Sarajevo did not reach England until the Monday morning newspapers.

When his mother's favourite brother, Uncle Willy of Greece, had been assassinated the previous year, George V was 'terribly upset'. Now he wrote in his diary: 'Terrible shock for the dear old Emperor.' The reflection that the Archduke was, after all, an irritating firebrand was left for later consideration. The King would drop into the Austro-Hungarian Embassy in Belgrave Square with a message of sympathy for Count Mensdorff; that would tie the matter up neatly, he decided.

The aged Emperor Franz Joseph had ruled the Austro-Hungarian Empire for sixty-five years. As the Kaiser had noted, his had been a life full of acute grief, and other victims of the assassin were only too well known to him. It was the Italian anarchist Lucchoni who had stabbed to death his wife, Elizabeth of Bavaria, 'a woman' – by his own account – 'who never hurt a soul, and only did good all her life'. 'Then I am to be spared nothing,' he had declared when news was brought of this event; and now, now yet more suffering, this time for his troubled empire. If *Simplicissimus* could draw the Slavs as rats overrunning and undermining a doddering old Austrian double eagle asleep in a chair, then equally no one could pretend that the sleep was a peaceful one.

In London, Lloyd George was dismissive. He was brought a red dispatch box from the Foreign Office at teatime on Sunday. Inside it was a telegram announcing the assassination. 'This means war,' he declared; but war in the Balkans was an everyday occurrence. An incident there, no matter how regrettable in itself, was no more than a very small cloud on the horizon, and to be expected. There were no perfectly blue skies in foreign affairs.

In Sarajevo, Catholic Croats paraded in the streets, singing the Austrian national anthem, soon to be joined by young Serb Muslims intent on breaking the windows of hotels owned by Orthodox Serbs. Who in England could be expected to understand such things?

Sir Arthur Nicolson, Under-Secretary of State in the British Foreign Office, wrote a blandly confident letter to Sir George Buchanan, British Ambassador in St Petersburg. 'The tragedy which has just taken place in Sarajevo will not, I trust, lead to further complications.' A letter displaying extreme lack of foresight, given his overall assessment of the international scene – as Ransom would recount. Perhaps his personal feelings were getting the better of him, for he had found Franz Ferdinand 'a sly and stupid man' when he had met him once at Windsor. Besides, looking back, he wasn't sure that – even with his experience of Germany's mood – he made much himself of what might have been a purely Austrian problem in the Balkans.

* * *

If so, he was wrong. On the eastern side of the peninsula of Jutland, near the Baltic entrance to the Kiel Canal, lay the chief naval centre of the German Empire. Kiel Week was a rival to Cowes and this year, 1914, was no exception. The Hamburg-America line rechristened the old transatlantic steamer *Deutschland*, *Victoria Louise*, for the occasion, and it was filled with non-German guests, mostly invited by the Empress. For nearly two decades no British naval vessel had been invited on a friendly visit to Germany; in close comradeship, soldiers and sailors from the two countries fraternized contentedly. Mr Armour, the Chicago meat millionaire, and the Prince of Monaco alike had made the journey there in their private yachts. For the moment, the sun shone in a summer sky, while the few patches of cotton-wool cloud were constantly harried out of sight by the invigorating sea breeze.

On the 24th, the Kaiser had arrived from the Elbe Regatta (where he had had a satisfying victory in the *Meteor*), via the newly deepened and widened Kaiser-Wilhelm Canal and a ceremony to open it, over which he had presided. The improvements to the Canal were of some significance to the Germany navy and – mixing business with pleasure – the Kaiser had inaugurated new locks at both the North Sea and eastern exits. As he arrived at Kiel, battleships in the harbour fired their salutes, the Imperial yacht made a wide sweep in the water and then steamed down the long double line. Crowds cheered, bands played, guards presented arms. Above, airships and seaplanes floated or soared in approving respectfulness.

At short notice Wilhelm made his first visit to a British Dreadnought – the *King George V* – and hoisted his flag as a British admiral. Sir Horace Rumbold, counsellor at the British Embassy in Berlin, was the immediate object of a high-spirited tirade for wearing morning coat and top hat on-board ship. 'If I see that again, I will smash it in,' the Kaiser declared, with his own fervent disregard for protocol. The British suggested that he might like to take a look at the gun installations. He declined, and even an observer without insight might have identified the beginnings of a distinct non-meteorological coldness in the atmosphere. Churchill had been keen to come, but Tirpitz had put a stop to that: he wasn't going to sit at the same table with 'that adventurer'. Von Moltke was off in Karlsbad taking the cure and while the French Prime Minister, Briand, had actually been discreetly invited via the Prince of Monaco, there was no sign of him.

For the moment, the Kaiser had other concerns as he stood in admiral's uniform underneath the awning on the deck of the *Meteor*: there were races to be umpired.

In the dingy of the *Sunbeam* early the next day, seventy-eight-year-old Lord Brassey went rowing, accompanied by a single companion, in order to ease his stiffness. On the far side of the Harbour he strayed into the Imperial dockyards. Challenged by a policeman who spoke no English, he was temporarily detained as a suspected spy, much to the amusement of the Kaiser's dinner party in the evening. Brassey maintained that his only reason for coming was his inveterate enthusiasm for friendly relations with Germany and especially for the German navy, in which he had innumerable friends. The Kaiser gave instructions that the police should deny the arrest; he had other irritations with which to contend – like the success of Herr Krupp von Bolen's *Germania* against his own *Meteor*.

At breakfast on Sunday the 28th, Prince Lichnowsky – summoned to Kiel by Wilhelm – and Rumbold sat on a terrace overlooking the harbour. 'I don't like the attitude *The Times* has recently taken up towards my country,' the German Ambassador commented (he was suffering, if the truth be told, from the aftermath of a migraine attack). 'Oh,' said Rumbold, 'I have not noticed any especially unfriendly articles. But what of the German

Professors in your own press?' Lichnowsky was impatient. 'Nobody cares or minds what the Professors say.' Lichnowsky was on edge, and would take his edginess back to London.

In the early afternoon of the same day, a coded telegram from Sarajevo arrived at Kiel for the Kaiser. Raising a spectacular spray before the onlookers, a motor launch set out from the harbour and soon overhauled the *Meteor*. Throttling back fast, it gave news of an urgent message for the Kaiser. Wilhelm wanted it over the loud hailer and then, very calmly, asked for the telegram itself to be thrown on-board. An empty cigarette case was used for the purpose. The Kaiser himself unfolded the crumpled piece of paper, which read: 'Archduke, heir to the throne, and wife assassinated by revolver shots.'

An aide said: 'Should we continue the race?' Wilhelm was a moment in answering. 'No, the Regatta must be cancelled. I shall leave immediately.'

In the evening, after a hasty change of plan, people were turned away from the gates of Prince Henry of Prussia's castle, where there was to have been a reception. The British fleet, itself under orders received from London, left for Portsmouth. Prince Henry, in the excitement of the moment, blurted out to the departing navy men: 'We are sorry you are going, and we are sorry you came.' Some of those present were sorry too. The Foreign Office in London, via the British Naval Attaché in Berlin, learned that the British had been thoroughly outclassed by their German counterparts in the competitive sports, football among them, that they had played.

On Monday morning, Kiel quickly lost the British flags that had adorned it. By that time the Kaiser, his sense of injury increasing by the hour, had become dangerous to those around him. The assassin was thought to be a young Serbian student – and it was Serbians who, just eleven years before, had murdered the last Obrenović and his Queen in Belgrade.

Wilhelm showed fatigue and stress. His pallor was white, and his eyes blinked restlessly. 'Only fourteen days ago,' he thought, 'I was with Franz and saw him in his happy family circle.' The wonderful smell of the famous roses at Konopischt came back to him. 'God comfort the unfortunate children and the poor old Emperor. There will be a final reckoning with the Serbs for this; there must be. They dare to kill a Royal prince, when even I am tortured with self-doubt about my plans. Can there ever be justification for killing the Lord's Anointed? What is the sign?'

It was strange that, whatever Ransom's doubts about the planned assassination of his own king, he could not have begun to understand how Wilhelm could be frightened at what he had proposed for his own quite different reason: the sacredness of monarchy.

For now, Wilhelm kept his uncertainty to himself: with whom, in any case, might he share it? That his people were behind him there seemed little doubt. There was always a resistance to crisis, of course. The Balkans were no more worth the bones of a single Pomeranian grenadier than they had been in Bismarck's time for those about to depart for the summer vacations, who read the news sheets handed to them as their crowded trams passed Nollendorf and Potsdamerplatz. Nevertheless, on Wilhelm's arrival back in Berlin, crowds lined the Friedrichstrasse in the approach to the Linden; shoulder to shoulder they sang 'Die Wacht am Rhein', 'The Guard on the Rhine'', or the hymn to Franz Joseph, 'Unser güter Kaiser Franz'. Outside the Russian Embassy in the Linden, the gestures were fiercer still: 'Nieder mit Russland', 'Down with Russia'. But was the assessment of the Serbian crisis in the German press correct? Russia, in theory always ready to extend her influence in the Balkans, was hesitant, and France anxious; and Britain was disinterested. If only that could be relied on. And if it could not? Well, then God's vengeance, 'die Strafe Gottes', must fall upon the British and their king.

CHAPTER FOURTEEN

Where does one belong?

O N the Sunday that Sarajevo was to take place, Ransom woke late, his head throbbing from the after effects of a Saturday night of drinking. A large Suffragette demonstration was in prospect for Trafalgar Square in the afternoon and he decided to get away from the centre of London for a few hours to collect his thoughts before facing the social chatter at Margot Asquith's for tea. Rosalind had gone to the country and he took a cab – in those days 8d for the first mile or ten minutes – in Berkeley Square. He told the driver to go south of the River Thames and settled back to read the Sunday newspapers.

The Salem fire, which had left 10,000 people homeless and caused $10,000,000 damage to property, was widely reported. On Friday, in a patent leather factory in Salem, Massachusetts, the fire from a chemical explosion had been fanned by the wind through the buildings. From this site, at the foot of Gallows Hill where witches had been hung two hundred and more years before, the flames had spread south-east to the heart of the city. Through the densely packed tenements to the seashore, to Colonial mansions and witches' houses, the devastation had stretched. The orphanage, the hospital had been burned, but not the birthplace of Nathaniel Hawthorne, the 'house of the seven gables', or the old Customs House of his novels. How people took comfort from literature, or even a mere literary association, as if it would purge the pain of those who had suffered!

He put his newspaper aside. Two million people lived across the Thames in an eight-mile stretch of the river. On Saturday nights, he supposed, they were all to be seen, nearly every one, in the streets, in the pubs, in shops, by stalls. Now, as his cab unquestioningly drove along unfamiliar highways, there was hardly a soul to be found. Some determined figures, hurrying to church or other place of worship, late for their ritual cleansing; isolated groups of boys, even more quietly defiant than usual; a tramp in the gutter. The pubs, with their faces brightly polished, gleaming like jewels amidst the decaying façades of the houses around them. The summer wind, silently rustling an extraordinary jumble of debris, much of it recently deposited in the midst of the previous night's entertainment: cigarette packets in profusion; pink scraps of the Saturday evening papers; odd pieces of clothing of every description – socks, boots, bonnets, unidentifiable rags. And the smell! Of rotting refuse, stale fish and chips, sickly jam, pressing up against one's nostrils in air that seemed close despite the breeze.

He could guess at the scene inside each house. It was far, far from his own world, but Anna had shown him its Jewish equivalent in the East End. Here, in the little terraced houses he was passing, there would be the treasured memories of the past enshrined in a higgledy-piggledy scene of photographs, souvenirs, trinkets – telling the tale of Bank Holidays and festivals past. Too little furniture for the lovingly collected rubbish that filled draws to overflowing. Weekday clothes carelessly thrown down, as if to compensate for the neat, sombre ware of Sundays. Plaster falling from the ceiling, its dust slowly settling to obscure what had fallen on the previous occasion. People living, people dying....

Enough. He did not belong here, and his life was cosily secure by comparison. He could communicate with his own acquaintances and friends and colleagues through a multitude of conscious and unconscious signals. He could travel with ease through the few square miles of Central London that were his home territory. For no more than an extra ½d he could have letters, delivered within a few minutes of the mail trains leaving, that would be sure to arrive at their far-flung destinations the following day. Through the 'Jaggers', the uniformed boys of the District Messenger and Theatre Ticket Company, he could receive tickets for the theatre, have his place kept in queues, have letters or parcels speedily taken wherever he fancied.

But not all this communicating power, nor all the problems of his present existence, could either make him or allow him to enjoy a comfortable crossing to the world on the other side of the great river in his home city.

Still far from the acres he knew so well, he left the cab after it had rejoined the north bank of the Thames and had taken him on to the Shepherds Bush Exhibition Centre. Here, since May, a century of peace between Britain and the United States was being celebrated amidst gardens and other amusements. It would not normally have occurred to him to go anywhere near such a site, but as the cab had been making its unguided way, beginning to show through its driver signs of impatience, his eye had caught a mention of the exhibition in the paper.

The noise of the band of the Grenadier Guards drowned all rational thought. By a large poster board, the loud, complaining voice of a middle-aged lady nearly succeeded in defeating it as she attacked a slowly growing but bemused crowd for its indifference

to the perils of modern advertising. 'We must abominate, I do
abominate the present flagrant methods which have been introduced by the American "boomsters", and which – like everything
American – are vulgar, offensive and pay little regard to truth or
honesty.' Pause for breath, then the beginning of the next tirade,
lost in the brass section of the Guards, until we could hear, '…a
vulgar method for exploiting all the frauds, quackeries and rubbish of the twentieth century…the *total* abolition of the hideous
sign-boards and figures that disfigure our towns and cities…every
quack medicine, pill, face decoration and hair *non*-restorer to be
boycotted….'

Why should the English think such eccentricity endearing?
Tolerate it? Of course. But without encouragement. It was with
something close to enthusiasm that he neatly avoided a little two-
seater Ford rushing along the road outside the Exhibition area,
hailed a cab and headed back to home territory for tea with Margot.
However much he might scorn the luxury in which the 'radical'
Tories indulged themselves at the newly opened Carlyle Club in
Piccadilly, however much he might disapprove of the plutocrats
at the Royal Automobile Club – the Hotel Nouveau Ritz, as they
called it – this was a civilization that (for the afternoon) he felt he
understood, that kept to rules and conventions to which he could
subscribe. Momentarily, he even put Anna from his mind in his
search for a foothold outside the threatening quicksand.

* * *

'Margot, how can I ask you to forgive me for being so late?' he
asked, inviting such forgiveness. It came: 'You poor darling. The
traffic is so terrible.' (He had said nothing of traffic.) 'You know,
it took us more than an hour to get from Hyde Park Corner to
the Lavery private view at the Grosvenor Gallery last week.' She

steered him into the centre of the gathering before he could comment, snatching a cup of tea from the maid's hands and pressing it into his own. 'And now you have missed our little après-midi de musique...German lieder, Grieg's *Im Kahne*, American folk songs, oh, and Professor Granville Bantock's *Lament of Isis*. Such delights.'

Margot was by no means as silly as this, but she seemed to be matching her mood to the somewhat undistinguished company of the day. 'We were just puzzling our heads over the new Futurist quarterly, *Blast*. What could it mean? Elizabeth's faithful little dictionary provided the answer: "a flatulent disease in sheep". At last, one understands.' Clever, but not very clever. Lady Ophelia Roper, next to them, was almost cross: 'How I hate the new painting – post-impressionists, cubists, now futurists, all those faces of emerald green, trees of Reckitt's blue, that horrible Bismarck brown. Anarchy, sheer anarchy.'

'Perhaps we should vote on their virtues: an appropriate answer to anarchy, don't you think?' he asked.

'So Murray of Elibank seems to think,' Lady Ophelia opined (whined, it seemed to him). '*He* suggests a referendum on Votes for Women.'

'Hum,' Margot commented. 'It depends on the women. After the latest of Mrs Patrick Campbell's weddings, Mr George Cornwallis-West was heard to bleat that it was *his* wedding too.'

'That reminds me,' Ransom said, thinking of the author of *Pygmalion*, in which Mrs Cornwallis-West was starring and which he had seen that week. 'Mr Bernard Shaw has joined Madame Tussaud.'

'*Well*,' Margot replied playfully, 'has nothing more exciting than *that* happened this week?'

'*Well*,' he said quickly, 'it is difficult to decide what would most interest the sophisticated lady of today.' This was easy. 'Financial affairs, perhaps? There is the Channel Tunnel, of course. The Movement grows apace and neither Rothschilds nor the Nord Railway Company of France need be downhearted. Or James Horlick's baronetcy. What a splendid tribute to the value of Malted Milk! Or investment? The City of St Petersburg loan issue, redeemable at par in sixty-seven years from the 15th of January 1915 – a splendid opportunity: the lists closed on Wednesday. No?'

Henrietta Carew, a diminutive form of no mean beauty, said – with mock seriousness – 'I think we would all prefer a little *esclandre*, don't you agree? A soupçon of gossip. Something, perhaps, about one of our high-stepping friends? Something to *épater les bourgeois.*'

Her husband Charles, an equally diminutive theatre owner, enquired: 'A trip to *Monna Vanna* at the Haymarket? Who would have expected *that* to pass the censor?'

Margot, drawing on her cigarette and thereby indulging in her own little bit of social scandal, was dismissive. 'The lady in question, who never wears less than a cloak, is more covered than most of us this Season.'

Ransom did not hear Carew's rejoinder, though it seemed to register in an almost imperceptible change of expression on the face of the maid. His mind wandered. He glanced across the room to where Henrietta's daughter was talking to some young man, and was reminded of seeing the same girl in the paddock at Ascot: her eyes sparkling under her sunshade of white silk, inset with replicas of paintings by Watteau and Fragonard, each framed with tiny frills of lace…. He realized what the attraction was – there was something of Anna in the face. How different everything would have been if Anna had been part of the only world he knew: it would translate her unapproachable mystery into manageable romance.

He strained his ears to catch the distant conversation of the young couple. 'The Prince of Wales to go back to Oxford after all…a third year at Magdalen…shy and nervous as I am…yes, he laid the foundation stone of a new church on the Duchy of Cornwall estate in Kensington last Saturday…his first public appearance, I believe….' Fascination with royalty: one of the hallmarks of this sort of gathering. Yet never quite as strong as sheer political ignorance – the ignorance apparently without inhibiting effect on the expression of opinions. There would not be much of the 'When I was a boy…' tirades in this Liberal gathering, but they were common enough throughout upper and middle class land. ('No pampering in those days, no Socialism, no Lloyd George. We didn't tax the rich to help the poor then. Too much sentimentality never benefited anyone: kindness simply makes them breed, you know…. The country cannot support it, I tell you. When I was a boy….') And when it was not mere ignorance, it was frivolity: joking about causes, or issues, or opinions that might involve life or death.

Anna had turned him into an outsider, with nowhere to go. He didn't want her world, and he no longer seemed to enjoy his own. And yet…too much time to philosophize was of no help at all. If only this wretched German business hadn't arisen, turning everything topsy-turvy, if only Anna was waiting for him in Clarges Street: we all have our own ideas of a stable universe, and we'd all like to get back there.

At tea on Fifth Avenue you would hear politics discussed about as often as Chinese conchology: it was bound to be different in England, where there was no division between the social and political worlds. You could go in a moment from Lady Ophelia cleverly (as she thought) identifying the strength of the stamp-collecting lobby – won over to Home Rule by the prospect of an 'absolutely sweet' set of new Irish stamps – to a quite sombre discussion of Lord Roberts and his mutinous speech in the House of Lords after the introduction of the Amending Bill. The Conservative press had been lyrical in their praise of the former army commander-in-chief's 'noble and memorable' lines, in which 'a soldier of unsurpassed experience, who has been inculcating discipline all his life, confessed that his idea of discipline is not something that turns a free man into a slave, but something which in essence recognizes that the disciplined man is a human being, a free agent, a person who has a right to call his soul and his conscience his own.'

'Tush!' expostulated Carew. 'It was an outrage. Would Roberts have allowed "conscience" to sanction disobedience when he was in command in Afghanistan? And what if there is – as threatened – a rail strike? Wages are bad, conditions are bad…should the army maintain law and order? Does Roberts stand with Tom Mann?'

This was more like it, and his wife was equally serious in her way. 'If it isn't Ireland, it's Europe,' she sighed. 'In Paris everyone was so down in the dumps – the Balkans, the Germans, the Mexicans: plenty of candidates for blame. I doubt they've sold an Old Master in the Place Vendôme, or a pearl necklace in the Rue de la Paix since Christmas.'

'That reminds me,' said Margot, light-heartedness (if that was the right word) breaking through with little difficulty. 'Hugo Johnson was over from the Paris Embassy this week singing the praises of the soup that was served for the King's birthday dinner: clear and pale, with jellyfish things floating in it. Looks horrid, tastes divine. He said there was a rage for exotic-looking soups in Paris this summer.'

'A little less Continental influence would not be a bad thing,' declared Ophelia. 'The Ritz is Parisian, the Carlton is Parisian, the Savoy is Parisian….'

'…. And there's that dreadful new German hotel in Russell Square,' Margot interjected.

It was time for Ransom to say something: he could feel that it was expected. Nothing said, but…. 'There's something more important than that. We owe *all* our best hotels to the *Americans*. No matter who built them, or in what style: it was American travellers who demanded better treatment.'

Carew was not listening very closely. 'Personally I'm all for ending any embargo on Continental invention. Why do we continue to think that bars are in such bad taste? Who would accuse Grand Duke Michael of Russia of lack of judgment because he accepts a martini from the hands of Charlie at the Cannes Hilton? Hum! I ask you.' The rest was lost, as he spluttered into his moustache.

If they occasionally pretended to be tired of food and drink and fashion and gossip, the pretence did not go very deep. They had all experienced strict upbringings, in preparation for the self-indulgence that was to follow. They laughed that afternoon at the mothers of Haverford, Pennsylvania, who had formed a club to nationalize and standardize the chastisement of children for their thoughtlessness, disobedience and moral turpitude. They were distanced from the sufferings of childhood, the memory of its privations ensuring that Henrietta could not remain unmoved by a mountain of cream peaches or Ophelia by the French convent-made lingerie from Madame Caroline's salon in the Place Vendôme.

Ransom understood this very well, felt it most of the time himself, but with more than a tinge of doubt. The fixed order of things was no longer so clearly identifiable.

CHAPTER FIFTEEN

Earnest discussions in several places

IN another part of London, teatime conversations of a more earnest kind were in progress. Inside Bonar Law's London home, Pembroke Lodge – 'a rather suburban looking detached villa…with a small garden', according to Asquith, 'and furnished and decorated after the familiar fashion of Glasgow or Bradford or Altrincham' – several prominent Conservatives were discussing tactics.

'The gilded tradesman', as Churchill called Bonar Law, was not offering sumptuous fare in any sense: abstinence was the keynote to his character, abstinence from alcohol, the pleasures of food, humour, even the more dubious delights of gossip. The only thing anybody seemed to know for certain about him was that he was a businessman: a strange background for a Conservative leader. He spoke clearly, concisely, precisely, without emotional subterfuge or subtlety of delivery, with contempt for what in a later age was to be called charisma. But he made a formidable opponent because of the speed with which he absorbed the essentials of an argument, and the forcible directness with which he expressed it, or argued against it.

He had before him a long memorandum that he had sent to important figures in his party the previous day. 'I believe, and I have been at some pains to obtain accurate information on the subject, that an appeal to the country now would result in a very considerable majority for our party...the electorate is clearly concerned that there should be an alternative to the Irish policy of the Government; it will not tolerate a continuation along the old lines.' He nodded in approval of his own document: the Home Rule issue was less divisive than Tariff Reform had been, and he at least was keeping a clear head on the issue – Central Office was even working away at comparing the electoral effects of the loss of various combinations of Ulster Counties.

Still, Carson – who had just left – had not been encouraging. There were many shades of opinion in the party and almost any course of action would be open to the gravest objections. He had some doubts about that latest leaflet they were using, the one in which a comparison was made between Unionists who had fought for their country during the Boer War and who were now in danger of being shot at, and those same Liberal supporters who had been in the camp of the pro-Boers and were the chief prosecutors. Even *The Times* had warned him about the explicitness of his language in the Commons – lest anyone should have excuse 'for pretending that he and the Unionist party are anxious to bring about the calamity of which they are only giving warning'.

When he looked at the others in the room, it was difficult to feel reassured: 'I am their leader,' he had once said of the diehards, 'I must follow them.' Just so. With people like Lord Londonderry to satisfy, anything might happen. Had Law enjoyed gossip, he might have appreciated what his Liberal opponents had heard in their clubs when Theodore Roosevelt had last been in London – that, as Roosevelt said, Londonderry had 'no more brains than a guinea pig, he was as obtuse as a lamppost; I might as well have talked to the chair opposite us. If the hereditary legislators are in the average like him in the House of Lords, then the Lord have mercy on England.' There was some muttering about the last sentence, but on the whole the men sitting in the leather-upholstered armchairs of the Reform Club were looking forward to the arrival of the ex-President on his latest visit – to take place in a week or two's time.

Major-General Wilson was becoming a doubtful ally, too. 'Unless Asquith agrees to the Lords' amendment – and there is no chance of that, since Redmond will not allow it – Carson will set up a Provisional Government and will take over such Government offices as he can.' Wilson seemed certain of it. 'There are good men behind it and they will soon get it in working order.'

'But what will the army do?' asked Law.

'Much depends on the way the picture is put to us. I do believe that if Carson and his Government are sitting in City Hall, and we are ordered down to close it, we will not go.'

'I still find it very difficult to judge how much Carson will be prepared to risk,' Law observed gravely. 'He is no solder, you know. Do you not think that when he says, "I will die in the last ditch rather than submit to a Home Rule Government", it is as if he is addressing the "Gentlemen of the Jury", rather than "Men of Ulster"?'

Wilson frowned at this apparent display of faintheartedness. 'I will give you that he is without kinsmen in Ulster. Indeed, he has never even lived there. I believe his father was not only a Home Ruler, but one of the signatories convening the meeting which started Isaac Butt's movement. Yet the man's a leader, a real leader – I'm with him.'

Whether this last comment was a deliberate aspersion on Bonar

Law's own abilities or not, it left the other man unruffled. Privately he had some confidence that Carson's talents, if formidable, were resolutely negative: take the wind out of his sails, and he would not have oars with which to row for the port. He was, perhaps, a showman who needed a script: that air of righteous defiance disguised an inability to build from nothing. Captain Craig might be a more formidable opponent in that respect: when he had said that the Germans and the German Emperor would be preferred to the rule of John Redmond, Patrick Ford and the Molly Maguires, he could at the same time play on the hostility felt by Conservatives for France ever since the days of the French Revolution.

And what would Asquith do? Wilson fulminated against 'Squiff' and his 'pestilent Government', yet the Prime Minister was clever in an unscrupulous sort of way – perhaps he had even closed his eyes to the army of Ulster Protestants in order to escape from the need to give Redmond his Home Rule. The Liberals were an unprincipled crowd! 'Off the platform, when the lights are put out, when Lloyd George goes home again, then he becomes Mr Lloyd George, and after the most eloquent tirade against the evils of luxury, he does not deprive himself of any of the little comforts to which many of us are accustomed.'

If it was so, then Mr Lloyd George had to be credited with a certain perception about Mr Bonar Law: 'the fools chose the right man by mistake,' he had observed. This Conservative leader knew where he was going. Bonar Law surveyed the faces in front of him: 'Now, listen….'

When Sir Edward Carson arrived back at his home in Eaton Place after leaving Pembroke Lodge, he passed without comment the Suffragette chained to the railing outside. Several times the police removed her, several times she had returned. Carson, who was deeply indifferent to women in general and coldly contemptuous of Suffragettes in particular, summoned his butler and gave him concise instructions. Presently the butler appeared on the pavement with a jug of water and, with some skill, laid a trail of embarrassment from the lady in question to the road. These antics were sufficient to attract a crowd and, as often in human affairs, success was achieved not by rational argument but by the creation of red-faced awkwardness. The maiden retreated. Carson, in his drawing room, lit a cigarette without glancing out of the window.

* * *

Monday was an uneventful day for Ransom. The impact of Sarajevo was not yet great and only the *Morning Post* and the uninfluential Labour *Daily Citizen* seemed disturbed by its implications. The Conservative *Morning Post* was in any case for ever ready to beat the drum. 'If the word mobilization is pronounced in St. Petersburg, Berlin and Paris, it will have to be pronounced in London.'

In the evening he went with Rosalind to Covent Garden to hear Caruso in *La Tosca*, joining the shouts and cheers as *E luce van le stelle* reached its close. Rosalind, with her quirky and unmatchable originality, compared the tenor's enormous Adam's apple to the throat of a canary, but she too revelled in the opportunities they could all experience in London that summer. There was an irony. When the pleasures of Caruso at Covent Garden were exhausted, Chaliapine awaited at Drury Lane. And in lighter but more modern vein one might drop into the Shaftesbury Theatre for *The Cinema Star* (a different kind of irony), with Cicely Courtneidge, Fay Compton and Jack Hulbert. All were playing to packed audiences the night they heard Caruso.

As the crowds streamed from theatres and cinemas all over London, snatches of conversation and comment could be heard connected to the news from the other side of Europe, but it was breakfast the following day before serious consideration was given to what the assassination meant. Ransom had himself met the Archduke twice, in formal circumstances – once at Edward VII's funeral and again only the previous year, when he had been a shooting guest of the King's at Windsor. He seemed to him a rather boring man, with staring blue eyes which some took as a sign of honesty without much other evidence. He was rather silent in company and did not appear to take to English society: one could see that there was a touchiness and rancour in his character that he found it difficult to control. Ransom heard him mutter, tactlessly, about the growing influence of the Jews; he was all for using Catholicism as the link to hold together the far-flung parts of Austria's disintegrating Empire.

Rosalind, as usual, focused on the most irrelevant byway of the whole story: the morganatic marriage of the Archduke to his wife meant that, while she could become Queen of Hungary, she would never have been Empress of Austria. Now she would be neither. The oddest things always aroused Rosalind's interest and she was to be found in the Speaker's Gallery, with a mixture of other sad, happy, complacent, excited, bored and flushed faces, when the House of Commons turned its attention to Sarajevo in the afternoon.

The absence of party strife, which – petty though it often was – provided the fuel for the particular atmosphere of Parliamentary gatherings, dulled the proceedings. At the best of times, there was very little speech-making of oratorical distinction and this was no exception. Sir Edward Grey, as ever, read without noticeable alterations of tone from his prepared speech, as if what he might say was of little moment and certainly no concern to others. That, at least, was the description given to Ransom by Winston, for he had lunched late in the Members' dining room and made no move when the roll of paper on which was printed the name of the Member addressing the House signalled that Sir Edward was in full flow.

Asquith spoke of 'one of those incredible crimes which make

us despair of the progress of mankind'. The aged Franz Joseph set an example of almost unparalleled assiduity in the pursuit of his duty. He was temporarily elevated in the Prime Minister's words to the role of unperturbed, sagacious and heroic head of a mighty state, a state 'rich in splendid traditions, and associated with us in this country in some of the most moving and previous chapters of our common history'. But there was no hint of any action, only of what was required by protocol.

One of the Tory backbenchers launched into a tirade against Serbia – 'A half-civilized and wholly waspish and disorderly little state, whose annals are a dreary record of incompetence, violence and political crime.' Had not King Edward VII, alone among Europe's sovereigns, taken diplomatic action against the regicides who had murdered the last Obrenović? This MP had already lost his audience, which was always more loyal to its own direct concerns than to abstract questions of right and wrong. 'Arising out of the Prime Minister's statement, may I ask…?' 'The hon. gentleman is trying to connect the unconnected.' 'Am I to draw the conclusion…?' 'The hon. gentleman may draw what conclusion he likes.' As the lobby correspondents noted, Asquith's heavy jaws snapped together, as if the questioner's head lay between them. He was in command.

* * *

The warm weather temperatures they had enjoyed for several days began to climb into the eighties as the Cabinet assembled the following morning. When Ransom arrived, Grey was sitting alone in his usual seat. He was secure in the knowledge that most of the Cabinet were surprisingly willing to concentrate on Britain's own problems and leave foreign affairs to him, with the Prime Minister and Haldane. Morley, Lloyd George and Harcourt, the Colonial Secretary, tended to take a pacific line, but there was no especial need for this Government to be influenced by its own Radicals, particularly because the Conservatives in Parliament could be relied on to support anything which helped the Entente between France, Russia and Britain. And most British politicians, inside and outside the Cabinet, were indifferent when it came to understanding the strange peoples who inhabited the Continent of Europe: as the popular press roundly put it, Mr Lloyd George did not have enough French to entertain a cat, while as for Mr Burns – he sounded like a Bank Holiday tripper to Boulogne.

That day stuck in Ransom's memory as the only time the Cabinet addressed itself seriously to what might happen if the international situation deteriorated. He listened rather than participated, self-consciously knowing that his own views had only been muddied by the pressure now upon him. Grey spoke sombrely: 'Events may move rapidly and, if they do, we may no longer wait on accident, and defer our decisions. If war were to come to the Continent, and the Cabinet were for neutrality, I do not believe I am the man to carry out such a policy.' Lloyd George, eager to interrupt, declared that he had consulted the Bank of England, the City, cotton, steel, coal producers…all were aghast at the very thought of war, which would break down the whole system of credit with London at its centre, strangle commerce and manufacturing, raise prices….

Here was Morley's cue. The old man was listened to in quiet. 'In the present temper of labour this tremendous dislocation of industrial life must be fraught with public danger. The atmosphere of war cannot be friendly to order, in a democratic system that is verging on the humour of 1848.' He looked straight into Ransom's eyes. 'Have you ever thought what will happen if Russia wins? If Germany is beaten and Austria is beaten, it will not be England and France who emerge preeminent in Europe. It will be Russia. Will that be good for Western civilization? People will rub their eyes when they realize that Cossacks are their victorious fellow-champions for Freedom, Justice, Equality of man (especially of Jew man), and respect for treaties.'

Grey's face showed his displeasure at this rhetoric. 'The French show no sign of wanting a formal alliance. The Russians, on the other hand, may help us to deter Germany.' Churchill assented: 'The Russian naval presence in the Baltic is now a force the Germans cannot ignore, and it allows us to reduce our Rosyth fleet.' Ransom later conveyed the strange, urgent yet archaic nature of the debate by explaining that this led Sir John Simon, the Attorney General, to make a complicated analogy with the Peloponnesian War, in which the highly disciplined military state of Sparta (Germany) fought the liberal-loving, mistress of the seas, Athens (Britain). Not for nothing were the shelves of the Cabinet room full of the great works of Classical civilization.

The general, but tolerant, impatience with Simon was expressed differently by Churchill, who took the opportunity to point to the backward-looking spirit of the army, lost in the mythology of past success. He enjoyed the chance to refer to his own experience in the Boer War – dubiously relevant to the discussion – and, through the inner logic of his own illogicality, finished with a peroration on the Channel Tunnel, the success of which was (he claimed) the fervent desire of the Board of Admiralty and of every well-informed person. The Prime Minister, sensing his moment to stop the rambles (rambles were always dangerous), firmly pointed out that, in his memory, no one of the slightest eminence had ever advocated the Tunnel.

* * *

Thus did Ransom's colleagues deliberate on the fate of Europe, a subject on which, it appeared, few of them had any sensible comment to make. It was of no help to him, though that was not unexpected. It was difficult to know which was more comprehensible: the strange language of diplomacy, with its careful and curious code-words to denote strength of feeling, or the knowledge that actions mightier than the subtlest diplomatic manoeuvring were in prospect. Nearly three hours could pass between the coding of a telegram in one of the European capitals, its transmission and then decoding at the other end – time enough, almost, for an army to be on the march, especially if the message conveyed had to be distilled through the complicated mixture of interests and intrigues on the domestic scene.

He lunched with his friend MacDonagh – the only journalist friend he ever had – and he was quite wonderful in his loving, cynical way about the use of 'silken phrases' to cover the brutal facts. As they sat on the terrace of the Savoy watching the lazily busy scene on the River Thames and (in MacDonagh's case) eagerly plucking the strawberries brought still growing on laden plants, MacDonagh gave his wine-induced account of a typical diplomatic report: 'His Excellency received me with the utmost cordiality. He assured me that his Government had sent no letter to the Panjandrum and have never entertained the idea of sending any. As I had myself read the letter which His Excellency had sent, I thought it best to express the utmost gratification at His Excellency's assurance, and I said that my Government had been guided by the same principles.' Then, with a final swallow of strawberry submerged in cream, MacDonagh concluded his little satire: 'I do not think His Excellency suspected that I had written to the Panjandrum first.'

As Anna had said to Ransom often enough, no one could join the Diplomatic Service without private means. The latest commission on the subject, MacDonnell's committee, had said as much. For Anna, it merely proved that there was nothing so dishonest as drawing-room society, or how else did the diplomats learn their ability to deceive and mislead? He had always thought that there was a sort of muddled honesty at work: if the Foreign Office tended to be anti-German, the India Office anti-Russian and the Treasury anti-war, they all had their good reasons.

Over cognac, MacDonagh tried to disabuse him of some of this. According to him, the Foreign Office itself was full of disputes – between Tyrell and Nicolson, Nicolson and Crowe, for example. Ransom told him that he had always admired the skill of Sir William Tyrell, Grey's Private Secretary, in being intimate with the Foreign Secretary: no one else managed it. 'There's the trouble,' said MacDonagh, with a disconcerting increase in the volume of his voice. 'Tyrell dislikes administration, paper, public meetings: what he and Grey plot together never reaches anyone's ears.' 'Not yours, you mean,' he countered, smiling, but without conviction. It was true, perhaps, that not much had changed since Lord Salisbury had run the Foreign Office as an extension of his country home and, as Ransom had observed in Cabinet, other Ministers paid scant attention to the affairs of Continental countries: some Foreign Office papers went to the Prime Minister but were not circulated to the Cabinet, many important memoranda – for all that he knew – never even reached the Prime Minister.

Eyre Crowe – the Assistant Under-Secretary – had once told him how badly informed (and feeble) the Cabinet was: a message, he gathered from MacDonagh, that he had somewhat freely broadcast. And since he clearly identified Germany as the main enemy of peace, perhaps Ransom should have listened more closely. But Eyre Crowe had always seemed so intemperate and extreme; it took someone with a German mother, as he had, to warn so fervently against German expansion. What's more, he seemed to have no desire to spread information more widely, merely to find the channels for his version of events – he had told Ransom himself how he 'deplored all public speeches in foreign affairs', as if the latter were no concern to the rest of them.

Nicolson, the Permanent Secretary, was also critical of the Cabinet. MacDonagh quoted him, a tetchy old man, suffering from rheumatism and arthritis, weary and bitter about the refusal of anyone to take responsibility any more, or to follow any policy which had at least an element of vigour and farsightedness. 'Grey wants to be rid of him, you know.' Ransom did not know: would he have been so ignorant when he was making his way a decade or so earlier (before he met Anna….)? It was all so complicated: the greatest intriguers also seemed to be the purveyors of the strongest criticism and advice – witness the aggressive behaviour of Churchill and Lloyd George towards Grey and his department.

* * *

It seemed to be the week for such earnest but desultory analysis: going round in circles was at any rate better than having to face facts. Things happened – but without pattern. In the afternoon of the same day as his lunch at the Savoy, it transpired (so Kell told him) that Roger Casement had left Ireland to follow a secret (but evidently not so secret) route via Glasgow and Canada to obtain American support for the Irish Volunteers. Kell did not give much for his chances with the aged Joseph McGarrity, the Philadelphian chairman of Clan-na-Gael: there were too many internecine feuds in the Irish community on both sides of the Atlantic and a cordial dislike of Redmond on the part of the Americans.

Other events, too, he found himself noticing or remembering. At the weekend, on Saturday, three men and a woman – anarchists, not Irish – managed to blow themselves up in a New York tenement: a premature explosion of their own bomb. In England – at Herne Hill – there was a demonstration against Home Rule; in France, at Lyons, the German Herr Lautenschläger won the Motoring Grand Prix; in Germany, on Sunday, five men were killed and two badly injured while 'amusing themselves by obtaining electric shocks from a broken power wire'.

The Irish, the Anarchists, the Germans…no absence of news about any of them. It did not seem to mean anything unless given a personal association, and then not much; he did not think of Anna when he saw a photograph of her American cousins in anarchy.

For Ransom, and for Rosalind, tragedy was found in less portentous guise. In this hot summer, river parties had become as common as falling leaves in autumn. Rosalind's younger sister, Lucy, had been among the revellers who had arranged impromptu for the steam launch *King* to take them from Westminster Pier for supper and dancing on Tuesday evening. This was no ordinary crowd of party-goers: among those the son of the Russian Ambassador, Count Benckendorff, had assembled were Lady Diana Manners, Iris Tree, Nancy Cunard, Mrs Raymond Asquith, Mrs Jasper Ridley…and Sir Denis Anson, whose principal achievement at Oxford had been to set loose in the Quad several sack-loads of rats, accompanied by all the terriers he could gather from miles around. The terriers had the time of their lives, as Anson must himself have hoped to when he jumped fully clothed into the Thames, only to be carried away by the strength of the currents to death by drowning.

Iris Tree testified that all members of the party were perfectly sober, but the consequences were the same.

Lucy cried. How she cried! They could not understand the depth of her passion for this wild man. Who, indeed, can comprehend the passion of one person for another? But they shared her grief, Rosalind suppressing her censorial disapproval of the company's behaviour, while Ransom – edgy, nervous – was content to find a channel for his own suppressed unease.

* * *

Meanwhile, the Cabinet having had its mandatory dabble in foreign affairs, it was left to the Foreign Office to concern itself with distant events. There was unanimity there on one broad matter only – that the problems of Empire (the consistent preoccupation of the immediate past) had given way to problems of European hegemony or balance of forces. The indications, uneven but impossible to ignore, were that Austria would press for revenge against the Serbs, and that Germany would support her. No one, it seemed, yet believed in the certainty of war, but the Foreign Office was well used to working out theoretical analyses in great detail.

Eyre Crowe produced a minute for Grey: 'Our interests are tied up with those of France and Russia in this struggle, which is…one between Germany, aiming at a political dictatorship in Europe, and the powers who desire to retain individual freedom.' Nicolson, with his carefully modulated pessimism, certainly identified the threat from Germany, but seemed more fearful of offending powerful Russia – 'such a nightmare', he said, 'that I would at almost any cost keep Russia's friendship.'

What was the Foreign Secretary to think? None of the advice encouraged action, and no action was expected to be necessary. Out of his office windows he could survey the pleasant prospect of St James's Park. It must all be neatly done, he thought, and there is no reason why it should not: the Russians to keep the Serbs under control, the French to put brakes on the Russians, the Germans to pull back the Austrians…. And the English? Well, they would offer – as they always had – wise counsel, and here, indeed, was the German Ambassador arriving to receive it.

Lichnowsky had had a depressing meeting with Beth-mann-Hollweg after news of the assassination of Franz Ferdinand had arrived at the Kiel Regatta. He himself had been optimistic, but the Chancellor was full of reports from the General Staff of the alarming size of Russian armaments. The armed forces were being increased by almost a million men, railway links with the frontiers of Russia were growing stronger and stronger – and Russia and England had plotted a naval agreement. English steamers might be expected to transport Russian troops to the coasts of Pomerania. Lichnowsky tried to shrug all this off: he had heard such reports for thirty years, he said – Russia was never going to be ready. But Bethmann was unimpressed; he made it clear that the Ambassador should protest to Grey on his return to London. Privately he had decided that Lichnowsky was not to be trusted, though – as Von Bode could attest – that was nothing new.

Lichnowsky's stubbornness was winning him little support. He had once served as Counsellor in the Vienna Embassy and had acquired in those days a low regard for the leaders of Austria. Should allies with such poor judgment be supported in hare-brained schemes, he asked Von Jagow. Von Jagow was unmoved: allies were few on the ground. Von Jagow, Von Moltke, Beth-mann-Hollweg – each member of this triumvirate, knowing fully the Kaiser's plan to incapacitate England through the murder of her monarch, reinforced Lichnowsky's instructions to be firm without fully arousing fears of war. The Prince, in his innocence and through a natural ability to play the part of the honest broker with men of civilization, fulfilled his role well.

Von Bode went on holiday the very day that Lichnowsky returned to London – a misleading sign to those watching that the Austrian clouds could not be too threatening. In fact, free of his official duties, he could give all his energies to the organization of the assassination. The decision made, it was not at all clear to those in London how it was to be put into action. Wilhelm asked only for success, not for the details. At the time, Ransom was puzzled by the awareness that nothing seemed to be happening – the events in Berlin had come so swiftly, and so suddenly, that any halt in the plot seemed unnatural. But it would be pointless now to try to reconstruct Von Bode's movements during these weeks – much that happens is, of course, lost to history for ever, and it is easier to understand Ransom's own feelings at the time by sharing his complete ignorance of the concrete plans that were taking shape.

As long as nothing did happen, Ransom was occasionally successful in the suppression of what he knew lay below the level of consciousness. It is unliveable with, therefore it does not exist: that was the rule by which they lived their lives, learned from home, school, army, and expressed in attitudes to social ills, sex, everything. It had usually seemed to work.

Visiting Sir Edward Grey in the Foreign Office, Lichnowsky was reserved, firm (as he thought) and polite. 'As a result of the murder of the heir to the throne, the relations between Austria-Hungary and Serbia have becomes so acute as to cause a certain amount of anxiety. In this period of acute tension, I would urge the British Government to influence St Petersburg to put pressure on the Serbs to be reasonable. Austria has no option but to take strong measures herself – and in these, I am bound to say, Germany will support her.'

Grey was stiffly reasonable in his reply. 'In any fresh Balkan crisis, you may be sure that Britain will work with the German Government as far as might be possible without moving away from France and Russia. The greater the risk of war, the more closely would I adhere to this policy.' If the situation deteriorated – Grey had already decided with Nicolson – he would propose a Conference; that had worked well with the previous Balkan crisis and the Ambassadors involved then – Cambon for France, Lichnowksy for Germany, Benckendorff for Russia, Mensdorff for Austria – would be able to show their trust in each other again.

In the privacy of his thoughts, Lichnowsky would have agreed. Even the great Bismarck, in his *Reflections*, declared that it was 'no part of the function of the German Empire to call upon its subjects to shed their blood and spend their substance in order to help its neighbours towards the realization of their wishes'. But that was not wholly the point: Berlin might be less keen on accepting Sir Edward Grey once again as saviour of the Balkans. And what might be expected of Russia? Serbia was not the only powder keg in which the Tsar was playing with lighted matches: in June he had visited Rumania, and deliberately crossed into Transylvania, with its three million Rumanians under the rule of Austria-Hungary.

'Will you permit me a private and friendly remark?' Lich-nowksy asked. Grey was silent in assent. 'It is not for me to ask indiscreet questions, but you have repeatedly declared that there is no secret agreement between England and a foreign power. It must be in your best interests to quash rumours that such an agreement may nevertheless exist.'

Grey spoke slowly but calmly. 'There are no secret treaties which in any way bind this Government, but I should like to think on what you have said and return to the matter in a few days' time.'

Lichnowsky nodded. He had not expected, nor even wanted, to get further. Diplomacy was for those who liked tidy answers, but not for those who expected those same tidy answers to be long-term solutions.

The statement that came from Grey before the end of the week seemed proof enough of that: conversations of a technical nature had taken place between the British and Russian naval authorities – they were not aggressive in kind and represented no menace to Germany. For the rest, Grey would not wish to mislead – British relations with the Entente Powers were 'very intimate'.

'I do not deny that "conversations" have taken place from time to time between the naval and military authorities', Grey told Lichnowsky. 'The first was as early as the year 1906, when – during the Moroccan crisis – we frankly believed that your Government intended to attack the French. Still, such conversations were about nothing definite and were absolutely without warlike intent: English policy is at *all* times for peace.'

Lichnowsky allowed himself a single ritualistic comment, smoothly delivered. 'May I suggest, Minister, that it would be desirable to keep such conversations to a minimum.

'Otherwise they might lead to serious consequences.'

CHAPTER SIXTEEN

Anna explains

SO far as a well-informed observer could discern, Asquith and his Government, indeed the entire political world in Britain, at this stage had some difficulty in noticing that 'the Eastern problem' existed at all. It was hindsight, Ransom supposed, and the desire to record all that happened, that made him dwell upon it when he decided to write down the unfolding story. The preoccupation with Ireland was so great that in the few weeks either side of the Sarajevo assassination he was fully stretched in keeping pace with the tortuous turns of policy and behind-the-scenes negotiations between political leaders of all parties. He had made it clear to the Prime Minister on his return to England that the unofficial encouragement given by the Kaiser to arms sales to Ireland was scarcely necessary; Germany's businessmen were not slow to identify opportunities and there was little to be gained by applying diplomatic pressure on the German Government.

Asquith, in private scathing about the Chief Secretary for Ireland, Birrell, could not afford a change of minister at this critical juncture, but there was need enough for help. Consequently, he was officially briefed to look at ways out of the deadlock. The key question seemed to be: if an understanding could be reached for the exclusion of Ulster from Home Rule (temporarily, permanently, whatever the conditions) could everyone be made to agree on the geographical boundaries of the newly independent province? The main difficulty surrounded the counties of Fermanagh and Tyrone – the issue being: should they or should they not be incorporated into Ulster? The Ulster provinces had never been solidly Protestant: Donegal, Monaghan and Cavan all had large Catholic majorities, Fermanagh and Tyrone small ones.

You could never tell with politics. What proved effective usually looked simple in retrospect – because it worked. Asquith, not a man for simple solutions, was unimpressed by Theodore Roosevelt when the former American President lunched with a group of them: he seemed full of platitudes and trite statements. Perhaps they were the prerogative of the elder statesman. Even so, 'I believe in liberty, but liberty with order' seemed for the Prime Minister an insufficient theoretical base on which to work out a political programme. Lloyd George, whose own instinct for telling simplification was unsurpassed, was not so sure. As he said to Ransom, 'Roosevelt thoroughly understands the racial questions upon which politics really turns in America. He knows what the Germans want, what the Poles want, what the Irish want, what the Italians want.' The last American census had revealed that there were more than 4½ million Irish Americans and no one needed reminding of the significance of that.

But how you made a policy to please all these disparate parties was not at all clear to Ransom. His colleagues were all noticeably subdued through these discussions, for – apart from anything else – his very earliest political mentor, as a schoolboy, had died that week. Later the bitter but impressive political foe of the Liberals,

Joe Chamberlain, had had a life which could only be interpreted in one way: if ever a career was a reminder that the rise to the political heights was often only a guarantee of ultimate failure, it was Chamberlain's. A month before, he had made his first public appearance since his stroke in 1906: a farewell to his West Birmingham constituents at a Highbury garden party – Unionist, of course, but the photograph of him in his bath chair, with Austen Chamberlain and his own two-year-old daughter in his arms, was poignant for political enemies as well as political friends.

Lloyd George, in an emotional outburst that would have sounded patronizing from anyone else, said: 'But Joe was a wonderful failure. He possessed courage, the greatest of all political qualities.' To have courage, Ransom thought, you need belief in one or the other of two things: in yourself or in what must be achieved. In a curious way, it was the sense of being part of something over which one had no control that threatened both these beliefs. Chamberlain never had that trouble. *Truth* summed it all up in its article on 'The Passing of Joe' – like Napoleon, the glory was his, if not the victory. He would be written about for his failures more than others are written about for their successes: he spoilt as much history as Gladstone made.

* * *

It was a time for such reflections. But then at last, on Monday, the 6th of July, something happened to make everything clearer. It was a day crowded with public events that were to be significant. At breakfast time the Kaiser left Kiel for what was said to be an extended cruise in northern waters. More or less simultaneously, King George V and his Queen departed from Buckingham Palace to take the Royal train from King's Cross: the beginning of an eight-hour journey – punctuated by stops at Grantham, York, Newcastle and

Berwick – before they reached Waverley Station in Scotland. During the ensuing tour they steamed slowly down the Clyde and inspected a number of ships – from super-Dreadnoughts to torpedo-boat destroyers – all in the process of being built: at the Fairfield yard the King saw the battleship *Valiant*, in preparation for its launch in September. He felt, Ransom supposed, secure and proud.

In Dundee, however, a city which had not seen a reigning monarch for seventy years, one of the grand, but lost, ironies of history took place. According to the report in *The Queen*, the monarch was greeted by blue skies, a breath of wind from the east and gay displays of buntings. From the moment of arrival at Tay Bridge Station 'there was not one discordant note in the wholehearted joy with which the people hailed their sovereign.' It appeared that 'Their Majesties displayed much interest in the manufacture of jute, to which the City had owed much of its prosperity....'

The irony was this. While Von Bode and a small group of German agents in London plotted and replotted plans, speculations, schemes, ideas for assassinating the English King, finding no easy solution, an old and bitter survivor of the jute mills, 6 a.m. to 6 p.m. for a short working life, had positioned himself in an empty building overlooking the Royal procession route, equipped with the rifle he had brought back with him from the Boer War. He coughed frequently, a sufferer (among many others) from the way jute's thick, ugly dust enters the lungs. The King and Queen approached in their open coach; he raised the ancient rifle and pulled the trigger.

Instead of sending its bullet straight to the intended target, the rifle exploded. The King survived; the noise was lost in the general noise; and the man – he lost an eye and, a year later (when his lungs gave up fighting), his life.

The forces of order seemed to be winning, though temporarily there was no shortage of adherents to the revolutionary cause. In

France, Ransom later discovered, two tramps carrying bombs had been arrested in Beaumont-sur-Oise; it never became clear whether – as was said at the time – they were intended for the Tsar on his next trip to France, or whether they were really to be directed at President Poincaré.

* * *

And so it was, on this portentous 6th of July, that the House of Commons passed the 2nd reading of the Amending Bill by 275 votes to 10, and adjourned for the day in respect for Joseph Chamberlain, whose funeral was to take place. ('For my part,' Chamberlain had once said, 'I believe in leaving the Irishmen to stew in their own juice': a fine sentiment from one who had brought down a Government on the very issue of Home Rule.)

After the funeral service Ransom returned home and sat quietly for a few minutes at the large and handsome desk he had inherited from his father. It was a peaceful moment and he started slightly as the bell of the telephone began to ring.

It was Anna.

Never before had she telephoned him at home. She was tense, and tenser still when they met in the early evening at Clarges Street.

He remembered feeling surprisingly calm, which at first made him seen cold and uncompromising. 'There is much to explain, isn't there?'

Anna, her black hair swept back from her face, looked much younger than her twenty-six years. 'Not so much,' she said quietly.

She showed signs that she would continue, and he waited. He looked at her and already his anger began to subside. Anna appeared miserable, but went on, very dispassionately. 'I told you that my family came from Hamburg twenty years ago. My brother Georg, older by ten years, stayed. In time he joined the anarchist groups there and worked to destroy the regime from which my parents had fled. That is, until Nicolai's men got him – two years ago. If I wanted to see him again, I was told, I had to do as instructed: initially, just to remain friendly with you.'

Ransom was silent. He did not doubt her, any more than he ever had – before the events of the last six weeks.

'At first I was distraught, utterly broken. Then it dawned on me – I still can't imagine why it took so long – that here was the means of achieving what I had always strived for. If I could actually help the great powers into war, at least show how unscrupulous they were in their grubby pursuit of power, then all sorts of other distant hopes would begin to become real. Destroy the system, and the people responsible for it; then find the better replacement.'

'Anna, my Anna. How can you believe that?' He held out his hands, pulled her up gently from the bed and into his arms. A solitary tear fell down one cheek, but she moved away with a firm, though not an unfriendly gesture. 'That's what you've never understood,' she said. 'I do believe it; and that belief gives form to my life and sustains me.'

'That's not *you* talking: it's the result of years of hearing nothing but the same, stale propaganda. You mix with the wrong people.'

'Don't patronize me! How would you know?' she retorted sharply. 'Life gets strangled at birth in Berkeley Square; none of you recognize companionship or compassion – you feed off each other's dissatisfactions.'

The fact that Ransom, or any of his immediate circle, would have been quite capable of recognizing the truth of this accusation was irrelevant. It did not make it any the more likely that he would abandon all that he had learned or inherited in the peculiar jungle that made up the world of the English upper classes. Yes, the meek and the gentle should inherit the earth – that sentiment was voiced by thousands of good Anglican people in thousands of England's reassuring churches every Sunday. But the way forward was not with any creed whose ideas were all theory and whose actions were all emotion: it was to behave decently, as decently as circumstances allowed, to be trusting and to be watchful.

You may judge whether, in his way, Ransom was able to show compassion without forcing the feeling. It did not occur to him that there was an inconsistency if he loved someone who despised the nine-tenths of his life that she could not spend with him at the same time as he patiently sought to uphold the values of the society in which he had been brought up – that, indeed, was how he had behaved ever since he had first met Anna.

'You must know how anxious I've been,' he said without malice. 'Did they tell you everything?'

'Yes, they told me everything. I don't know what I really thought, but I suppose I wanted to give you the chance to decide what to do without any pressures....'

'No pressures! Anna, I love you!'

'I thought...I believed if you could think that I would betray you, then that might be best for you. You would go your way – you would have managed it unscathed – and I would somehow go mine. Killing is not so terrible in my world if the motive is right, but I knew you would never be able to feel the same.'

'Yes?'

'I didn't take account of everything. I forgot how selfish love is. And, Walter, I wanted you back. I needed you.'

'And your brother,' he said softly.

She nodded. 'I have to ask you to help me. Please. I can cope with everything they might do to me. But I could never forgive myself for abandoning him. You understand?'

He sighed, took two steps to the room's solitary chair, sat heavily down in it and sighed again. Of course he would do the decent thing. The question remained: what *was* the decent thing? Should he betray his country or the person he loved? And how could he live with either decision?

There is a point in human affairs when emotions dictate actions, muddling them perhaps, offering temporary truth only perhaps, but launching men and women from the traps they make for themselves and providing at the least the prospect of landing somewhere new.

Such a point came as Anna gently ran her hand through his hair and he looked up into her eyes. Then they made love with a mutual tenderness, warmth and relaxation that was oblivious of everything else. It was not that she was offering herself to him in return for his support; this was a joyful, free and human affirmation.

For an hour afterwards they lay contentedly in each other's arms, until at last reality seeped its way back into their unwilling consciousness.

Anna said, quietly: 'I'm going now. I don't think you should decide anything immediately but you know there won't be much more time.'

'I know,' he replied, not eager to say more. He made as if to stop her going, but then allowed her to leave. She looked round once.

He was back with his dilemma, losing sight with astonishing speed of any sense of exaltation.

Now, certainly, like the frightened schoolboy waiting to return to school, he might allow himself some genuine self-indulgence in an attempt to ward off tomorrow. It was two hours later that he let himself out into the street. He did not notice the man watching in the shadows opposite. If he had, he might have wondered at the coincidence that took the same man to the club in quiet, badly lit Greek Street – off Soho Square – to which he had walked. The commissionaire took Ransom into the hall, where he signed the visitors' book and went into a darkened, smoky room in which a band was playing 'Hitchy Koo' with rather more enthusiasm and skill than those on the dance floor could manage.

He sat down at one of the tables. Next to him was an unaccompanied woman wearing a short, narrow pink skirt, split in front, diaphanous stocking, satin shoes laced criss-cross up her long, lean legs, corsage cut exceedingly low. They smiled at each other. Her eyes seemed calm and – to his surprise – undemanding.

He ordered two bottles of *oeil de perdrix* – pink champagne. Tonight, for once, he was out of control and pleased to find himself in that condition. The band struck up again – 'O you beautiful doll'… 'Waiting for the Robert E. Lee'… 'He'd Have to Get Under, Get Out and Get Under': all belted out with as much gusto, if not as much ability, as if the lead singer was Ethel Levey on stage at the Hippodrome.

His head began to spin as they joined the dance floor. They all joined hands and danced round in two concentric rings, controlled by a whistle from the leader of the band. The general idea, quickly learned, was to dance off with whomever one found oneself opposite. The resulting hilarity seemed timely, but he was none the less glad to return to his new-found companion.

They launched into the Rouli-Rouli, an import from Paris which was supposed to reproduce the movements of a steam boat and the sensation of the passengers aboard. Now feeling very drunk, he had eyes only for the rhythmic movements of the young girl – for such she had turned out to be – alongside him.

Across London Sir Edward Carson pushed aside an empty plate that had contained his favourite ice cream, drowned in a thick syrupy sauce, prepared to light a cigarette and decided to pen a note to Captain Craig.

'I am not for a mere game of bluff, and unless men are prepared to make great sacrifices which they clearly understand, the talk of resistance is of no use. The day on which we shall be compelled to order mobilization will be the day I shall love best.'

CHAPTER SEVENTEEN

The hour of no illusions

ON Saturday, the 11th of July, the Kaiser Wilhelm anchored the *Hohenzollern* in Sonjefjord, near the Norwegian town of Balholm. The journey had not been a very pleasant one for him – for large parts of it he had lain white-faced in his cabin, overcome by the wretchedness of being seasick.

The Kaiser had considered carefully whether he should take the trip in the aftermath of Sarajevo. Bethmann's advice – that since it was widely known that the cruise was planned, it would imply that something was afoot if it were abandoned – seemed cogent. Besides, it was intolerable not to be on the move: as the joke had it, Wilhelm I was the Greise Kaiser, Frederick III the Weise Kaiser – and Wilhelm II the Reise Kaiser: the old, the wise and now the travelling ruler.

Before his departure he had secret discussions with his ministers in Potsdam. The general way forward was clear, was it not? Germany's recent history proved that war and the use of force were the means to advance the State. Napoleon, the English, the

Tsar – none of them had scruples about taking what they wanted, pursuing a policy of domination. Why should Germany be denied? Why should she have to make excuses for wanting what was rightfully hers?

And yet, a modicum of subtlety had its place too, especially with the English. Ballin should be sent to see his friend Haldane to encourage pro-German opinions within the Liberal party. The English must be tied in knots, softened by confusion.

From the bridge of the *Hohenzollern*, the uncomfortable sailing at last over, Wilhelm could see a quiet prospect of forests, mountains and farmhouses. The Norwegian newspapers, he was told, spoke of war preparations by the Serbs. Germany, as ever, was not receiving a good press, its motives in question. He tossed papers into the waters of the fjord. 'These filthy journalists… never taking the trouble to understand me…vile, rotten people who do nothing but insult me. Whatever I do is wrong according to them.' Then more anguish, reading from a dispatch in which Tschivschby, the German Ambassador in Austria, had warned the Austrians against hasty steps. 'Who authorized him to do this? It is idiotic. It is none of his business…. We must clear the Serbians out of the way. Forthwith.' The Slav 'Wasp's Nest' was overdue for extermination: 'Those dogs have added murder to rebellion, and must be made to knuckle under.'

More reflective, he murmured. 'The Tsar will not take the part of the regicides. In any case, we strike first. We must.' Austria was a problem, to be sure. The old Emperor had talked weakly of his hope that 'everything would continue as peaceable as ever' when he had visited him in the Spring: only Istvan Tisza, the Prime Minister of Hungary, seemed strong enough, and Franz Joseph distrusted him. The Archduke Franz Ferdinand, it was true, had wanted to reorganize the Austro-Hungarian army on German lines, but the new heir to the Empire, young Karl, was hopelessly inexperienced.

At least Wilhelm had given the Austrians a formal promise of support against the Serbs before his departure. The time for mere rattling of sabres was over.

None the less, Berchtold – the Austrian Chancellor – seemed to have evolved a good plan: send the Serbs an ultimatum so formidable that they would have to reject it. The murder had been plotted in Belgrade…. Serb officials had supplied bombs and arms…. Serb frontier guards had allowed terrorists into Bosnia…. Austrians must be allowed to enter Serbia to investigate…. Propaganda against the Empire must cease…. Anti-Austrian officers must be dismissed….

That would do it, surely?

Later, Wilhelm fell into a restless sleep, with strange dreams. The Archangel Gabriel awaited Christ, in the guise of Wilhelm, on his return from this world to Heaven. Gabriel asked what arrangements had been made for the government and increase of His Kingdom upon earth. Christ replied: 'The control of My Kingdom I have given into the hands of a few simple and sensible men, and I have instructed them to inform others until at last the whole world shall know that I have died for them.' The Archangel questioned Him: 'What if these men should fail in their duty? What arrangements have been made for the propagation of the Kingdom in that case?' Christ replied, 'I have made no arrangements. I am counting on them.'

Nothing could calm the anger of Wilhelm against the regicides who had killed Franz Ferdinand; and nothing could totally calm his inner doubt about his own plans for his cousin, George V. It was with the *Kaiseridee* that he must take refuge: the absolute sanctity of his own role as God's anointed, in care of his people. Barbarossa was at last freed from his long entombment, his spirit reborn in this new, and greater, Emperor.

'Looking upon myself as the instrument of the Lord, without regard for daily opinions and intentions, I go my way, which is devoted solely and alone to the welfare and peaceful development of the Fatherland.' Not that practical considerations had been ignored. The army was ready: the businessmen were prepared. 'No one will be able to reproach me again with want of resolution.'

And yet…could he be certain? Wilhelm's face was wracked by neuralgic pain, and there were long hours of tossing and turning without rest.

* * *

In death, it usually transpired, all the dreariness, all the pain, all the failure, all the hatreds of life could be forgotten – at least by those left behind. The Requiem Mass for Franz Ferdinand in Westminster Roman Catholic Cathedral that week had seemed proof enough. The high altar was flanked on both sides by immense candles. The Austrian Ambassador, alone, sat on a carved, gold-coloured chair. Prince Arthur of Connaught was there as the representative of the King, as he had been at the funeral itself; Asquith and other political figures, including Ransom, were also present. The American Ambassador, distinct from all the other uniformed Ambassadors from many nations since he wore ordinary evening dress, did not puncture the magnificent solemnity of the occasion as Bishop Butt intoned the words of the Mass. There was no ritual like the ritual of death.

Still, the mood passed as quickly as the ceremony. The Ransoms left London on Friday morning for a weekend in the Sussex countryside. After breakfast on Saturday house guests lounged in over-cushioned chairs and read the newspapers, with intervals for croquet. The talk was serious – in a paradoxically desultory sort of way. The Oxford victory over Cambridge by a margin of 194 runs at Lords. The 'Accidental Death' verdict in the Anson case. Eton's victory over Harrow by four wickets, also at Lords. The decision by the Church to give women votes and seats on Parish Councils. What the House of Lords was doing to the Amending Bill. The narrow Government majority of 23 when Asquith applied – for the first time – a closure on the Budget Finance Bill. Everything in fact except the possibility of a European war – they could all read the firm pronouncement in *The Spectator* if they cared to wander into the library: 'The field of foreign affairs is this week barren of important events.'

Some slept the afternoon hours, to rouse themselves only when cream and jam and cakes announced their presence. For the slightly more energetic, a short journey through archways of glorious roses could take them to the tennis lawn. A few, disregarding the lateness of the hour at which they had arrived the previous night, had left early for golf; the same enthusiasts would be the first to the billiards room, or the bridge table, if it should rain. For others, who preferred their minds to wander, there was the memory of the wonderfully long summer of 1911 (the cold and wet of the following year discounted) and the fond hope, fuelled by the imagination, that 1914 was going to emulate it.

Ransom felt in a way a homecoming. For him, the country house and its ways were the symbol of the only life he understood. The social hierarchy was underpinned with the strongest of foundations – the servants. The housekeeper ruled one empire: the maids, engaged or recruited by her, were her domain. The butler exercised similar control over the male servants. Their employer encouraged them; it freed him of the bother and it showed the value of the status quo to those who might just have the ability to question the system.

Jakko Henderson, their host, had given up his seat in the House of Commons to concentrate full time on playing the squire near Pulborough: better, he had decided, to dominate the country scene rather than pretend to an influence he did not have in Westminster.

Despite the fact that his wealth was recent (his grandfather had died en route to England from the Warsaw ghetto), he played the role of Lord of the Manor to perfection – so unlike what George Sturt called the 'Resident Tripper', a common breed, who rode roughshod over the local people, yet hadn't the discrimination to know how distasteful they found his loud, discordant, incomprehensible behaviour.

Jakko enjoyed every day of his life at Waterfield, from the cup of tea his butler brought him before his bath, to be followed by a single cigarette, through the irrational pleasure of breakfast dishes kept warm for hours on end in silver dishes, from these early morning joys to the last savoury morsel and last drop of port after midnight. On his rather rare trips to London, he travelled by carriage and pair the short distance to Pulborough Railway Station, where the Stationmaster would flourish his top hat in greeting and usually manage to gather a small but respectful crowd to attend his departure. Perhaps the same people, like the retainers of old, turned out to join the army of beaters at Jakko's shooting parties, allowing themselves the occasional glance at the long and richly decorated table which appeared through the hard work of yet more hands when the hour of luncheon approached.

There was no shooting this weekend. As Jakko sombrely remarked, it was plausible that half of them would be shooting at the other half in Ireland at the beginning of the grouse season. His mother, impassive in her chair at the prospect of something that had threatened many times before (Ireland was always in crisis), enjoyed the Victorian security and fixity of her costume – her black silk dress, lace cap and strings of pearls.

The weather was discussed endlessly; today it was hotter, colder, less humid; this afternoon it might be much colder; tomorrow it might rain. Ransom's father had once told him: 'It is not manly to show your feelings. You should not show affection to your mother.

You must display reserve at all times.' According to country-house rules, even falling in love did not seem to be permitted without engaging in the more important activity: the game. And when love came, after tennis or badminton or croquet, it found that it was only an act of duty, after all. Ransom wasn't really complaining – life seemed easier, more settled that way. But it left limited room for pleasure, none for passion. So it must have been with Rosalind in the beginning; it was difficult to remember. Long ago….

In his room, overlooking the gardens at the back of the house, he surveyed himself in the mirror. All seemed in outward good order, the smooth line of his suit spoiled by nothing more serious than a prominent silk handkerchief and that little globular container which would spring open at a touch to reveal four gold sovereigns. He fingered the Smith and Wesson pistol that Kell had specially ordered for him by post from the Paris gunsmiths Gastinne-Renette. Where did that go down in the budgets, he wondered. And more to the point – would he have to use it?

* * *

It would not have been surprising if the answer to that question was furthered in some way by Ireland. While the Kaiser wrestled with his problems, and Ransom with his, history was unwilling to come to a stop. Sir Edward Carson arrived on Irish shores aboard the Liverpool steamer to celebrate the anniversary of the Battle of the Boyne. Union Jacks could be seen waving in all the villages along the shores of the Lough. Crowds cheered and jostled. A mill girl opposite the door of the Ulster Club, hatless and wearing a black homespun shawl, clutched a bunch of orange lilies carefully wrapped round with newspaper. Pushing with a fevered desperation through the throng, she thrust them into Carson's hand.

Inside, the men of the Orange Lodges, in bowler hats, dark

suits with orange sashes, and white gloves, sat waiting. Embroidered banners containing likenesses of William III hung round the room; drums were beaten with hypnotic regularity, the sheepskin of the drumheads stained with blood from the bruised hands of the drummers.

Ironically, the Battle of the Boyne had been fought more than two centuries before on the first, not the twelfth, of July. The reasons for it falling on Irish soil were almost fortuitous and both the dethroned British king, James II, and his Dutch opponent, William of Orange, made extensive use of foreign troops. As monarch, William III scarcely noticed the existence of the country, except to endow his favourites – mainly Dutch – with huge grants of confiscated Irish land.

But today, Sunday, the 12th of July, 1914, the toast was, like every year, to 'The glorious, pious and immortal memory of the great and good King William, who saved us from Popery, slavery, knavery, brass money [James II's finances] and wooden shoes [James's French allies].' History, as ever, was far too serious a matter to be left to the historians.

Carson, in his speech, would have no truck with ingenious political solutions, the idea that you could test opinion within the counties and if necessary divide them, with one representative coming to Westminster, another to a new Dublin assembly. 'By Ulster, I mean Ulster,' he roared to the approval of his audience. 'I see no hopes of peace. I see nothing at present but darkness and shadows. We must be ready. In my own opinion the great climax and the great crisis of our fate, and the fate of our country, cannot be delayed for many weeks…until something happens – when we shall have once more to assert the manhood of our race.'

As he spoke, on the other side of Europe the Foreign Minister of Austria worked on the ultimatum for delivery to Serbia.

After he spoke, he presided over a smaller gathering: the

members of the Ulster Provisional Government. The plan was to take over post, customs, internal revenue – all the offices of the Crown in Northern Ireland – and to hold them 'in trust for His Majesty the King'. James Craig explained that a coded telegram from London would be the signal for action. 'All difficulties have been overcome', he said, 'and we are in a very strong position.'

At Larne the service was conducted by the Bishop of Down and the Moderator of the Presbyterian General Assembly. Carson's voice was distinct in the congregation as all sang, 'O God our Help in Ages Past', just as it was later when troops, equipped with rifles and fixed bayonets, drilled on three sides of the square, supported on the fourth by a double row of Volunteer Nurses.

It looked like a disciplined force, but there would be others to face it. In the South, Sinn Fein's own volunteers, farm labourers and 'corner boys', had also come together, a hundred thousand strong.

* * *

Ransom had taken the train back to London early on Sunday afternoon, leaving Rosalind to follow the next day. He said that he had a busy few days ahead, which was true enough, though he had nothing planned for the evening and gravitated in the direction of the Chancellor's residence in Downing Street. Lloyd George never minded being disturbed: it gave him an audience. As he entered, the Welshman was in the midst of practising a speech, the words being faithfully recorded by his secretary – and devoted lover – Frances Stevenson. He did not stop immediately:

'What is poverty? Have you felt it yourselves?' he asked his two substitutes for a crowd. 'If not, you ought to thank God for having been spared its sufferings and temptations. Have you seen others enduring it? Then pray God to forgive you if you have not done your best to alleviate it. The day will come when this country will shudder at its toleration of this state of things when it was rolling in wealth. Apart from its inhumanity and its essential injustice, it is robbery, it is confiscation of what is the workman's share of the riches of the land.'

His resonant tones faded from the room – slowly.

'I trust that you are not offering your support to one of our candidates again,' Ransom said, almost sourly. 'The last time you told the voters that they were half-starved slaves, horribly oppressed, worked to death for the enrichment of those already rich enough, I may remind you that we lost heavily.'

'Hush, man. D'you have no feelings? This is the truth. This is a rich country. It is the richest country under the sun; and yet in this rich country you have hundreds and thousands of people living under conditions of poverty, destitution and squalor that would, in the words of the old Welsh poet, make the rocks weep.'

'Then they should rouse themselves,' Ransom said irritably, knowing that the comment was unworthy as he said it.

'Rouse themselves! If these poor people are to be redeemed they must be redeemed by others outside, and the appeal ought to be to every class of the community to see that in this great land all this misery and wretchedness should be put an end to.'

Ransom appeared lost in thought. His nerves were on edge and he had come here to relax, but there was going to be no respite in this conversation.

'A drink?' asked Lloyd George, as if all was quickly forgiven.

'Thank you. I think not, after all,' he replied. 'I can see I'm interrupting.' Frances Stevenson blushed: Lloyd George's speech-making *was* a sort of love-making. Ransom was fond of his colleague's wife, Margaret, and he didn't think he understood the significance of all this at the time. He made a rather graceless exit: they would see each other tomorrow, talk then.

As the door clicked shut, Lloyd George was already in full

flow again: 'There are faint hearts to sustain, there are hotheads to restrain….'

* * *

In London behind-the-scenes negotiations extended in every direction as the new week began. For the umpteenth time in recent months, *The Times* invited its readers to admire the exemplary restraint of the Ulstermen. The only restraint they had shown, some muttered, was in not massacring their Catholic neighbours or marching against the British army that was so much in sympathy with them. But the Government could not completely close its eyes to what the newspaper said. The words – one might almost say the facts – were powerfully convincing; 'Not even the most absorbing tragedies in our neighbours' houses can be allowed to distract us from the tragedy which threatens our own. The strain in Ulster is already almost at breaking point. The risk of an outbreak, comparatively slight in the disciplined forces of the Continent, has been magnified tenfold by the appearance everywhere of a rival organization which has arms and numbers but neither leadership nor restraint. The National Volunteers complete a picture of accomplished anarchy and almost inevitable disorder. For all practical purposes the Imperial Government has simply abdicated its function in Ireland.'

Ransom was deputed to talk to Bonar Law and, if he could, with Carson; Asquith, with Birrell, met the Nationalist leaders, Redmond and Dillon. The latter, Asquith complained, seemed as intractable as ever, bad tempered and adamant that the Ulster counties that contained Catholics must be part of the Home Rule scheme.

In Cabinet they had, as Asquith later said, a dreary time trying to solve the problem of how to get a quart into a pint pot. He himself had seen Carson in the end, and reported to them. 'It showed how little progress the negotiations had made. He is quite anxious to settle in my judgment, but makes much of his difficulties with his own friends. Threats seem non-productive: he knows that the Metropolitan Police have been asked for 2000 volunteers to go to Ireland as reinforcements; he knows that the Army Reserve men in the police have been warned to hold themselves ready to rejoin their colours.' Asquith shrugged. What else could he say?

Meantime, Speaker Lowther was also trying to adopt the role of honest broker. He wrote to both Redmond and Carson. 'If you think that any good purpose would be served in bringing about an arrangement on the Irish question by a meeting, I should be very glad to place my services and the use of my library at your disposal. My library is neutral ground and remote from the public eye; and as to myself, I would either be present at, or absent from, your meeting as you may think best.'

Redmond was unmoved. 'I have no information which leads me to believe that a meeting such as you suggest with Sir Edward Carson would at the moment be fruitful.'

Carson was obliquely intransigent. 'If the basis for discussions could be the exclusion of "Ulster" I would be prepared to enter into them.'

For the moment the Speaker returned to more pressing matters of diplomacy: the dinner party and ball at his house for Slatin Bey, famous as a long-time prisoner of the Mahdi after the death of General Gordon in the Sudan. Ransom drank too much there that evening, Wednesday the 15th of July, mainly in fear of the ordeal of the following evening – another ball at Buckingham Palace. He had heard nothing more, but the idea of being in a public place with the King was quite sufficient to increase his nervousness.

Through the thudding pain of his headache on Thursday afternoon, the House of Commons seemed to have succumbed to amused hysteria over the Irish question. While the Empire was falling to pieces, as one of the observing journalists noted, the feeblest of witticisms provoked a roar of admiring laughter. A weary Asquith had to face the insistent questioning of Mr Hogge as to why the Union Jack (how much trouble the Celtic associates of England have brought her!) should be flown over Holyrood Palace, in preference to the Red Lion. Later, when they assembled at the Palace, the Prime Minister commented that he had wished he had replied by an expression of puzzlement – the Red Lion, in London at least, usually being a public house, not a national emblem.

The facts were these: by the time the House of Lords had given a Third Reading to the Amending Bill the previous day, the original Bill had been drastically changed in at least one important respect – Ulster was permanently and entirely excluded. The Bill would go back to the Commons the following Monday, but it was certain that neither the Government nor Redmond would accept it. Asquith at last felt impelled to act, though his decision – for a Constitutional Conference called by the King – was not one with which he felt happy. He was too skilled a politician to ignore all the facts: he would talk to the King at once.

The Court Ball had been postponed for a little more than two weeks because of Court mourning for the Archduke and his wife. There was no talk of European war that evening, however, and some were already beginning to discuss the plans for celebrating Queen Alexandra's seventieth birthday in the Autumn: the Kaiser and Kaiserin, the Empress Marie of Russia and assorted Scandinavian royalty had already expressed the intention of coming. It was not that there was nothing happening on the Continent; there were always 'incidents' – they expected them, and in their priggish way, they made light of them. So Rasputin had been stabbed at Tobolsk, his Siberian home; so the Russian minister in Belgrade had died in mysterious circumstances when visiting the Austrian legation…

such matters were of no concern in London. Even now Ransom could still share the mood.

Ireland was a different matter. As *The Spectator* columnist dourly remarked, Ireland was not like the rest of the world, for there the maxim that three-quarters of a loaf of bread is better than none did not apply. Even Winston seemed quite sober on the matter when he spoke to members of the Cabinet, Ransom, Grey and Asquith among them. 'Carson and Redmond, whatever their wishes, may be unable to agree about Tyrone; they may think it worth a war, and from their point of view it may be worth a war. But that is hardly the position of the forty millions who dwell in Great Britain; and their interests must, when all is said and done, be our chief and final cause.'

Asquith nodded. For once he did not disagree. Moreover, it would not be difficult to persuade His Majesty to hold a Conference. Since the King himself had first discussed the idea (to the Prime Minister's initial irritation), a patriotic article in the *Daily Telegraph* had suggested that the King alone was 'outside our quarrels and above our conflicts'. If his office forbade him to interfere, it did not forbid him to act as 'mediator and moderator'.

So it proved. Asquith found the King in a tent in the garden and they talked for half an hour. His monarch contentedly quoted Queen Victoria at the time of the Boer War. 'I refuse to allow my house to be made a melancholy house,' she had said. There was need for seriousness, for good feeling, but none for long faces and canting talk about the end of the world and the destruction of all that is worth having. 'Besides,' the King mused, 'Mr Redmond is afraid of his American supporters and Sir Edward Carson is afraid of his Orange fanatics. We can build on that.'

Asquith found himself applauding the King's suggestion that the Speaker should preside and he agreed to write a memorandum advising a Conference. A cordial reply would be made.

After Question Time in the House of Commons the next day, Bonar Law agreed to meet the Prime Minister in Sir Edward Grey's room.

'I must urge you, Mr Law,' the Prime Minister said to the Conservative leader, 'to accept that the Nationalists should at any rate receive part of Tyrone. I see no solution otherwise. Failure to settle will mean a General Election with considerable difficulties for whomever should win. The King, as you know, is very distressed about the whole matter. Only yesterday Stamfordham telephoned to complain that the Lords had treated Ireland as if it were a butcher's joint to be carved to suit their own palette.'

Bonar Law, able to assume that – despite their disagreements – the King was pro-Unionist, was equally firm in his reply. 'It may be that Irishmen prefer the logic of a fight to the logic of a compromise, whether or not they are likely to win the battle or to be beaten. The plain fact is that the men of Ulster will not submit to rule either by your Government or by the heirs of the cultural tradition they detest in the South. If there is a drop of blood shed in Ulster, then we will win overwhelmingly any election that may follow.'

'I'm sure you would agree, nevertheless, that it would be a crime if civil war resulted from what is in effect so small a difference – whether a county or two in the whole country were part of Home Rule, or not?'

'You might care to argue that our intransigence creates such a position, but frankly the people of Ulster know that they have a force which will enable them to hold the Province; and – with opinion so deeply divided as it is here – it is quite impossible that another force could be sent against them which could dislodge them. I must tell you,' Bonar Law continued, 'that they know that they can force their own terms and that they would rather fight than give way on such a point as this.'

He had not quite finished. There was a moment's silence and

he continued: 'Put yourself in the position of an officer. He believes in his heart and conscience, as I do, that the Government is doing this thing without the consent of the country, that in pressing it forward without the approval of the country they are as much a revolutionary committee as President Huerta and the governors of Mexico.'

Asquith was unmoved. 'Suppose there was to be no time limit on the exclusion of Protestant Ulster from Home Rule. Would that make the difference?'

'I do not believe so, Moreover, I fully expect that the Ulster Provisional Government will be set up within a few weeks if your own Government has not come to some agreement.'

This time Asquith did not comment immediately. Then he observed: 'Perhaps the King should, after all, be asked to convene a Conference of all the parties?'

'I would not welcome it, Mr Asquith, and I would not expect it to bear fruit.'

The Prime Minister sighed perceptibly. Bonar Law continued. 'I will go so far as this: should you make it your responsibility to give an invitation to such a Conference in the name of the King I would be bound to accept it.'

'For that I give you my thanks,' Asquith said with a weary decisiveness.

* * *

He recounted this conversation to Ransom as they dined a little later at the Ritz. As they sat, next to one of the large, elegant windows in the dining room, they could look out on one of the delights of London – Green Park. To their right, at the far end of the restaurant, Father Thames viewed – ogled it seemed to Ransom – a voluptuous lady. Already slightly drunk (a common experience for him in these weeks – this time from the effects of most of a bottle of Heidsieck Dry Monopole 1898), he declared that the lady (he believed) represented the Ocean. If he was going to say goodbye to the good life, he might as well drown his doubts in its delights.

M. Charles, the manager of the restaurant, walked quietly across the splendid carpets from the Marie Antoinette Room which adjoined it and which, this evening, also contained diners. It was on his recommendation that they had the Filet de Sole Romanoff, with apple, artichokes and mussels: 'My brain', said Asquith, 'needs serious feeding,' but there was not the usual twinkle in his eyes as he spoke. 'Well, Walter,' he went on, 'we shall have Cabinet tomorrow to agree on the details of the Conference. I am not confident, but I see no other way.'

'Certainly if it ever became known that the King had desired it, that Redmond and Carson were willing to attend and that we had hindered it, we should be held responsible in the event of civil war breaking out.'

'Redmond and Carson seem the only ones in complete agreement,' Asquith commented with heavy irony: 'They at least seem totally clear about what they could not expect the other to accept.' He continued: 'We must handle the announcement with some care; it must be seen to be of importance, but – in case things go wrong – I'm wary of allowing leaks in all directions. My inclination is to give an exclusive to *The Times*.'

'Lloyd George could talk to Northcliffe after the Lord Mayor's banquet for the bankers tomorrow,' Ransom suggested.

'Not a bad idea,' Asquith mused. 'It will mean, of course, that the *Mail* has it too. But it wouldn't be a mistake to have Northcliffe on one's side.'

'It won't please many of our own people.'

'That's manageable,' said Asquith, as mistakenly confident as he always was about discord in his own camp. 'Reports from the constituencies are bad, especially the working-class ones,' he added, almost with relish. 'Trevelyan says that the whole of the Liberal working class is on the point of revolt. "They have never approved of leaving Carson alone, they were more angry about the gunrunning, and they will be quite furious about the Conference." Those were his exact words. They give me confidence that we will win through.'

They both smiled. Then a pause to enjoy the Pêche Belle Dijonnaise, with its blackcurrant ice and cassis; this civilization, he reflected, saw no contradiction between pleasure and the pursuit of power – there was merely some doubt about which came first.

'Of course,' continued the Prime Minister, 'some of our backbenchers will continue to complain. It remains very clear that Sir Thomas Whittaker and his supporters are for Redmond.'

'There are a substantial number of them, too,' Ransom observed. 'And what is your view about the Labour Members? Should they be represented at the Conference?'

'I think not. This is a national matter – not for a sectional interest. If we invite Labour we might as well invite Big Business.'

Again the simplification disguised the complex political calculations involved.

'As for Europe….' Ransom began hesitantly.

'I'm not worried,' Asquith said. 'When the Court went into mourning two weeks ago for the Archduke, I suppose there were fears of a new Balkan conflict, but I believe now that the worst of it can be an Austro-Serbian war. And that will be short if Germany gives Austria support.'

'I bumped into Benckendorff today, outside his Embassy. You heard about his son's boating accident?' Asquith nodded. 'He did not even seem to be thinking that his government would be involved,' Ransom continued.

'No, the Russians will keep out,' the Prime Minister said. 'This is all a local affair of little concern to us. Besides, we have our hands full with our own local difficulties.'

He wondered if Asquith was right. If he was, it put a very different perspective on his own plans. The Kaiser's plea to keep Britain out of a conflict between Germany and those who threatened her was unconvincing; he had read the desire for conquest in his expression more or less at once. So, sooner or later, Germany would act: it would be for him to make sure that – if the assassination was successful (oh, what a strange word to use!) – Germany would be linked in the plot. Then the conflagration would be bound to grow: England might be drawn in and, as far as he was concerned, that would at least mean giving the right side the chance of coming out on top.

At that moment, several things suddenly became clearer to him. He was in an impossible position, but that did not mean he was totally unable to influence what happened. The strain was terrible, yes, but there was no point in trying to shrug off a burden that would not go away. He had to help Anna – he had to; and if he was slow-wittedly playing in a game where he had no understanding of the rules, well, at any rate the game had a good way to go yet. Despite himself, he felt something close to exhilaration.

Asquith was looking at him. 'Are you all right?'

He shrugged, smiled, and said: 'Yes. Yes I am.'

They walked through the Winter Garden of the Ritz, with its impressive marble pillars, gilt in abundance, great decorated mirrors and fountain surmounted by golden cupids. Everything in the Ritz – the silver, the china, the glass, the gilt-bronze garlands which represented the decorations at one of Marie Antoinette's feasts – was in the style of Louis XVI: the King whose life ended on the guillotine.

They emerged outside the vast white stone building in the middle of the arcade. Ransom gave an involuntary chuckle, and then – as if in reaction – an involuntary shiver.

He declined the Prime Minister's offer of a lift in his car and walked a little unsteadily down Piccadilly – a purposely circular route home towards Hyde Park Corner. Outside the German Officers' Club, he bowed low and halted a moment before moving on. At the stall on Hyde Park Corner, lit by paraffin lamps, you could buy hard-boiled eggs, bread and butter, penny buns and a cup of Camp.

The night was misty, the lights glowing faintly all around. At this time, a while after midnight, only the odd cab passed. A few drunks, anxious prostitutes – by now a trifle desperate and despairing – a couple of soldiers – potential customers – a cart with street cleaners, the unexplained presence of a solitary woman porter from Covent Garden with empty flower baskets on her head…. Mostly silence.

This was the hour of no illusions.

CHAPTER EIGHTEEN

Kriegsgefahrzustand: the imminence of war

THE newspapers reported: 'The King is to travel from Victoria to Portsmouth Station this morning, and he will embark on board the Royal Yacht *Victoria and Albert* for conveyance to Spithead. His Majesty is to remain afloat until Monday afternoon, when he will be obliged to return to town. He will not be able to visit Dartmouth and Plymouth, as had been hoped.'

His reasons for needing to return to London became formally known when the Prime Minister rose to speak to a crowded House of Commons on Monday at precisely 2.30, though – according to plan – *The Times* had carried the story that morning.

In the English Channel, the King had passed between the assembled line of his impressive fleet, assembled at action stations and stretching almost all the way from Spithead to Cowes: battleships and cruisers, destroyers and submarines. Above, the bright yellow airship *Astra Torres* crossed the South Downs and flew west to join the silver-grey *Parseval*, which had come up against the wind from Aldershot; in greater number aeroplanes flew into sight and then slowly disappeared over the horizon. At night, searchlight beams lit the sky on both land and water.

The King paid a genial visit to the *Collingwood*, on which the Prince of Wales was serving, and the officers and midshipmen were presented to him. To the Commander-in-Chief, Home Fleets, a satisfying telegram was given: 'After the review of the Fleet today, and my visit to some of the ships yesterday, I should like to express to you, and through you to the flag officers, captains, and officers and men under your command, my high appreciation of the efficient and splendid appearance of the Fleet. I am impressed by the keen spirit of all ranks and ratings in every branch of the service, and by the promptitude with which the reservists returned to duty. I am proud of my Navy.'

Behind the scenes, some of the discussion was less bland. Everyone was conscious of the strength of the German fleet and some were alive to the effect of Russia's growing army on the balance of power – one and a third million men already available, according to a report in *Le Temps* just telegraphed by the British Ambassador in Paris, a million more in five or six years' time at the present rate of growth. The First Sea Lord, Prince Louis of Battenberg, pondered the wisdom of dispersing the elements of the Fleet as the King joined the London, Brighton and South Coast Railway at Portsmouth Dockyard, en route to Victoria Station, early on Monday evening.

By then, Asquith had long since finished facing the Commons, though the consequences of his statement were being debated all over London. He had received no resounding applause from his party, at best a frigid cheer, and he kept strictly to the point. 'In view of the grave situation,' he said, 'the King has thought it right to summon representatives of the Parties, both British and Irish, to a Conference in Buckingham Palace, with the object of discussing issues in relation to the problem of Irish government.' He looked from face to face, and added, 'Mr Speaker will preside.'

Mr Hogge, the Member for East Edinburgh who had been so solicitous for his country's flag the previous week, immediately rose to his feet. 'Can the Prime Minister say whether any of those taking part in the Conference attached any conditions to their entering the Conference?'

'I cannot say.' Mr Hogge, together with Winston Churchill, Keir Hardie and others who felt that they should have been there, were not invited. The omission of any Labour Member encouraged the left to see the Conference as constitutional interference by the King, intended to defeat the Parliament Act. One Labour man even suggested that if he himself had made Carson's speeches he would have been invited to the dock rather than to Buckingham Palace.

Bonar Law had made a brief statement merely acknowledging that he had loyally accepted the King's command. Redmond deliberately disclaimed responsibility for the Conference, but indicated that since the invitation was in the form of a command from the King, he too had accepted. His 'supporters' were less kind: Mr Ginnell, the Irish Nationalist Member for Westmeath N. asked the Prime Minister what authority he had for advising the King to place himself at the head of a conspiracy to defeat the House of Commons. His question was ignored both by Asquith and by the Speaker, but at worst public opinion was going to identify in the whole business 'a Royal *coup d'état*' (as the *Daily News* called it), at best it would be thought that the Liberals were exploiting the monarchy. It was all very well for the Prime Minister to declare that 'His Majesty the King throughout this matter has followed the strictest constitutional precedent'; but if the Conference failed, what would the world make of the statement that the King 'has not taken any step from the beginning up to now except in consultation with, and on the advice of, his Ministers'?

Now that Ransom had had the opportunity to analyse the affair (how curiously easy it was for him to be detached and involved at the same time, he thought), he could see that he might have used his influence to argue against the Conference.

Still, he could imagine Asquith arguing back. 'What is the alternative?' he would ask, each word and syllable carefully weighed.

And did it matter while the King's life was in danger? Should he, even at this late stage, take someone into his confidence. Asquith? Kell? Someone else?

It could not be done. Political friends are not true friends. How would he begin to explain? There was no way back – and yet the subsequent record he left showed that he found himself in surprisingly good spirits. The waiting might soon be over.

* * *

At the Conference there were to be just eight delegates, each supported by two secretaries. For the Liberals, the Prime Minister and Ransom; for the Conservatives, Bonar Law and their leader in the House of Lords, Lord Lansdowne. Representing the Irish Nationalists, Mr Redmond and Mr Dillon; representing the Ulstermen, Sir Edward Carson and Captain James Craig. The omens were all discouraging. Lansdowne had written to Stamfordham saying that he undertook to do his best to promote a settlement, but equally he would have thought that some bases of preliminary agreement might have been ascertained before summoning the Conference. It was a fair point.

For those involved, Ireland had become almost the sole preoccupation of the moment, though the primary concern in certain Society drawing rooms seemed to be fears of what might happen to the Dublin Horse Show. Elsewhere, Lady Julia Affleck was practising her smile before the cameras in preparation for the hearing of her decree nisi against Sir Robert Affleck. She was just one of five well-known ladies bringing their matrimonial affairs before the London courts this week. In Paris, on the other hand, the whole population was preparing to goggle over the sensational Caillaux trial, staged following the murder of M. Calmette of the *Figaro*. In Russia there were preparations for something else: strikes in St Petersburg, which were to deteriorate into fighting between Cossacks and the strikers after a lockout was decided upon.

And in Berlin, for those who knew or who could identify the signs, something much more serious was in the air.

Bethmann-Hollweg and Von Jagow had had confirmation the previous Saturday, the 18th, that Austria intended to present Serbia with an ultimatum that was almost a declaration of war. If her intention was to wipe out the Serbs, as it clearly was, Germany would support her, even – perhaps especially – at the cost of war with Russia. Yet Russia was a worry: her railway communications network would make her a serious threat to Germany's eastern frontiers. German intelligence intercepted the following report by the Russian Foreign Minister to the Tsar: 'I take the liberty of submitting for the indulgence of Your Imperial Majesty the enclosed analysis of the pressing political questions on the chance that Your Imperial Majesty might deign to refer to them in your most exalted reply to the King of England…. It is absolutely essential to see beyond the limits of the present complication, and to face the fact that it is now a question of the maintenance of the balance of power in Europe which is seriously threatened. It is to be hoped that England, whose policies for centuries have been directed at the maintenance of this balance, will likewise now remain faithful to the legacy of the past.'

There was only one solution: act first, knock out the French and free resources for the real battle to come.

Geography had not been kind. But Von Moltke had long been clear about that. There was yet an answer to the dilemma – and it lay several thousand years in the past with the lesson of the Battle of Cannae. Outflank the enemy. If in the south there would be delays in the Jura, Belgium and Luxembourg had to be the keys: it could be six weeks – less probably – from the Belgian frontier to the streets of Paris.

Von Jagow drafted an urgent dispatch to Klaus von Below-Saleske, the German Ambassador in Brussels: 'The Imperial Government is in receipt of reliable information relating to the proposed advance of French armed forces along the Meuse, route Givet-Namur. This leaves no doubt as to the French intention to advance against Germany through Belgian territory. The Imperial Government cannot help being concerned over the probability that Belgium, despite the best of intentions, will be unable to resist a French advance without assistance. For Germany it is a dictate of self-preservation that she anticipates a hostile attack. It would therefore fill the Imperial Government with the deepest regret should Belgium view as an act of hostility to herself the entrance of Germany upon Belgium's soil, should she be forced by the measures of her opponents to do so in self-protection. If, on the other hand, the Belgian attitude is friendly, Germany will be willing, under an arrangement with the Royal Belgian authorities, to buy for cash all the necessities required by her troops, and to make good every damage that may possibly be occasioned by German troops. Should Belgium oppose as an enemy the German troops, and in particular throw obstacles in their way by the resistance of the Meuse fortifications, or by the destruction of railroads, roads, tunnels or other artificial structures, Germany would be obliged, to her regret, to regard the kingdom as an enemy. The future regulation of the relations of the two nations to each other would then be left to the decision of arms.

'Your Excellency will communicate this matter to the Royal Belgian Government in detail and in the strictest confidence, and will request the transmission of an unequivocal reply within twenty-four hours.'

Only one question remained: the English – what would they do? The ultimatum to Serbia would be presented on the evening of the 23rd of July. Any action to throw England into confusion would have to be taken by roughly the same time.

* * *

As Von Jagow dictated his instructions, the issue was at last coming closer to its resolution. Before going to hear Asquith's statement in the House of Commons, Ransom had met Von Bode for lunch at an unprepossessing German restaurant in Regent Street. This in itself started to worry him, for he had to make an impromptu excuse for missing Margot Asquith's own luncheon party; the rare and wonderful collection assembled there – Cambon, Chaliapine, Lady Diana Manners and Count Kessler among them – seemed more appealing than usual. The Prime Minister, he gathered afterwards, had been somewhat gloomy: an unguarded moment in which he expressed the hopelessness of the impasse – an impasse with unspeakable consequences and one which to English eyes seemed so small.

Slightly hysterical at the absurdity of his own lunchtime meeting place, given the need for secrecy, he had been firmly – almost brutally – advised by Von Bode that, outside the realms of popular spy fiction, the only real asset was to keep calm and act normally. He retorted that if anything was better calculated to panic him than their present surroundings, he would be surprised. Von Bode nodded. He too was evidently worried about Ransom. Would his nerve hold?

Through the revolving doors, set between marble pillars, he had arrived in an oddly rectangular room, with dark wooden panels and heads of game on the walls. Here men sat noisily drinking. Beyond was the main restaurant, like a medieval hall, with dark wood-block flooring, more brown panels, formal, unfriendly, leather-backed chairs. Rollmops, goose soup with dumplings, Munich beer – this was the staple fare. Through the coloured windows, patterned with coats of arms, he could just see Glasshouse Street. Wooden carvings of the heads of wild animals – boars and bears, eagles and elephants – looked down on an accumulation of decorated beer mugs belonging to regular customers, past and present.

Von Bode was concerned. The motives for involving Ransom in the first place seemed as good as ever. The implication of an English Cabinet Minister, with an anarchist mistress, in a plot to kill the King of England, seemed a winning ploy in all circumstances; if anything went wrong, the blow to English morals and the inevitable anger against traitorous behaviour, would distract attention away from Germany and might even be almost as effective as the assassination itself. But the desire to push him further, get him directly to help, or to cover for, the man who would carry out the shooting – that might be too much of a risk? The Kaiser had been impressed by Ransom, it seemed, but the Kaiser had never been the best judge of a man – if he was, why had Lichnowsky been given the Ambassador's job?

Von Bode decided that Ransom must be told something, but not everything. The plan was settled, he said. King George V was to die during the Conference called in his name to resolve the Irish question. It was best that he did not meet the assassin, but he should at least be prepared to add to the confusion in which the man might escape.

'But how will he get to the King?' Ransom asked.

Von Bode was silent for a moment. Convincing possibilities

were few. An intruder might get over the wall from Constitution Hill or, on the other side of the Palace, from Buckingham Gate. But what then? There might be an underground route through the sewers, but still there would be no guarantee of being able to reach the King. No, the only solution was the one they had adopted: the assassin must not only be present in the Palace when the Conference opened, but his being there must not arouse any suspicion. Ransom would be able to work that out for himself, if he was clever enough: it still wouldn't tell him who was involved.

Von Bode parried the question, emphasising the need for secrecy. The less Ransom knew, the safer it was for him. They ate then in silence, each of them preoccupied with his own thoughts, and took a curt departure from one another afterwards.

It was simple for a man like Leon Czolgosz, the Pole who had shot President McKinley a dozen or more years before. However much the American police had wanted to find a string of associated plots, however hard Czolgosz tried to affirm his anarchist beliefs at his trial, the facts were starkly simple: an introverted neurotic, feeling the world's injustices on his own shoulders, had decided to end the life of the supreme symbol of power – and hence op-pression – around him.

The irony was that you didn't actually get the power from po-litical success. Oh yes, it was splendid to receive every night that tough leather dispatch case, which marked one's membership of the Cabinet and which promised – when unlocked – to reveal the secrets of the world. But what did it amount to? Wasn't Northcliffe right when he told Ransom that any Editor of a great London journal or newspaper would always have more power at his disposal than the strongest of political leaders.

But more. To be tied to someone, anyone, by love or blood, was to lose power over one's own destiny. Would he have found himself faced with the dilemmas of the moment if he had chastely rejected his involvement with Anna?

It was not the grand passion that you remembered when questions like that were asked, but all those little things. One morning, a stolen breakfast in Clarges Street, nothing more: the simple joy with which she had made an American treat. Before her, carefully written out, the recipe: Indian corn and wheaten flour and caster sugar, bicarbonate and salt, cupfuls of cream. Twenty minutes of excitement, then laughing, crying, in anticipation; the masterpiece emerges: Cream Johnny Cake. Was anything ever more perfect for the solemn middle-aged?

Such a muddle of feelings, wishes, wants....

As he walked towards Berkeley Square, cars, cabs, broughams jostled with one another, carrying the fortunate from lunch to tea, and then – later – it would be on to Caruso and Melba at Covent Garden, or Chaliapine as Boris Godunov at Drury Lane, to candle-lit suppers or sumptuous dinners.

This was again a moment of dejection, as quick to arrive as his unbalanced elation at the Ritz. He peered unfocusedly around him. There through the chemist's window in Brook Street were bottles and boxes, pots and capsules: manicure sticks, digestive tablets, jujubes, face cream, smokers' cachous; poison, too, if needed. Everything and nothing.

He fled on, quickly past the front door of his home – comforting in the spaciousness and luxury that was not apparent from the street.

There seemed no chance of working for what was left of the afternoon, and he decided to retire early.

CHAPTER NINETEEN

The conference meets

WHETHER through fear of the approaching moment of action itself, or through nervous over-indulgence in unfamiliar food, he slept fitfully that night – the eve of the Conference. He dreamed, too: of a bleak, treeless island, surrounded by giant cliffs and punctuated by vast rugged quarries. He relived the horrors of a magazine article he had read as a child, but which remained with him still.

Through chilling double gates of an unpleasant stone-built complex of buildings, watched by uniformed guards: here was prison, the prison of his mind. Marching in line past sentries, loaded, cocked rifles at the ready, seen at all vantage points; past the Principal Warder, with ugly sabre attached to his belt. Just visible to the left, the railway track – only access to the one beaching point, fragile link with the outside world. To the right, the bay, resting in it the formidable shapes of several giant battleships, at either side of them cruisers, torpedo boats and destroyers. On to the stone-floored chambers, with four or five tiers of cells running down the two sides, each tier of cells fronted by an iron gallery. Strip, a humiliating search, a foul bath: into worn, ill-fitting prison garments. Up iron staircases to the gallery on the top tier; the door swings open.

Inside, an iron cubicle, no more than seven feet by four. On one side a rudimentary bed, just two feet wide, above its head a single shelf with plate, knife, fork and pannikin; all of tin, polished like silver. A little fold-down table; a four-legged stool, slate and pencil: nothing more to be seen. Dim light from outside through a narrow fluted glass window; in the gallery a gas jet burns all night and most of the day. The heavy door locks as it closes and is then locked again. An eye peers through the hole revealed by swinging the iron plate from side to side.

No visitors here, no letters. No hope.

Inside the 'jewel room' now, all of stone save the door, hand-cuffs, chains, leg-irons on the wall; ready waiting the long-handled, nine-thonged whip, with lashes of hard cord, not knotted but whipped round the end with fine tough twine....

Into Ransom's nightmare there came an intrusive sound, which gradually roused him into wakefulness. The telephone was ringing insistently.

'Walter.'

'Anna.'

Anna was sobbing – but not with despair. Georg had escaped from his prison, managed to get out of Germany and though she did not know exactly where he was, he was evidently safe.

It was far too much of a personal release for her to want to think about what this meant for the assassination. Given a choice in calmer circumstances, he felt deep inside, she would not really want to be the cause of another's death, would she? The truly violent were their own breed and you might find them anywhere, using the loyalty of the faithful. Anna was surely one of the faithful.

He seemed to grow the calmer in response to her excited state and pondered only moments before outlining what he proposed. Anna must not move from Clarges Street. While there was a chance that he could not only stop the German plan, but implicate the culprits, he must take it. It was risky, especially as he did not know exactly what was to happen at the Conference, but if he told everything to Kell or Asquith now, the likelihood was that the Conference would be cancelled. The Irish troubles were too finely balanced for that, and it was also time, surely, that the Kaiser was brought out into the open. He would deliver to Anna a note of explanation, addressed to Kell, which she was only to pass on if the worst happened.

Outside, as he spoke, dawn was already breaking over Berkeley Square.

* * *

The delegates arrived at Buckingham Palace in separate carriages shortly before ten o'clock the next morning – the day the Shah of Persia was to be crowned in Teheran. The Irish Guardsmen at Wellington Barracks cheered Redmond and Dillon as they passed and made far more stir than the two forlorn Suffragettes who tried to enter the Palace. The Speaker was unmistakable in a white hat, set slightly at an angle; he greeted everyone with a cordiality that was not shared by the different parties facing each other. Judging by their clothes, a number of the Irish delegates were not used to meeting their sovereign. Carson and Craig wore ordinary cut-away morning suits, Dillon an indefinable long garment with tails, Redmond at least a frock coat, but a singularly ill-fitting one. Somehow the very gravity of events focused attention on such trivia.

At every door and stairway inside the Palace, impassive pikemen passed silent judgment on the mere mortals who passed by them. A stray Court official, in white silk stockings and breeches and gold-laced coat, hurried along, intent – it seemed – on some private pageant. They were to converse in a large room to the right of the Grand Hall of the Palace – on the ground floor adjoining the Ballroom, and overlooking the garden.

When all the delegates were assembled, the King – quiet in manner and dress – joined them. Speaking without notes, unsmiling, he said:

'Gentlemen. It is with feelings of satisfaction and hopefulness that I receive you today, and I thank you for the manner in which you have responded to my summons. It is also a matter of congratulation that the Speaker has consented to preside over your meetings.

'My intervention at this moment may be regarded as a new departure. But the exceptional circumstances under which you are brought together justify my action.

'For months we have watched with deep misgivings the course of events in Ireland. The trend has been surely and steadily towards an appeal to force, and today the cry of Civil War is on the lips of the most responsible and sober-minded of my people.

'We have in the past endeavoured to act as a civilizing example to the world, and to me it is unthinkable, as it must be to you, that we should be brought to the brink of fratricidal strife upon issues so incapable of adjustment as those you are now asked to consider, if handled in a spirit of generous compromise.

'My apprehension in contemplating such a dire calamity is intensified by my feelings of attachment to Ireland and of sympathy with her people, who have always welcomed me with warm-hearted affection.

'Gentlemen, you represent in one form or another the vast majority of my subjects at home. You also have a deep interest in my Dominions overseas, who are scarcely less concerned in a prompt and friendly settlement of this question.

'I regard you, then, in this matter as trustees for the honour and peace of all.

'Your responsibilities are indeed great. The time is short. You will, I know, employ it to the fullest advantage and be patient, earnest and conciliatory in view of the magnitude of the issues at stake. I pray that God in His infinite wisdom may guide your deliberations so that they may result in the joy of peace and settlement.'

For two long days, there was little sign of such guidance. It had seemed much easier the year before at the Conference of Ambassadors called by Sir Edward Grey to settle the frontier between Serbia and Albania than it was to cope with matters so much nearer home.

Bonar Law and Redmond kept notes, but no official record was to be maintained. It was as well. A long-drawn-out debate on the protocol to be observed if the Conference were to fail made for a discouraging start. Then followed a bad-tempered argument on what should be discussed first: the area to be excluded from Home Rule, or the time limit on exclusion from it. In the event the issue of the time limit was not formally put at all, a whole day being spent on the intricacies of the mix of Catholic and Protestant populations in individual counties. Ransom wished he could have felt more involved, though he managed to do what was necessary. In a moment of exhaustion late on the first day, these overbearingly articulate men, some of them passionately involved in the matters at hand, found themselves staring at each other in an embarrassed, and momentarily unbreakable, silence.

It could not go on indefinitely. Asquith decided on one last proposal: that the six north-eastern counties of Northern Ireland should vote for or against Home Rule. Redmond was firm that he could not agree to this any more than he could to the exclusion of the whole province of Ulster. Carson was more scornful: how could he renounce the two million male 'covenanters' in the three remaining counties of Cavan, Monaghan and Donegal? The only agreement seemed to be on what the opposing parties were not going to accept and it seemed likely, moreover, that any deviation from negativity would need to be referred back to the headstrong supporters of both sides. Never was a better case made for the inevitability of conflict – the only thing that might alter events was an even bigger issue impinging from outside. And of that Ransom was only too conscious.

On the fourth morning it remained only to decide how the impasse should be announced. The King had not joined them again, and all Ransom could do was involve himself as best he could and wait. At last the Speaker sent the King a short note: the Conference, 'being unable to agree, either in principle or in detail upon the area to be excluded, had brought its meetings to a conclusion'.

As they left the room, Redmond approached Carson. 'I shall ask you to shake my hand for the sake of the old days on the circuit.' The gesture was accepted. Craig shook hands with Dillon, but neither man spoke. Asquith whispered to Ransom a homily on the sheer folly of supposing that they could ever hope to understand the Irish. Even at such a time, he was quite ready to comment on the foibles of human nature.

The King was to say goodbye to them in groups. He had prepared himself to tell Redmond that he was not to be seen as an enemy of Home Rule – which was bound to come eventually – but that his overriding concern was for peace. This was true – and might at least have some propaganda value with the Irish leader.

Ransom was by now somewhat off his guard. As they waited in the anteroom, the Speaker's eye caught the first page of the lunchtime paper. It brought news of the Austrian ultimatum to Serbia, but after a passing remark to the Prime Minister, he – like the rest of them – lapsed into weary silence.

Craig, Carson and co. Then the turn of the Redmond-Dillon camp. The Conference was breaking up with a resumption of the same formal intransigence with which it had begun. The door opened and Redmond went in, followed by Dillon, together with their two aides, Michael Mulliner and William O'Connor.

The action came suddenly – certainly for Ransom, since by then he had almost, if not quite, suppressed all thoughts of what was supposed to occur. He caught the eye of O'Connor as the other man disappeared from view. With this came the thunderclap of recognition: William O'Connor was the figure he had seen for that split-second back in the Koenigergratzerstrasse on his visit to Germany.

With the inspiration of shock, he launched himself past a startled Asquith and threw open the door.

An extraordinary amount of time seemed to pass as he surveyed the scene. The King, standing towards the window, showed only puzzlement, then slightly more active confusion in his eyes. How different he seemed to the Kaiser, the noisy reincarnation of Barbarossa. This was an artless, almost humble figure, summoned by a sense of duty to fight his retiring nature, adopt uncomfortably the demeanour of ruler, and support the weight of a millstone that was not his own choosing.

Now O'Connor was raising a gun to point at the King, as Ransom reached for his own. The others, halted in their polite approach to their sovereign, were frozen into a tableau.

Outside, as they recovered from their surprise and moved forwards, the Prime Minister and the Speaker heard three distinct shots, a second between each. It was exactly ten minutes to eleven.

CHAPTER TWENTY

The future can look after itself

FOR some while previously, agitated telegrams, hasty coded signals and messages had been compiled and dispatched across the Continent of Europe. German troops had crossed into Luxembourg shortly after breakfast. Troop trains – hundreds of them in the full day – made their way at frequent intervals across the Rhine bridges at Cologne and Coblenz, moving west, on to the Belgian frontier. Here the ironic conqueror's cry was 'Vive la Belgique'. In countries far distant from one another diplomats hurriedly began to burn sensitive papers.

For rich Englishmen, on their way to holidays in Homburg or Carlsbad or Marienbad, there were stormy days ahead. In Berlin, an excited mob – fresh from stoning the windows at the British Embassy – gathered at the Old Palace to call for the Kaiser.

Eventually, Wilhelm appeared on the balcony. Dressed for battle, he looked tense and tired. His people cheered. Gaining strength from them, he raised his hands and called for silence.

'I commend you now to God,' he shouted. 'Go into the churches, kneel down, and pray for help for our soldiers. Germany is at war, a glorious war. I can no longer see parties – only Germans.'

Forgotten were any doubts, forgotten even the qualms about the English. Good news would be on its way from there.

From Paris information came of a pleasing confusion, despite the immediate imposition of martial law and the appointment of a military governor. The German manager of the Astoria, found sending wireless telegrams to Berlin, was strung up outside his hotel, but the reckoning would soon come for that. And if a thousand voices took up the words of the Marseillaise and prepared to win back Alsace-Lorraine, the lost children of the French, a thousand more babbled hysterically as they blocked the Gare du Nord in a frantic effort to escape from the capital.

From the Tsar came a satisfyingly weak telegram, with its emphasis on Serbia. The Kaiser smiled as he read it. 'In this most serious moment I appeal to you to help me. An ignoble war is being declared on a *weak* country. The *indignation* in Russia, *shared fully by me*, is *enormous*. I foresee that very soon I shall be *overwhelmed* by the *pressure* brought upon me, and be *forced* to take extreme measures which will *lead to war*…. I beg you in the name of our old friendship….'

The Kaiser was happy as he dictated a reply. Bethmann-Hollweg's last-minute doubts had been a nuisance, but he could feel confident. The nation was behind him. His troops were well armed. The plentiful early harvest was gathered. It was fully time to show the strength of his hand. 'In my endeavours to maintain the peace of the world,' he wired to Tsar Nicholas, 'I have gone to the utmost limit possible. The responsibility for the disaster that is now threatening the whole civilized world will not be laid at my door…. Nobody is threatening the honour or power of Russia, which can well afford to await the result of my mediation. My friendship to you and your Empire, transmitted to me by my grandfather on his deathbed, has always been sacred to me....'

In London, however, all had not gone to plan. On Monday, the 20th of July, the day the Irish Conference was announced, the Special Branch of Scotland Yard quietly arrested Anna. Working in close conjunction with Kell's men from MI5 – as they often did – they handed her over to him. No formal charges were made. Anna and Ransom had been watched ever since his visit to Germany had been planned, but more recently it had not only been without Asquith's approval but in secret from him. Kell had learned little from these observations and yet was left with the instinct that nothing properly added up. The Prime Minister, in his own way and in his own time, had come to a different, but firm, conclusion: that Ransom was in love with Anna; that is was possible that the association, if made public, could do harm to his Government; that, nevertheless, it was very unlikely ever to come into the open; that, if it did, Ransom would resign quickly and there would be no lasting repercussions. Ransom's behaviour recently had had some strange features, but he was of some use in sorting out the Irish morass.

Through Monday and Tuesday Anna refused to reveal anything. Isolated from any news, she could not be sure when the action would begin, but the fact that Kell kept on at her seemed proof that nothing had happened yet.

At first Kell's questioning had merely provoked the most stubborn hostility in her. He was a skilled interrogator, who mixed promises with threats, but – when it came to it – what was going on independently in Anna's thoughts was the key. Suppose something went wrong – after all, Ransom had been given so few of the details. They could not have trusted him – and would have done so still less once Georg had escaped. Finally, and with a certain bravado, she told Kell to go and find in Clarges Street what the Special Branch had missed: Ransom's letter – secured in a bag attached to the outside of the skylight.

Kell's fury at the dangerous meddlings of amateurs was for the moment suppressed as he rushed to act on what he had read. Goddamnit, the switchboard at Buckingham Palace must be out of order: there was nothing for it but to drive straight there.

On arrival, he found people rushing in every direction. Pushing his way through with the aid of his identity card, he came upon the strangest scene he had ever encountered.

Open-mouthed, the King of England sat at his desk staring distractedly out of the window. His Prime Minister, the Speaker of the House of Commons and a Cabinet Minister were bent over something hidden from view. As he strode into the room, he saw what they were looking at – the lifeless form of William O'Connor, blood spreading from wounds in his head onto the carpet.

The newspaper headlines changed rapidly from that point on. The European news was too unexpected wholly to replace the tea-time CONFERENCE ENDS IN FAILURE – TRAGIC DEATH IN SHOOTING ACCIDENT. Asquith had calmly, if not very creatively, invented the story. Following the end of the Conference, the King had been showing O'Connor some new guns en route to Sandringham for use in shooting there when one of them had accidently gone off. It was a plus that the King's interest in sporting guns was well known; and it would have been too much to hope that, with all the publicity focused on the Conference, O'Connor could be made to disappear without some reason being given. His motives, in retrospect, were easily pieced together: what better disguise for a fanatical Irishman, driven by hatred of the English, than to be associated with that most reputable of the Irish extremists, John Redmond?

There was no serious probing of the official account because of what followed. Anna, when brought up to date with recent events, quickly outlined all that she knew. Britain was technically tied by treaty to come to Belgium's aid, but any doubts the King or Asquith may have had about the wisdom or morality of declaring war on Germany were dispelled by the account of the Kaiser's plan. The Prime Minister, relieved perhaps to find he had to act under the pressure of events, directed operations from Downing Street. 'I have sent a precautionary telegram to every part of the Empire informing all the government officials that they must prepare for war,' he said contentedly to Margot. No doubts here, it seemed, about what war might do to the Liberal creed, to belief in progress or rational processes.

Other members of the Cabinet were not told the full story, and a few resignations followed. Lloyd George, who might have had doubts, sensed correctly the prevailing mood of the country. For the moment, most opposition ceased. After a meeting of Unionist leaders at Lansdowne House, near to Ransom's home in Berkeley Square, Lord Lansdowne's chauffeur delivered a letter to 10 Downing Street:

Dear Mr Asquith

Lord Lansdowne and I feel it our duty to inform you that in our opinion, as well as that of all the colleagues whom we have been able to consult, it would be fatal to the honour and security of the United Kingdom to hesitate in supporting France and Russia at the present juncture, and we offer our unhesitating support to the Government in any measures they may consider necessary for that object.

Yours very truly
Bonar Law

In the House of Commons, Grey's manner seemed to show a

peculiar indignation that the whole world should be out of joint and afterwards, in greater privacy, he was to crash his fists to the table in the only emotional action Ransom ever saw from him – 'I hate war!' But there was no mistaking the reaction he and Asquith received in Parliament. Redmond rose to declare that Ireland would set aside her own quarrels and join England in the fighting. 'Today there are in Ireland two large bodies of Volunteers,' he averred. 'One has sprung into existence in the North and another in the South. I say to the Government that they may tomorrow withdraw every one of their troops from Ireland. Ireland will be defended by her armed sons from invasion, and for that purpose the armed Catholics in the South will be only too glad to join arms with the armed Protestant Ulstermen.'

The Speaker was asked for permission to sing the National Anthem: it was the first time that 'God save the King' had ever been sung in the House of Commons.

Excitement was not confined to the political world. Ransom joined the huge crowd in the Mall, surrounding Buckingham Palace and growing larger by the minute. Only happiness and exhilaration was visible in their faces. 'We want our King': the cry continued into the early evening, long after the King and Queen had appeared on the balcony for the last time. Ransom too added to the great roar of approval and acclamation: who could have resisted the joy and power of the occasion?

By the Duke of York's steps in the Mall, he experienced a kind of elation as the windows of the German Embassy were smashed until police arrived on horses to restore at least a sort of order. Harold Nicolson, son of the Permanent Secretary at the Foreign Office, walked across Horse Guards Parade to deliver a British ultimatum to the German Ambassador. Lichnowsky, apparently abandoned and certainly uninformed by this Government, declined to receive him.

As Ransom left the scene, a small group of pacifist demonstrators was in some danger, their singing of the Red Flag drowned in the excitement. It was a good time for those who liked to take the lead. Mr Kent, of the New York Bankers Trust Co., formed an American Citizens Relief Committee, taking the best part of the Savoy for the purpose. And everywhere he found evidence of Winston rushing hither and thither in high spirits. The more everything moved towards catastrophe and collapse, he told Ransom, the more 'interested, geared up and happy' he became. The sailors at his command were 'thrilled and confident' and the enemy could look forward to 'a good drubbing'. What he didn't say was that – just in case any of them became fainthearted – he was going to make soundings of Bonar Law over the possibility of a Coalition Cabinet. As it happened, he got nowhere, but the political battle could never finally be lost while the military battle had still to be won. Lloyd George felt the same, Ransom was sure.

Viscount Morley, one of those strong-minded 'faint-hearts' who resigned from the Cabinet over the war, was more angrily passionate than Ransom had ever seen him. 'You think it was inevitable, do you?' he asked fiercely. 'Of what war has that not been said since Hannibal?'

Whatever else, the inevitability depended on a number of people exercising their will in a particular way. And yet Ransom's own part in the story seemed proof that great events cannot be controlled. If it had happened differently, would history have recorded a very different story? Ransom doubted it. Apart from anything else, the peculiar official ability to hide the unfortunate, the awkward, the embarrassing in public life often disguises what really happened. The public record, the human desire to believe, the sanctification of the historians – powerful medicine.

There is no one left to ask whether it is even plausible, as history has it, that the Kaiser Wilhelm II lived on well into his ninth decade without himself ever being the target of the assassin. For Ransom, the considerations were different that Summer of 1914. He had a shaken King and a relieved Prime Minister only too anxious to make him the hero of the moment: provided no one knew. If the full story came out, he would at the least have had to resign and, whatever Kell thought, there was no necessity for that, was there? The members of the Conference were given a limited account of events; and Redmond was content to overcome his shock that one of his entourage was a traitor by joining in the new sense of national unity against the common enemy.

Anna, at Ransom's insistence, was released, though Asquith warned, politely, that now was an excellent time for him to be a little more conscious of his position in the relationships he enjoyed. Everyone, he advised, needed the passion – and he meant it – but that was not what kept the world in motion, or won a war.

He did not argue; like Anna, he was struck by the sense that a whirlwind of events could reveal so much to them about each other, and yet in an extraordinary way leave everything unchanged.

With whether the future was to be just as unpredictable, or just as inevitable, they would both be unconcerned for some time to come.

Acknowledgments

I have consulted sources of many different kinds in piecing together the historical background to this story. Here I would like gratefully to acknowledge my specific indebtedness to the following:

For Wilhelm 11 and Germany in 1914: D. Chapman-Houston (ed.), *From My Private Diary – Daisy, Princess of Pless*, London 1931; Virginia Cowles, *The Kaiser*, London 1963; Immanuel Geiss (ed.), *July 1914,* London 1966; D.J. Goodspeed, *Ludendorf: Soldier, Dictator, Revolutionary*, London 1966; O.J. Hales, *Publicity and Diplomacy*, Virginia 1940; D.J. Hill, *Impressions of the Kaiser*, London 1919; James Joll, '*The 1914 Debate Continues*', *Past & Present*, No. 34, July 1966; Gerhard Masur, *Imperial Berlin*, London 1971; Alan Palmer, *The Kaiser: Warlord of the Second Reich*, London 1978; Sir Horace Rumbold, *The War Crisis in Berlin, July–August 1914*, London 1940; Charles Sarolen, *The Anglo-German Problem*, London 1912; George Malcolm Thomson, *The Twelve Days*, London 1964; Ann Topham, *Memoirs of the Kaiser's Court*, London 1914; Barbara W. Tuchman, *The Proud Tower,* London 1966; Tyler Whittle, *The Last Kaiser*, London 1977.

For King George V and Queen Mary: J. Wentworth Day, *King George V as a Sportsman,* London 1935; Christopher Hibbert, *The Court at Windsor*, London 1964; Edward Legge, *King George and the Royal Family*, 2 Vols, London 1928; Harold Nicolson, *King George V*, London 1952; James Pope-Hennessy, *Queen Mary, 1867–1953,* London 1959.

For London: William J. Fishman, *East End Jewish Radicals, 1875–1914*, London 1975; Lloyd P. Gartner, *The Jewish Immigrant in England, 1870–1914*, 2nd ed., London 1973; E.V. Lucas, *A Wanderer in London*, 15th ed., London 1915; Alexander Paterson, *Across the Bridges*, London 1914; Rudolf Rocker, *The London Years*, London 1956; Paul Thompson, *The Edwardians: The Remaking of English Society, 1865–1914*, London 1975.

For Secret Intelligence: Richard Deacon, *A History of the British Secret Service*, London 1965; B.P. Holst, *My Experience with Spies in the Great European War*, Boone (Iowa) and Chicago (Illinois) 1916.

For Sarajevo: Theodor Wolff, *The Eve of 1914*, London 1935.

For Ireland: George Dangerfield, *The Damnable Question*, London 1977; St John G. Ervine, *Sir Edward Carson and the Ulster Movement*, London 1915; H. Mongomery Hyde, *Carson*, London 1953.

For the political scene in 1914: Robert Blake, *The Unknown Prime Minister*, London 1955; Randolph S. Churchill, *Winston S. Churchill*, Vol. 11, *Young Statesman*, London 1967; Edward David, *Inside Asquith's Cabinet*, London 1977; Sir Almeric Fitzroy, *Memoirs*, Vol. 11, London [1925]; Robert Rhodes James, *The British Revolution: British Politics, 1880–1939*, Vol. 1, London 1976; Roy Jenkins, *Asquith*, London 1964; Michael MacDonagh, *The Reporters' Gallery*, London 1913; Michael MacDonagh, *In London during the Great War*, London 1935; Kirsty McLeod, *The Wives of Downing Street*, London 1976; William Martin, *Statesmen of the War: In Retrospect, 1918–1928*, London 1928; Gilbert Murray, *The Foreign Policy of Sir Edward Grey*, Oxford 1915; Lord Riddell, *More Pages from My Diary 1908–1914*, London 1934; Peter Rowland, *Lloyd George*, London 1975; H.A. Taylor, *The Strange Case of Andrew*

Bonar Law, London 1932; George Woodcock, *Anarchism*, Harmondsworth 1962.

For contemporary events and social life: John Burnett (ed.) *Useful Toil*, London 1974; Lieutenant-Colonel Newnham-Davis, *The Gourmet's Guide to London*, London 1914; Donald Read (ed.), *Documents from Edwardian England*, London 1973; and *passim Bystander*; *The Graphic*; *Harper's Weekly*; *Illustrated London News*; *John Bull*; *The Nation*; *New Age*; *Pearson's Magazine*; *Punch*; *The Queen*; *Review of Reviews*; *Saturday Review*; *Spectator*; *The Tatler*; *The Times*; *Truth*; *Vanity Fair*; *Annual Register.*

Warmest thanks to Helen Farr for keying the manuscript, to John Hawkins for cover and imprint design and wise advice,and to Alan Cooper for preparing the files.

15264264R00151

Printed in Great Britain
by Amazon